978-0-9926161-2-0

Copyright © 2021 by Warwick Paul Davis

The right of Warwick P Davis to be identified as the author of this work has been asserted in accordance with sections 77 and 78 of the Copyright Designs and Patents Act 1988.

All rights reserved. This book is sold subject to the condition that it shall not, by way of trade or otherwise, be lent, re-sold, hired out, stored in a retrieval system or transmitted in any form or otherwise circulated in any form of binding or cover other than that in which it is published or represented and without the permission of the author

This book is a work of fiction. Any resemblance to actual persons, living or dead, is entirely coincidental and highly unlikely.

28479

INTRODUCTION

Wil Kingdon is whisked onto the world stage from his quiet but important life in Eastbourne. He is key to trying to solve the potentially catastrophic disaster that faces the world. As events unfold he tries to explain the situation to his small band of friends raising many controversial health and historical topics that Wil thinks are associated with the problems everyone faces today. Myths and legends associated with Sussex are used to illustrate some of the issues and highlight why the region is important.

Coincidentally the names of all the characters are derived from the names of places in and around Eastbourne and East Sussex.

Can technology be a deadly double sided sword that, instead of supporting and enriching society, will actually bring society to the brink of catastrophe…….or maybe over the brink?

ONE

It had taken a long time in the preparation but it had been worth it. All the, now peacefully sleeping, folk that had spent hours decorating, hanging trimmings, moving, stacking, cleaning and polishing had retired to their bedrooms anticipating an excited day tomorrow. The room they had left was a picture. Even Dickens could not have envisioned a better, more perfect Christmas room. A huge log fire had burned gently in the grate but now it was reduced to throwing a soft flickering orange light into the room. The remaining embers and glowing logs shifted occasionally as they settled deeper into the iron grate sending delicate showers of sparks up into the darkness of the chimney at the same time releasing soft sighs of air and blue flames dancing up between them. The aroma of the burning logs mixed with that of the pine leaves of the tree and the holly and fir fronds scattered around the room. The large room was warm and cosy being lit only by the fire and the strings of lights draped around the huge Christmas tree each casting their coloured light into the darkness. Even the moon, full and bright, shone in through the floor to ceiling windows that were framed in heavy red velvet curtains. Snow fluttered past the window laying silently on the frames and lawns outside lighting up the countryside reflecting moon light into the room. Every flat surface inside the room was covered with sprigs of holly and fir branches amongst which nestled greeting cards, photographs and candles. The thick, soft cushions scattered across the sofas and chairs still had the imprints of their recent occupants. The cups, saucers, glasses and plates from a late night supper sat on the small tables and would have been waiting to be cleared in the morning if the dog had not enthusiastically already cleared the remnants of the sausage rolls and mince pies when no-one was looking. Piles of neatly wrapped presents were layered under the tree also waiting for the morning. The mince pie left out under the tree for Santa had also already been enthusiastically cleared up by the dog who was not in the least interested in the carrot or the sherry.

Aside from the crackling of the fire and the deep, regular bass ticking of the grand-father long clock in the corner of the room everything was quiet. Even the dog, stretched out full of tit bits and fast asleep in front of the fire only whimpered quietly as he dreamed of chasing rabbits across the snow covered fields outside. Occasionally his ear would twitch as the fire crackled but he was soon back to his chase. Annoyingly his slumber was soon terminated as he, at first, raised his head and then slowly sat up with his ears pricked, listening. He looked about the room peering with acute eyes into the gloom concentrating and rotating his ears trying to pick up and locate the sounds that had disturbed him. Shifting his body weight he sat bolt upright, hackles rising, still listening until he rose to his feet, looked round to the fire, licked his lips and walked quickly to the door which he opened with his nose before walking briskly out of the room without looking back.

Behind him the tall church candle that had been burning on the fire hearth went out.

TWO

Henry had worked on the railways all his life. It was hard work but at least it was work and having been a long, long term employee there were not many dodges and skives that he did not know about. He was prepared to do his bit, earn his crust, but he liked to feel he was a bit of a rebel sometimes and the odd skive helped him to feel that way. Diddle the boss, cheat the system a little bit, and get one over on the establishment when it wasn't looking. It all helped to make the day go by a bit quicker. He knew his supervisors knew what he was like but he also knew they thought he was a good worker and they could rely on him to put in a fair days work. Most days. Anyway supervisors came and went just like the trains. He had seen dozens in his time but Henry was not going anywhere, just like the rails he was supposed to be looking after.

Today he had reported to his supervisor at the main line station and after checking in and getting his work schedule he had been sent to the small wooden hut they used as a base a couple of miles from the small branch station deep in the Sussex countryside. Being away from the station there was always a good chance to catch up with the gossip, have a fag and a mug of tea and waste an hour or two before getting down to work. The small sturdy huts they used as their base were set into the steep grass banks a short but safe distance from the rails. Their brick walls and tin roof were a God send in the winter when the heat of the small wood burning stove could thaw the frozen limbs in minutes and heat the kettles even quicker. In the summer it was nice to take the old wooden chairs outside and sit in the sun, quietly resting until the trains came hurtling past in clouds of dust, discarded rubbish and decibels of noise or until just before the supervisor happened past all steam and noise himself.

This day Henry had been assigned to walk through the nearby tunnel checking the line for loose plates or cracks by inspecting them visually and tapping them with his long handled hammer. The torch he wore strapped to his helmet was of little use in his inspections and he relied heavily on hearing the right sounds from the tapped rail. He had become quite accomplished at distinguishing the different notes that rails in various stages of disrepair made. On bad days he fancied that he might be able to retrain as a piano tuner but hands as big, bruised and calloused as his had become would not sit well on piano keys. Perhaps if he could whack the piano with his hammer he could manage. But maybe not.

Checking the lines was fine, at least there was some skill involved, but he did not like the clearing of the rubbish from them. Periodically teams of rail men would scour the lines for rubbish that folk had left and he was amazed at the number of bins they could easily fill. They were used to the rubbish that people threw from trains in the open but how they managed to throw stuff out of the windows in the tunnel was always a bit of a mystery and why was there only ever one shoe of a pair on the line. What did the people do with the other one? But, in his time, he had found all sorts of things himself. Anything from a prosthetic limb to a coconut could be found although he had never found a purse or wallet or piece of jewellery. Perhaps people were a bit more careful with those. Anyway human rubbish was the least of his worries. His worst find was when a cow had wandered into the tunnel and had been hit by one of the fast expresses. The body was dragged the length of the tunnel with parts of its body being torn off and scattered the whole way. It had taken days to find all the pieces and by the time they did they were smelling to high heaven. Rather the odd beer bottle, shoe or sandwich box than that.

All those years ago the busy old Victorians had driven the tunnel in front of him through the chalk hills and built the elegant stone, superb, façade. It and the brick lining was superb although rather covered with algae, age old soot and decades of air pollution. But in their eagerness to get trains down to the south coast the builders had rather neglected the drainage systems so Henry also had to check for pools of water as he traipsed into the gloom with his hammer slung over his shoulder. Nothing worse than a day working with wet feet except the day the water disguised a particularly deep hole and a leg disappeared in it up to the knee. As Henry disappeared into the gloom he felt the warmth of the sun leave his shoulders and the dampness and coolness of the tunnel take over. The bird sounds disappeared and he was plunged into a world of his echoing deep breathing and blackness. He paused and he swung his hammer into place and started tapping the rails as he slowly walked into the darkness. Tap one line down the track and the other on his return journey. Two taps per step around five thousand steps each way today so twenty thousand taps.

It was a long tunnel and he was acutely aware that he did not want to end up like the ill-fated cow so he kept a close eye on the tunnel entrances one of which gradually shrunk and one of which gradually grew while often checking his silver pocket watch for the next train. When the time approached for the next train he stepped off the track and made for one of the small brick recesses that had been designed into the wall of the tunnel at regular intervals to be used as a shelter. Not only were the recesses just the right size but the builders had thoughtfully incorporated a small brick shelf just high and wide enough to sit on. Propping his hammer against the side of the shelter he squeezed into the gap plopped himself onto the seat and rummaged in his pockets for his cigarettes. Safely inside he took a roll up from out of the tin and put it between his lips. The flare of the lighted match illuminated the tunnel for a second but as he raised it to his cigarette the light went out. He tried again, and again. Running out of matches he cursed his luck but then one match stayed alight long enough for him to draw on his cigarette. His lungs drew gratefully on the smoke but even before his intake of breath was complete the match and the cigarette both went out and he felt a strange tingling in his lips.

Normally being on his own in the dark of the old tunnel did not bother him but on this occasion he felt uneasy. He moved a little as the express thundered past him. As soon as it had gone he popped out of his shelter and started to make his way back to the entrance and the sunshine walking a little quicker than usual still tapping as he went but looking about him for what he did not know.

THREE

Typical. One minute everyone is having a wonderful time, having a drink and then another drink and maybe just one more then. Chatting loudly and amiably, worrying about how many calories had been in that Christmas dinner, comparing presents and wondering who would be the first one to start dancing. A small group gathered by the fire, another by the table loaded with the snacks no-one wanted but no-one could resist and a third by the bar. Out of the din of excited chatter some bright spark had suggested playing a game of hide and seek and, like a Mexican wave, it rapidly spread around the room. In the next minute you find yourself in a fusty old cupboard somewhere in one of the rooms off the kitchen feeling rather stupid and wishing everyone had chosen charades instead of hide and seek. Susan Roads was no good at charades. No-one could understand her mimes even if she could think of what to do. And she could never remember the names of the films or books or whatever the others were miming apart from Gone with the Wind and everyone always did that and sniggered. But for some inexplicable reason she had been selected as the first person to hide and as she sat in the dark, on her own, it seemed charades might have been the better choice.

Feeling a bit like a naughty child who had transgressed some unwritten social protocol she found herself putting down her glass and leaving the room to go and hide. The house was enormous so the game had been limited to the ground floor but even so there were many rooms to hide in. Eventually she found a small room off of the large kitchen. Quite what it was supposed to be was a mystery but it did have a huge walk in cupboard, almost a room within a room within a room. She stepped inside with the uncomfortable feeling that she would either step straight through and into the winter of Narnia or bump into a few animal carcasses hanging and waiting for butchery. The single, empty shelf in front of her looked wide and sturdy so she sat herself down swivelled round pulling her legs up onto the shelf and reached over pulling the door to and waited. She hoped she would not be in there too long and wished she had brought her glass, no, the bottle of wine with her. It was quite a large cupboard but the feeling of claustrophobia was not far away and the smell of the cupboard was not very pleasant. She was convinced the resident spiders were watching her every move and waiting for their chance to attack. She resolved that should there be the slightest bit of evidence that there was a mouse sharing her hiding place then the game was going to be well and truly over and some other idiot could go and hide.

Soon after sitting down she took her mobile phone out of her pocket to check the time. The light from the display illuminated some of the space but the darkness resisted the light and apart from the cobwebs and a few empty hooks there was nothing to see. Time seemed to pass very slowly and she began to think that the others were playing a joke on her and would not be bothering to come and look for her. She imagined them carrying on the party, laughing and joking about her being hidden away somewhere unpleasant. She shivered and resolved that if no-one had come to find her in the next few minutes she was going back to the room and tell the others what she thought of them.

Whether it was because the effects of the drinks was wearing off she started to feel cold and shivered. A very fashionable and expensive party dress that exposed a little too much flesh was not the thing to be wearing in a dull, dark and chilly cupboard. The hairs on her arms stood on end and she rubbed her arms with her hands to warm them and pulled her knees closer to her chin. The darkness and cold started to feel more and more uncomfortable and she started to feel uneasy. Panic started to take over as she peered between the cracks of the doors to see if anyone was coming. No-one was there but she decided she had had enough and pushed at the doors but they would not open. The old, rusty but still operable latch had slid down and fastened the door shut as she had climbed in. She pushed harder and rattled the doors getting more panicked as they failed to open. It suddenly started to get more difficult to breathe and her lips started to tingle. The oxygen seemed to be being sucked out of the room and she panicked more. Suddenly the door flew open and she fell, inelegantly, off the shelf and into the room.

"What the heck's going on?" asked Anthony as he was almost knocked over as Susan fell out of the cupboard.

"I don't know. One minute I was stuck in the cupboard and it was difficult to breathe and the next minute I was on the floor here. Let's go back to the room I don't want to stay here. It's scary and they can stick the damn stupid game."

FOUR

Jev's hand flew to the back of his neck as his head snapped back sending a shooting pain up and down his spine. He gasped briefly but looking in his mirrors he could see people still getting on and off of his underground train. It was just a micro nap but as he gathered his thoughts he cursed his brother in law for tempting him out the night before. When he had come round to Jev's flat he had said he only meant to stay for a coffee but they had got talking and eventually talked themselves into going down to the pub for a single pint that turned into several pints that, inevitably, turned into the post 'a couple of pints hunger' that could only be assuaged by a kebab or two. That all took time and enjoyable though it was Jev knew he was storing up trouble for himself.

His early shift on the London underground started at 5am which meant him getting up at three thirty which meant only a couple of hours sleep after his brother in law had eventually gone home. Despite the fact that he had promised himself an early night he actually made it to bed just after midnight and then he did not sleep well with the kebab seemingly to have been particularly indigestible. Now he was tired, very tired and he had a long day ahead of him. He glanced in his mirrors again and swore never to have another late night kebab. Not until next time anyway. He rubbed his eyes and put another piece of chewing gum in his mouth hoping the chewing would help him stay awake.

"Why the hell can't they let people off the train before trying to get on?" he said to himself for the millionth time as he watched the seemingly unequal struggle of hordes of commuters trying to get off the train at the same time as hordes of commuters were trying to get on the train.

The cab he was sealed from the throng in was warm and quiet and that was not helping his torpor. There was not a breath of air and his seat seemed unusually comfortable. As he waited the minute of two before he could pull away again it seemed to be getting more difficult to breathe. So much so that he reached for his inhaler and drew deeply on it.

He sat up straight and rubbed his hands over his face again to try to wake himself up and took a swig from his water bottle. He looked down to his power gauge on the dashboard and was puzzled to see it flick into the red zone even though the train was stationary. Unless his eyes were playing tricks on him he resolved to report it at the end of his shift.

The train was quickly filling up and he had to get a move on. As the saying went there will be another one right behind.

He looked into the darkness of the tunnel ahead of him and his imagination briefly wandered to his home island of Barbados. To the beaches of Barbados. To the bars on the beaches of Barbados. He had grown up on the island only coming to England when he was a teenager. His parents still lived on the island and had a small four roomed breeze block and red tile house close to one of the wide sandy beaches. He could literally step out of his bedroom and be practically on the beach. A step or two more and he was standing in the warm, clear waters of the Caribbean. The local small town he called home was only a short bicycle ride away and the sun never seemed to stop shining. The difference in his life now was extreme, London always seemed to be cold even in the summer and instead of stepping onto sunny beaches he stepped onto crowded pavements, heaving stations and dark trains.

"One day, one day," he promised himself under his breath. One day he would go back to Barbados and sit in the sunshine far from the dark, snaking tunnels in which he seemed to spend so much of his life.

The buzzer went off in his cab and the power indicator went off the scale again flicking from red and back to green. He would definitely report it when he finished. He shook his head in incomprehension and licked his tingling lips. It was time to move off and he with his hundreds of passengers slowly moved towards the tunnel and disappeared into the dark. Jev was completely unaware that he would never see the island of Barbados again. Nor would he even see the end of the tunnel.

FIVE

Harvey and Lewis had worked as a team for the cleansing department for almost five years. They had developed a good relationship over that time despite being completely opposite characters and occasionally getting on each other's nerves. Harvey was in his fifties, a family man settled and content with his lot. He wanted to do a good job and took pride in his work. Although, in the grand scheme of things, he reckoned his job was not very important and that his clients could not care less about what he did he always felt that if someone was doing the job for him he would want them to do their best and do it properly. He took pride in walking into a dump of a place and walking out leaving a clean and tidy place. He had a strong sense of order and cleanliness but strangely and to his wife's annoyance that only seemed to apply to other people's houses. Despite years of reminders or nagging as Harvey would have put it he still left the seat up, left his dirty clothes on the floor, left empty toilet rolls on the hook and seemed incapable of shutting any cupboard doors. His shed at the bottom of the garden was best to be avoided at all times.

Lewis, on the other hand, was less committed to his or any work. In his late twenties he had been through many departments in the council in a very short space of time. In each one he had contrived to fail by actually working harder at being useless than if he had tried to be useful. Turning up late, often not at all. Being mildly insolent, slapdash and idle and having no end of exotic illnesses, family and pet bereavements that required time off. He knew he was not cut out for any of the jobs he was given. He didn't actually know what he was cut out for but he knew it would be terrific and he knew he had not found it yet. Ideally he would have been able to sit at home all day glued to his phone scrolling through app after app doing nothing productive or maybe playing on ever more challenging games machines. Basically doing everything that was enjoyable while waiting for the ideal job, the golden opportunity, to come knocking at the door. But when his stomach became as empty as his fridge usually was he knew he had to do something no matter how grudgingly just to keep body and soul together being ready for the big break when it came. Eventually meandering through all he opportunities the council had put his way he had found himself working with Harvey. But even on the first day he had resolved it was only going to be another short, tedious interlude until the dream materialised.

Five years on and he was still waiting and dreaming. It came as a surprise not to mention an annoyance to Lewis that he had actually spent five years doing the same job and had not been sacked or moved on. He blamed Harvey for, despite not exactly enthusing him about the job himself, he at least made it bearable. Most of his previous supervisors had given up on him after only a day or two but Harvey had been different and, in turn, encouraged him and teased him but in a constructive and friendly manner. Despite this five year inconvenience he knew the big break was still just around the corner or maybe even the big win on the lottery although despite many, many attempts that pot of gold had also not materialised. Nevertheless despite the lack of rescue he was constantly planning and vowed to be ready for it when it appeared. But over the time Lewis had developed a respect for Harvey despite the fact that they were chalk and cheese and they bickered a lot and it was quite apparent that he exasperated Harvey. Lewis would never tell Harvey that he had started to look up to him and saw him almost as a father figure but it did worry him that he may be settling down and becoming "normal". He swung between being depressed about being stuck in the job and taking the same pleasure Harvey did from doing a good job. So for five years they had muddled along, a traditionalist and a dreamer. The Council's own odd couple one of whom at least was horrified that in weak moments he almost admitted to himself that he might, just a little, be enjoying his work .

Their job would certainly not have appealed to many people. It was just as well they had stuck at it as replacements were hard to find. Harvey had actually been with the council for twenty years and there was not much he hadn't seen and been challenged with. He had done the bins, street cleaning, graffiti cleaning which annoyed him the most, litter picking which he liked, dog shit cleaning which he hated and now house clearing. Once, due to an injury which needed rest to recover from, he had tried a desk bound job which seemed to consist of answering the phone all day and shuffling endless pieces of paper from one side of the desk to the other. He knew he should read them but could never quite summon up the interest to do so. He never took to it and never quite knew what it was all about. All he knew is that he went to the same place every day, sat in the same chair at the same keyboard engaged a furious activity but never actually seemed to achieve anything other than having a very tidy stationery store in his desk drawer.

Harvey had quickly summed up Lewis when he was paired with him. Over the years he had seen plenty of Lewis' and they had quickly come and gone. But despite his initial impressions and despite Lewis's best intentions he was a quick learner and catching on fast and much to his obvious annoyance was getting very good at the job. Looking out of the van at the windows of the house they had been sent to they felt pretty confident they were up to the task. Just another job.

Lewis looked down at the clipboard he was holding to check the address. Number eighty six. Correct house. From the outside it initially looked like a typical late Victorian small villa typical of those that lay back from the smarter, larger ones that in turn were set back from the truly elegant villas of the Eastbourne parades. Eighty six was slightly drabber than its neighbours. The white paint was not quite so white, the curtains not quite so clean and the front garden, steps and iron gate definitely in need of some attention. At one end of the long, straight terrace the house had seen the ground floor converted, like many in late Victorian early Edwardian times, into a shop which having been through many identities was now an up market delicatessen. At the other end of the terrace the same had happened and the ground floor of the house was now a rather chic wine bar. Typically stylish for Eastbourne. The electric bike and maroon convertible Mercedes motor car parked outside suggested to Harvey that lunch today would be taken in the van and on the sandwiches his wife had made for him. Lunch would definitely be of the packed variety rather than the liquid one. Harvey flicked over the page to check the number on other sheets and it was correct. Number eighty six belonging to a ninety three year old DDA. An abbreviation for discovered dead alone. There were a couple of other details about where the body was found then NKR – no known relatives and, at the bottom of the sheet CED, clean, empty and disinfect. Beneath that there were endless sheets with risk assessments, standard operating procedures and lists of questions with boxes to be ticked. Lewis skipped over them.

Harvey and Lewis had at least one of these a month. An elderly person found dead, alone in their home. Sometimes the death had been a recent one but others had not been found for months and they were very traumatic even when the body had actually been removed by funeral directors. Decomposed bodies left smells, stains and blue bottles which were difficult to clear from the scene. The body, whenever it was discovered was removed and if there is no-one to take responsibility for the property it was handed over to Harvey and Lewis's department. Initially they were sent in to search for any clues about the occupant that may help towards finding any relatives, wills or funerals or if there was no evidence of family to arrange for the contents of the place to be sold. They then had to make it ready for sale or to be handed back to the council. The longer Lewis had worked at the job the more he began to feel sadness for the people who died alone with no-one caring about them or worrying about them. Not even anyone to pick over the pieces and maybe inherit something. Almost insidiously over the years the feeling that Harvey and Lewis were the clients closest relatives crept up on him.

This was the next one. Number eighty six.

Lewis looked along the weed covered and crumbling front path to the front door with its peeling paint and tatty looking door furniture. Scrooge's front door as described in a Christmas Carol came to mind. On the doorstep there was a small collection of empty milk bottles with different levels of green rain water gradually mouldering away inside them. Although the deceased had ceased only a few days before it appeared the bottles had been left uncollected from some, long since, terminated milk round and had, over time, slowly become more of a garden ornament than a grocery item. Harvey and Lewis looked at each other and their hearts sank. Neglect. They just knew that neglect on the outside meant neglect on the inside. How much cleaning and maintenance could a ninety three year old man have been expected to do? How did he even look after himself? It didn't look, from the paper work as though he had any family or friends or they wouldn't be here. It didn't look as though he had any help at all. As they climbed from their van and walked up the path for the initial inspection they braced themselves. Even after five years the first exposure could still be a shock. Standing in their new white coveralls, slightly misting up their goggles and sweating into their heavy duty protective gloves they drew a breath and prepared to go in.

Harvey took the key from the plastic wallet attached to the clipboard and slid it into the lock. It turned easily enough and he pushed the door gently open. He had to lean on the door to make it move pushing back whatever was leaning against the door. As it opened a familiar smell hit him. A smell of neglect. Fusty, damp, mouldy, dirty and old but at least not a smell of death. No windows had obviously been opened for years. The air inside could have been the same air that blew in fifty years ago and circulated round and round ever since never escaping.

They stepped over the pile of leaflets from the take away pizza parlours, Chinese and Indian take aways and looked down the long and high hallway. Floor to ceiling there were boxes in various stages of collapse. Some were split with bits and pieces of bags all seemingly stuffed with papers and the odd dead spider spilling out onto what used to be a carpet. As they went in the boxes seemed to lean into the hallway narrowing the width and creating an arch meaning only one person at a time could walk down the hallway and even then they would have had to hunch their shoulders if they were anything over five feet tall. A thick film of dust had settled everywhere and the pattern on the excuse for a carpet had been obliterated. Between gaps in the boxes a high level shelf could be seen displaying plates and books held together by cob webs, grime and dust.

They inched down the hall through the teetering piles wary that they might collapse at any minute and peered into the front room which was presumed to be a gloomy sitting room as that was all it could be. To call it a living room would have been a travesty as it was more like a suspended animation room. Something from a long deserted movie set. Piles of boxes and papers tied with coarse string lined the walls some two of three boxes thick. Against one wall was a sofa but it was loaded with boxes as was the low table in the centre of the room. On this boxes were arranged almost artistically into a tall thin pyramid meeting just below a dusty light fitting. There was no other furniture other than a single, rather comfortable looking even though dusty, wing backed chair in the corner. Around it were some newspapers scattered about as though the person reading them had just dropped them and walked out of the room. Light battled to get through the grimy windows but was almost beaten by the equally grimy net curtains. The only chance was for the light to squeeze through the holes in the curtains but then it only managed to light the gently swirling dust in the thick, static atmosphere of the room. Harvey was worried that the chair had been where the man's body had been found so he checked his clipboard again. Bodies tended to attract maggots when they were left to decompose and if there was one thing that Harvey could not abide it was maggots. With some relief he noted the body had been found in the kitchen.

"You carry on down here and I'll go and check upstairs," said Lewis.

The two split up and as Lewis inched back along the hall to the foot of the stairs he tried to climb them without disturbing the boxes piled to the sides. He heard Harvey trying to push his way into the large back room with a high ceiling and long windows looking over a quite large and very overgrown garden. It might have been used as a dining room as the only piece of furniture in the room was a large oval, curiously highly polished and very clean oak table. Even the brass decorations on the table legs were polished. No other furniture was in the room.

No chairs. No sideboard. Of course there were the obligatory boxes but they were only two of three high and they did not stretch all around the room. There were no pictures hanging on the walls and nowhere for any pictures or photographs to be displayed. Harvey thought it was odd and recalled there were no pictures next door either, at least none that he could see. There was a worn track of carpet beneath the table and a pair of thin but intact curtains drawn across the window. It all seemed a bit odd but at least there was not too much to clear out and most of it would just go straight to recycling. Maybe an extra big skip for the dust.

Upstairs Lewis was forcing his way into the front bedroom. There were supposed to be three and this was the biggest and he presumed the old man's bedroom. Harvey was pleased that Lewis had volunteered to go upstairs. In his experience the worst room in the house was either the kitchen or the bathroom and he could handle kitchens better. Just as he thought, as he pushed his way into the kitchen he could see all the surfaces piled with rubbish. Empty food containers, tins and bottles were everywhere. The cooker was covered in pots and pans that needed cleaning. The sink was filled with plates and cutlery. Somewhere under the sticky floor must have been some sort of floor covering but it was not immediately apparent what it was unless it was made of some sort of fat. Harvey was pleased he was going to be able to throw the whole lot out and not try to clean it all. He opened all the cupboards and found tins and packets of food, many tea bags and several packets of chocolate biscuits. The fridge also had food in although some of it was no longer the colour it should have been and would probably have moved of its own accord if prodded. Not too bad though. Quite manageable and nothing seemed to be looking at him or moving of its own volition.

As he backed out of the kitchen mentally scheduling the work and calculating how long it was going to take he heard a call from Lewis.

"Harvey, get up here. You're never going to believe this".

SIX

Norman Bay had lived in number eighty six all his life. It had always been warm and, when he was a small child, it always seemed to smell of either cooking or washing depending on which day it was. Monday was always washing day because it was thought the air was cleaner on a Monday because the factories that belched out the dirty, sooty smoke were closed on a Sunday. There was a slim chance the washing could be dried and taken back in cleaner than it had been when it was put out and even when the factories had gone Monday was habitually wash day. Often he had watched his mother with a pinafore tied tightly around her waist and her sleeves rolled up exposing red raw arms as she plunged into and out of the hot water pummelling the dirt out of the clothes. The washing was done by hand or with either a dolly and tub or a copper boiler and wash board with it all going through a hand mangle afterwards to get as much water out as possible before hanging it out to dry. He remembered when the first washing machine had been delivered. For weeks after the machine had been installed his mother would just sit and watch the washing going round not quite believing it was actually washing and not quite knowing what to do with the time it was saving her. To her dying day she maintained that the machine did not clean clothes as well as she had done. Most other days the place smelled of cooking. Mother was a good cook and always cooked things from scratch and it was always delicious. Sundays was always the best with a roast and potatoes. Evenings were spent reading or listening to the radio or watching television. While his mother was alive the house was always a home but after she died it just became a house and the smell of dust had taken over.

Initially the home was part of a small neighbourhood with other houses and people melting into a community. They would pop in and out of each other's houses and his mother was often to be found chatting in the street as folk passed. The small school was always busy as was the church and, of course, the pub. The few shops were essential community hubs where gossip as well as money could be exchanged. He remembered dashing up the street to get a loaf of bread or some milk. Strangely, it always seemed to be sunny and warm. But gradually the people he had known all his life moved away or died and fewer people moved in preferring the new houses on the estates being built around the town. The small amount of industry in the area closed down or was taken over and moved away.

Jobs were lost and so was the community. Gradually the houses that had been built for prosperous families who could afford servants that were housed in the basements or attics became converted into flats as they became too expensive to buy and maintain. The turnover of people increased and it became more difficult to know the neighbours so everyone became rather more isolated.

As Norman got older so the fabric of eighty six deteriorated and it made him sad. The happy, clean and smart house his mother took so much pride in was turning into a dirty, untidy place with an overgrown garden and crumbling façade. He regretted it but knew there was nothing he could do at his age to stop the rot. His was still a complete house with one occupant but it would, eventually, soon, be like all the others and that would be that. Anyway he was far too busy to look after the house even if he could and he had far too many calls on his unique skills and talents to worry about the paint work.

He didn't go out much, only to the grocery shop that was round the corner and stocked everything one could imagine. But he didn't need much just basics, chocolate biscuits and cigarettes, maybe a bit of tea or milk and he was always glad to get back to the house. Even after all his years he could still see Marley's face in the knocker on the front door. It was straight out of Christmas Carol and he was pleased to remember reading it year after year at Christmas time. He reckoned he could see spirits in the hallway as he opened the ghostly door but then, for him of all people, that was not really very surprising. It seemed no time at all since he was a young lad running errands to the shop or running more slowly to school, dashing up and down the wide staircase or playing in the garden.

Now he spent most of his time in the dining room or the back bedroom. Working. There was no such thing as retirement for him although he often wished he could just stop and sit. Take life easy and rest. He so wanted to rest although he was never quite sure what he would do when he did rest. He had never really had any hobbies, no outside interests to keep him busy even if he did retire. But, anyway, there was no chance of that as incidents still kept happening. If anything, more were happening now than when he started working and that was a great concern to him. He had kept a meticulous log over the years and plotted graphs and maps of incidents and they were definitely increasing not only in his area but around the world. Over the years and even before he had taken up the tasks file after file had been filled and carefully indexed and stored on the shelves. Maps had been pinned up and incidents highlighted so much so that the plaster beneath the wall paper had started to come away. Paper cuttings had been removed from the newspapers and journals he had collected and he had equally fastidiously filed and catalogued them all. Because he knew that the reports in the newspapers were often not accurate or did not display the real causes and reasons for the incidents he had resolved, many years ago, to keep all the papers just in case he had to refer back to them. He was well aware that the journalists who were recording the incidents could not possibly have known what was actually going on and it was partly Norman's job to make sure that they never actually found out. The almost obsessive storage of the papers had paid off on the odd occasion when there had occurred some otherwise hidden coincidences. But he frequently wrestled with himself wanting desperately to clear the house of some of the piles of papers that were becoming dangerous and restricting but he just could not bring himself to clear them. Not yet. Not today. Maybe tomorrow.

At least he did not have to travel so much now. Although he had enjoyed the travelling in his youth it was always becoming so much more difficult and the hustle and bustle of the trains, the overcrowding and pace was just becoming too much. Because he had been away so often and for so long in the early days it meant he had never really made any friends in the area much less met anyone to marry and have a family with. One of his regrets was that he never had any children and no-one to hand the business on to but it was way too late now. But at least he had a succession plan and could leave the travelling to Wil and he could concentrate on the paper work. Hopefully, Wil would take over the whole business when the time came.

There always seemed so much to do and more needed doing as time passed. Irritatingly it always seemed to take longer to do what was needed to be done now. Even the trips up and down the stairs took longer and the, now indispensable, afternoon naps became longer. When he remembered he needed a break he would fix himself something to eat in the kitchen. Fortunately he had the appetite of an anorexic gnat and his stomach had long ago accepted that any meals it did get would be small, unconventional, badly prepared from whatever was about and highly irregular. With a plate of something just about edible but probably unrecognisable he would go and sit in the front room in his favourite chair reminiscing or just day dreaming thinking about his situation and trying not to fear for the future. He would often think of the world outside and the role he had played in it for the last nine decades and treat himself to too many chocolate biscuits as he thumbed through paper after paper in case there was something he had missed.

On the whole Eastbourne had been good to him. He had heard all the jokes about it being God's waiting room and that people would retire there to die and then forget why they went there. It was an attractive town and, when he was younger, he had often walked along the promenade taking tea in one of the little cafes and maybe a chip supper on the pier. He would watch the day trippers and holiday makers doing the same thinking how lucky he was to have all this on his doorstep and how horrible it would be to be stuck in a little flat in London especially on a warm summer day. He often thought to himself how little people who said it was God's waiting room knew and what they would say if they knew the truth.

SEVEN

While Harvey and been looking downstairs Lewis had been through the front and second bedrooms and they had been much the same as the sitting room. They had a warm, dusty feel to them. The walls covered in boxes of papers, the carpets rather worn and tatty. Only the bed in the front room was made up and that was not very appealing. Presumably where the old man slept. There was a cupboard and small chest of drawers in the front room but there were very few clothes in them. Looked like the old man was not a follower of fashion. Unless it was the fashions of the fifties. There were a couple of photographs of, presumably, his mother on the chest and a small glass bowl with cufflinks, a watch, a couple of expired credit cards and some cash and a pair of bicycle clips collecting dust on the bottom. There was a small gas fire with a walking stick leaning against the wooden mantel piece and a small bedside table with an electric alarm clock and radio. It was all very sparse and dated but felt curiously comfortable.

But the back bedroom. Well that was something else and it was what had prompted the call down to Harvey. The room was absolutely immaculate. There was no carpet but the wooden floor was clean and polished and creaked warmly as it supported the weight of his feet as he walked into the room. The walls were covered in a neutral patterned wall paper and the ceiling was a clean whitish colour. Pale cream curtains hung down either side of clean windows and the light in the centre of the ceiling was clean. In one corner there was an old but simple desk again highly polished and clean with wooden trays holding piles of paper balanced to each side of a writing area. On this there were scattered pens and pencils, rules, envelopes, pads of lined paper and graph paper. Each pedestal had three drawers with polished brass handles and in the knee well a wicker basket with what looked like many chocolate biscuit and Kit Kat wrappers in it. To one side was a well-used high backed swivel wooden chair with a red leather seat cover and a battered looking red velvet cushion. Obviously not that comfortable but the worn varnish on the arms attested to its heavy use.

Along two of the walls were three shelves. On the bottom two were rows of neatly arranged box folders all neatly catalogued with letters and numbers. They did not appear to be in any sort of order and they were obviously from different periods of time with ornately labelled files at one end passing through time to new, modern folders at the other end. On the top shelf were rows of books in no particular order but many of them looked very old with most being leather bound with faded gold lettering on them. One thing that was not on the shelves though was dust. Clean as the day they were put up and they even smelled of polish.

Against the other wall was pushed a table with a couple of small wooden boxes on top but what took Lewis's eye were the charts pinned to the wall with unusually large shiny, brass tacks. Some seemed to show a collection of haphazard lines with tables of numbers down the sides and other tables and scribbles on pieces of paper randomly pinned around them. One, in particular, grabbed his attention and that was a rather old Ordinance Survey map of Eastbourne and East Sussex. It also had marks all over it. Some crosses, some circles, some numbers and other stars all in different colours. Down one side was a number of post it notes with writing and numbers on. As he was looking at the map Harvey came into the room.

"Hells teeth," exclaimed Harvey "look at this room. Is this different or what?"

"It's something else isn't it? Look at the files, look at the charts and maps. It's immaculate and not just a little bit weird".

Harvey walked into the room half expecting the old man to follow him in. He went over to the table and started picking up the boxes that were on it. Inside them were what looked like some sort of scientific instruments, technical drawing kit or things with an unknown function. Some just looked empty. He had not the slightest idea what they were for but they looked old and very interesting.

"God knows what these are for but it looks as though they might be worth something. Wonder what they are. Any ideas?"

"Not a clue," said Lewis "but this is not just any old house if you ask me."

Harvey walked over to Lewis and looked at the map of Sussex. His attention was drawn to a red circle that had been drawn several times. He looked closely at it and recognised the area as being that of the Long Man in Wilmington, just outside of Eastbourne.

"I don't know what is going on here," said Lewis "but I think we need to get this place checked out before we do anything".

"Good idea. But who would we get?"

Lewis had the measure of most of the management of his department and he was pretty certain no-one would have a clue about all this. All they would do is dismiss it and tell him to get on and clear the place. It was an old, empty house that needed to be cleared out and cleared off their books. There were targets to be met you know.

After a few minutes thought Lewis came up with an idea.

"I know. There was a girl I worked with when I was at the local museum for a while. She knew quite a bit about the local area perhaps she could shed some light on all this. I'll give her a call".

"OK, while you're doing that I'll phone in to the office and tell them it is going to take a while to sort out the mess here so we will need another day or two. Should give us some time".

EIGHT

Lottie Bridge had helped out at the Eastbourne museum in her vacations while she was at university but since graduating with a slightly disappointing 2:1 she had worked there full time for almost two years. She was a local girl, born and bred in Old Town, and had read Religious Studies and History at Durham university with a view to eventually moving away from Eastbourne to a city with a bigger museum and better prospects. After she had graduated she decided not to travel the world much to her parent's relief and moved back home with her degree certificate and a large student debt. The plan such as it was, was to use the family home as a cheap base from which to apply for the jobs that would pay off her debts and get her started in the world.

The first part had worked well but she recognised she was getting rather too comfortable in the cheap base and with the easy availability of her old school friends, who were doing much the same thing. She enjoyed a jolly social life but the student debt was not going down and the savings were not going up. Applications for jobs ever more outlandish and further removed from her planned trajectory were sent but she did not get to follow them out of the home so she had stayed and made herself happy at the museum while she waited. Although it was only supposed to be temporary Lottie found herself getting more and more interested in her little seaside town and she made the most of her enforced residence. She might be treading water but at least it was interesting water and her head was high above it. That's the attitude.

With her background of religious studies she was often given tasks relating to local churches and she was planning an exhibition of them and their history. She had spent a lot of time researching her local stamping ground of Old Town frequently cursing the local planners who had decimated the historic area when they widened the unfeasibly narrow Church and High Street. All that had been left was the Napoleonic Cavalry barracks that were used between 1809 and 1815 until they became part of the old St Mary's Union Workhouse and then the now demolished St Mary's hospital. Further down the street was the Lamb Inn which must have been as much of a welcoming sight for the cavalrymen or the horse carriage passengers coming across from Brighton and heading for the ports. Lottie had also frequented the pub frequently, sometimes with her history research hat on and to that end she had been able to explore its cellars which were built In 1180 and the subterranean passage used for monks to move from the crypt under the old coaching inn to the Old Parsonage. Or was it used for smuggling? Then there was her favourite, St Mary the Virgin church which she had spent many hours visiting and collecting information. Originally dedicated to St Michael it had been built in the 12th century with Caen stone from Normandy, curiously where her great uncle had been killed in World War 2. There had been much discussion about the size of the church when it was built being unusually large for the potential congregation and then there had been the interesting graffiti found around the church which posed more questions than they solved. By the fourteenth century a square tower had been added which Lottie had spent time observing sitting under what was claimed to be the oldest tree in Eastbourne, a yew tree, in the churchyard. Eastbourne's parish church was definitely to be the centre piece for her upcoming and break through exhibition. But then the phone rang.

When the call from Lewis came she had been trying to visualise the exhibition, making sketches and listing titles for displays working out how to make it interesting enough to pack the crowds in and make her name. The Great Exhibition it would not be but it would be a great exhibition. All being well.

She had met Lewis in the Dolphin pub one lunchtime after spending time in the Town Hall. Technically, both being local government employees they felt they had something in common if only the feeling of being exploited and taken for granted by an uncaring management. Since then they had met a few times and stayed friends. He knew a bit about the history of Eastbourne and had learned plenty more while researching his family tree. He was an out and out Eastbournian with a tree stretching back to the founding of the town itself and beyond back into Kent where many of the residents of Eastbourne had come from as the town grew. He was as keen to learn from her as she was to learn from him. Nevertheless the call and especially the content came as a bit of a surprise to

Lottie because she was pretty sure Lewis's job was rather tedious and uninteresting not to mention dirty and disgusting but from what he was telling her this sounded different and she was intrigued.

Making an excuse to her supervisor, who seemed less than interested in anything Lottie did, or what he did for that matter, about having to go and research a local church she slipped out of the office and made her way on her bicycle to the old man's house. When she got there the front door was ajar so she pushed it open and ventured in. Being a little shorter than Harvey and Lewis she almost easily squeezed herself into the hall and hearing voices upstairs she made her way to the staircase. As she made her way up to the next floor she suddenly felt a little bit apprehensive and was pleased to see Lewis and Harvey on the landing waiting for her. Lewis had not really explained what he had found, partly because he could not, and all she knew was that the old man had recently died in the house. Maybe she had seen too many horror films but strange empty houses and recent deaths often seemed to bode ill for the rest of the people. Why did people go into haunted houses without turning the lights on? Why did they go into them at all? There was always a monster of serial killer behind the next corner. Please do not let there be a cellar. Trying not to brush against any of the boxes, disturb any of the dust or think of vampires she walked towards the men and as she entered the back room she stopped and her mouth fell open. This was not what she was expecting at all.

"Wow, this is incredible. Is the rest of the house like this?"

"No, the rest of the house is nothing like this. It is more like the hall and stairs and best not mention the kitchen," replied Harvey. "This room and the dining room downstairs are very different to the rest and the one down stairs is quite empty except for a single table. No charts, maps or paperwork or anything like there is up here."

She looked around the room in a state of wonderment. Lewis and Harvey looked at her in a state of expectation.

"Well, what do you make of it?" enquired Harvey.

"It's incredible," she repeated. "It looks like a really elaborate, fantastic museum display". She walked around the room touching the boxes on the table and opening some. She looked closely at the box files and especially the books taking one or two out and quickly leafing through the pages. When satisfied she went over to the desk. "It looks almost as though the man just put down his pens and walked out of the room". Slightly spooking herself she looked towards the door almost expecting the man to walk back in and start work again.

"It's all so neat and tidy. I would be impressed if this was a museum exhibition but I presume this is where the old man," she hesitated not really knowing what he did but continued "worked. If what he was doing was actually work. Perhaps it was some sort of hobby".

She walked slowly round the room looking at the maps and charts occasionally lifting a note to see underneath or to read what was written on it. Back at the boxes she picked each one up and opened it looking inside.

"What is in all these files? What do all these charts mean?" she asked still slowly walking past them and staring at them.

"We hoped you were going to be able to tell us that," said Lewis with a slight hint of impatience. He was the one with all the questions and was hoping Lottie was the one with all the answers. "We only got here an hour or two ago", he looked quickly at his watch to check, "maybe a bit less so all we have done is look at all this. We really don't know what to do with it."

She stopped by the OS map pinned on the wall. It looked the most familiar and at least she recognised the area. She pointed to the area where the house was and then traced a line towards an area of the map that had obviously been touched more than other areas. Around it there were several tables of numbers pinned to the chart and quite a few lines coming from it and pointing around the rest of the map.

"This looks as though it was important to someone for some reason," she deduced. "Look at all the marks here".

Harvey and Lewis dutifully looked but did not really understand any significance.

Looking a bit more closely she said "It's Wilmington. The Long Man. Wonder why that was so important?"

"Maybe he liked to walk there. Perhaps it was his favourite spot," Harvey said trying to be helpful. "Why would an area like that be important?"

"Get away, he was ninety something years old and it looks as though he could barely walk to the end of the garden let alone the Long Man".

"Maybe, but why are there so many lines around the area and what do all these numbers mean? It doesn't look like a hikers map and, anyway, if he was local he would know the area, he wouldn't need a map would he? Anyway, how old did you say he was?"

"Around 90," Harvey said.

"You're right I don't think the average 90 year old is going to be trekking up the Long Man. Have you seen how steep the hill is?" she asked rhetorically.

"What is the Long man supposed to be anyway?" asked Lewis thinking he should know the answer really as he had seen it often enough.

"It's a bloody great hill carving of a man with two poles," chipped in Harvey helpfully.

"Well, yes it is that" agreed Lottie "but it is a lot more than that. Did you know it was the largest man made hill carving in the world? I think I am right in saying the next largest is in Cerne Abbas in Wiltshire. No-one knows who carved it or why they carved it or why they carved it where they did".

"Maybe they had time on their hands," chipped in Harvey hoping to be helpful again and failing.

"One legend goes that the carving was representing the Saxon God of Peace and the poles that he was holding were the gates to Vastrand which was the Saxon version of Hades," Lottie delved deeply back into her memories surprised that she could remember this but also surprised that she needed to.

"So he is holding the gates to hell in his hands," Lewis tried to confirm "that would be handy next to Eastbourne. And there was me thinking the gates of hell were actually the doors into the council offices".

"Yes. There are other representations of the figures holding the gates to hell but often the poles have been lost or covered over so the picture has been lost but this one is still intact. He was seen as the gateway to the other world".

"Right, so this old boy had a fascination with the Saxon gates of hell. Big deal." Harvey was happy to take the story at face value and get on with the job at hand.

"Yes," Lottie said slowly still peering at the map and the lists of numbers "but I think there is more to it than that. Let's have a look at the rest of the things a bit more closely". She was getting excited by the find. She had no idea what it all meant but felt it must mean something and maybe she could find out what it was. Whatever, she was going to have a damn good try.

NINE

Norman's last trip had only been a couple of months ago and he had only taken it because it had been in Tunbridge Wells, not far from home, and because his "assistant" Rod Mills had been there to drive him. Rod was a very distant relative. The sort who was actually more of a distant family friend of an aunt long forgotten who occasionally looked in on Norman to see if he was alright. He would give him lifts if he needed to go to the hospital or to the doctors and would occasionally bring him round a take away. Norman was particularly fond of a nice Chinese take away. Rod had never shown the slightest interest in what Norman got up to and Norman had quickly given up the idea that Rod might take over from him when the time came. Nevertheless he had his uses and today was to be one when he would be useful.

After it was over he experienced the same feelings he had felt after all the other incidents. Hearing the door shut behind Rod as he left Norman had slumped down in his chair at the small desk in the back room with a very weak cup of tea and a handful of chocolate biscuits and started to write the account of the incident. Over the years he had written up accounts of many of his experiences and even written several treatises on the subject. They were not for general publication but purely for others in the business to learn from.

In the early days it was all pen and ink and although he had progressed to a type writer he had never got to grips with computers. When each account was written if was filed in one of the growing numbers of box files. Occasionally, when Norman had time he would sort them and have them bound in a ledger. On the top shelf was his collection of books which he had accumulated over the years and they stretched back through the centuries and must have been the most comprehensive account and record of incidents through history as well as explanations and theories. They were written in Latin, French, old English and a couple of them in languages long forgotten but all were fascinating and Norman would often leaf back through them marvelling at the artistry of some of the accounts, the beautiful writing and illustrations in some. Many were so magnificent he felt embarrassed at the comparatively tatty type written and un-illuminated pages he collated. He often would try to imagine the circumstances that had caused them to be written and he would think about the people who were doing then what he was still doing now and how they tried to understand and explain what was happening. Perhaps it was all so much easier then when the church had so much power and scientific theory had yet to be invented.

He had been reading one of the old accounts on that day and it was as he read that he began to feel the now all too familiar feeling rising up inside of him. It was almost a different sense, a sixth sense, a bit like that attributed to dogs when they can sense danger or to twins if they think the other twin is in danger or having problems. It wasn't an unpleasant feeling but he did know it meant there was a problem on the horizon. It never occurred unless there was a problem. Sighing slightly he carefully closed the book he was reading and replaced it on the shelf and then walked over to the table. Taking the largest of the polished wooden boxes he went downstairs to the back room and placing it on the round table he flicked down the brass latch and opened it. Inside the wooden box there was thick, red velvet padding that protected a smaller brass box. This was covered in intricate carvings and filigree work. It was very old and quite worn in places through frequent handling but it still looked very impressive. He gently lifted it out of the padding and put if down on the table and closed the wooden box.

Holding the lid between thumb and fore finger he gently opened the lid supporting it all the way back until the hinge bulged gently as it took the weight of the lid. At first glance the box appeared to be empty but on closer examination there was a black plate just below the rim of the box. It had the appearance of a magician's box. As he looked into the box the plate appeared to be at the top and the bottom at the same time. The box was simultaneously full and empty. Norman reached into the lid of the box and took a small brass flask that was attached to a clip by a short, thin chain. Very gently he flipped open the flask and sprinkled a little powder across the black plate. Snapping the lid closed he replaced the flask in the lid.

For a moment nothing happened but then, just as iron filings move when a magnet is drawn across them the grains of powder moved across the plate. This continued for a minute or two and then the grains stopped. Norman peered at them long and hard. He was pretty skilled at interpreting the patterns but it still took time and he needed to be right. He often felt he was only a step away from being a necromancer studying the entrails of dead animals to try to divine a message. He could see himself in ancient Greece, in Delphi, looking for hidden messages in the warm guts of a goat spilled on the hot, dusty ground. The trick with this was to let the eyes focus deep into the box which seemed bottomless looking past the grains until everything became clear. And it duly did.

The message was a sort of code, a cross between a grid reference and a location description. To the untutored eye, even if they could see a message, they would see a mixture of what appeared to be different shapes a bit like the tea leaves when fortune telling from a used cup of tea. Norman had taken paper and pens from his desk and he noted down the symbols he could see. He knew they were actually symbols from an ancient language and not random characters. It was highly complex and even Norman was not entirely fluent. He often had to refer to his books to work out the meaning.

Happy that he had divined the entire message he very gently wiped the grains of powder from the plate ensuring that it was perfectly clean. As he did he could not help smiling to himself that although Rod had tried many times to explain e mail and blue tooth to him and tried to get him to use them he actually had a communication device that was far, far more powerful than anything that had been invented recently. This was old, so very old and it did not need electricity or satellites and Rod would never understand it and he never got spam or a weak signal and he didn't need a password. The fact that Norman did not know how it actually worked either was of no consequence. He just needed to know that it did work.

Gently closing the lid he put the brass box back inside the wooden one and took it and his writing back upstairs. After consulting a couple of his reference books he decided he had worked the message out and he wrote it in English on a yellow post it note and pinned it to his map. This time it was Tunbridge Wells but there was little information about the incident

He called down to Rod who had been trying to bring some order to the kitchen and he rushed outside to start the car and they set off. So keen was Norman's sense and so accurate his interpretations they often got to the location before anyone else and so it was in this case. But in this case it was because it was not the first time they had been to the same location. Although incidents could happen anywhere they were most likely to happen in areas of inherent weakness and this was such an area. Rocks were frequently featured in incidents. The best known, of course but for other reasons, was Ayres rock or Uluru in Australia but in England there were places like Avebury, a mystical set of stones in Wiltshire, which Norman had visited more than once in his life. There was Stonehenge and other man made stone edifices like the Easter Island heads but there were other natural rock formations one being close to Norman being Beachy Head. Of course these had come and gone over the millennia but right now Beachy Head was a strong source of incidents and was a strong magnet to some. It was fortunate that most of the areas of weakness were somewhat remote and people were rarely involved but with the advent of skyscrapers and ever larger monumental buildings the danger was that they would come to act in the same way as natural rocks and it had to be only a matter of time until they did. In fact there were theories that some of the ancient "lost" cities all had large, usually religious building, often pyramids and they had been the source of the problem that caused the populations to disappear.

This time though a single human had been affected. A climber exploring the rocks had become wedged in a narrow gap just like the American guy they had made a film about. This one though had not been completely trapped. The gap he had been trying to squeeze through was not quite large enough and to get out the man had started to unclip the climbing paraphernalia about his waist dropping it to the bottom of the rocks but during the process he had died. Until he had been rescued and investigated no-one would know why he had died. It might have been a heart attack or panic attack brought on by being trapped. Norman, though, had other thoughts.

Norman had sensed the rupture instantly and the drive had taken less than an hour so it was likely the person had died minutes before Norman and Rod had arrived. Norman got to work. It would only take minutes to get the process started but resolving it could take some time and they would do that back at home. The incident was relatively small so they did not need to hang around. It was much easier when there were no people involved but that was not going to be the case this time. Norman used his mobile phone to alert the rescue services just before they arrived. He did not want to be hanging round when they arrived and closed off the roads getting them stuck for hours. He had to be careful not to keep using the same mobile phone in case it was traced. It was much easier back in the phone box days but now even if you could find one it was generally just a box with the phone having gone long ago and been replaced with graffiti, books or pot plants neither of which were much use in an emergency .

As they drove back to Eastbourne they heard the local radio news saying there were huge traffic jams in Tunbridge Wells as rescue services were recovering a body from the rocks. They appealed for the person who had contacted the services about the body to come forward and that the initial cause of death was thought to be a heart attack.

Norman was pleased to hear the cause of death had been put down to a heart attack. At least that explanation would not disturb all the other residents of Tunbridge Wells.

TEN

The giant catamaran could have been on dry land for all the movement there was. The Aegean was calm, flat calm. Not a breath of wind disturbed the surface. Not so much as a ripple was to be seen. Wil sat on the top rung of the short aluminium ladder that led down from the left hull into the crystal clear blue sea. It seemed almost pointless that he should be sitting weighed down with two oxygen cylinders on his back and a mask that was already hurting his ears and giving him a headache when he could almost see the bottom of the sea, some twenty feet below him, from where he was sitting. Why go to all the bother of diving when he could sit warm and dry on the step watching the fish swimming below him. But he was keen to get back into the water even if it was only to get out of the heat of the sun. He sucked in a few last deep breaths of the warm, lavender scented Greek air with his face set towards the sun. Prepared he climbed down the steps as best he could trying not to look too ungainly gradually immersing himself in the warm water. Letting go of the bottom step he pushed himself away from the boat sucking on his respirator and trying to adjust the pinching face mask. He floated for a moment or two before pushing his head below the surface and kicking down towards the rocks on the bottom of the sea bed.

Greece had always been his favourite holiday spot. He had done most of the islands and a lot of the mainland. He could not get enough of it. It had always seemed so peaceful, the people were a joy, the history interesting and stimulating and he loved the dramatic scenery. Blue never seemed as blue as in Greece and the light just made everything special.

While sitting on the deck of the boat he had looked towards the thin ribbon of land that separated the blues of the sea and the sky. He could just see the row of harbour side taverns in which he had spent rather too much of his time looking out towards the catamarans, one of which, he was now on. In his mind he could see the characters from the Ray Harryhausen movies like Jason and the Argonauts that had so influenced his view of Greece. Even without closing his eye he could see the mythical giants walking through the sea and out from behind the rocky headlands. An imaginary trireme sailed round the spit of land a bright white sail helping the rows of oarsmen pushing the ship through the water. Gods looked down from their thrones on Mount Olympus onto their feeble subjects dashing about on the land. It was a country swathed in myth and mystery. Gods and heroes stalked every inch with one just out of sight around every corner. Adventure and history everywhere. Wil loved it.

Initially he had almost felt a bit guilty leaving Norman alone with no local help especially as the numbers of incidents seemed to be increasing but he knew Norman could cope and there were always others not too far away. He also knew that Norman knew more about the subject and had more experience than he could ever get so he reassured himself that all would be well. He also relied on the fact that he and Norman seemed to have an almost telepathic connection. It was almost as though they were twins. Twins with the best part of sixty years between them but twins indeed. The only niggle was that Norman was getting really old now and a bit less capable.

So it was that he slipped beneath the surface in a cloud of bubbles.

It was as Wil descended, gently kicking with his feet that Norman had first felt the stabbing in his chest. Norman did not eat a great deal so he was rarely to be found in the kitchen. Reasoning that he did not eat much and only used a few pieces of cutlery he also rarely needed to wash up or put stuff away so the surfaces were always cluttered. Making tea, an essential lubricant, though was always a good excuse for stepping away from his work and so it was today. The kettle was boiling and he was looking towards the sink of washing up hoping to see an empty and half clean cup. Now was not the time to be thinking about doing the washing preferring instead to delay it until tomorrow. Much better to free a couple of chocolate biscuits to have with the tea. He looked up quickly and stared out of the window with a frown spreading across his forehead. He grabbed at the pain that seared into his chest hoping to seize it and throw it away. His knees gave way slightly and he grabbed at the side of the sink to steady himself. But the pain stayed and his expression changed. He screwed up his eyes and ground his teeth together as the pain gradually took over his heart and then stopped it. Within seconds he had released his grip on the sink and he had fallen to the ground. His facial muscles relaxed and his mouth fell slightly open. Seconds later he had passed across the partition he had so diligently guarded all his life. As Norman grabbed at his heart Wil was running his hands over the smooth pebbles on the bottom of the sea but immediately the warm sea around him suddenly felt cold. He needed to breath faster and copious numbers of bubbles rose lazily to the surface. He tried to stand on the sea bed and then pushed himself to rise to the surface. Something was wrong but, as yet, he was oblivious to the drama that was unfolding at number eighty six.

ELEVEN

Wil started to get even more concerned as he looked down onto the south coast bathed in early morning sunshine. From his window seat in the plane he could see far out to sea and far inland as the plane banked, turned and descended slowly over the South Downs on its way into Gatwick airport. Brighton, Newhaven, Eastbourne then north to Tunbridge Wells and Crawley it all seemed so familiar. He never usually bothered to keep in contact with Norman when he was away but since getting back on board the boat from his dive he had phoned dozens of times and never received an answer. Something was badly wrong and he gently cursed Norman for not having any other form of communication although he feared that Norman was not going to be contactable on anything. He really wanted to get his mobile out and try one more time as if being closer might have helped but he felt he was under the beady eye of the cabin crew who were just waiting for him to reach into his pocket and tick him off.

The circling, landing and taxiing to the hard stand seemed to take forever although not as long as it took to walk the long interminable corridors of the terminal. Up this one, down that one, up that escalator, down that one, along that travellator, follow that sign, turn here, another turn there and eventually spew out into the giant passport control hall with the hundreds of folk who had all arrived at the same time from all over the world. Frustration as the queue he joined always became the slowest one and the person in front of him was always the one who could not work out the right way to insert their passport into the electronic reader and needed help from the officer who was always at the other end of the line. The urge to line jump was almost unbearable but Wil knew very well that as soon as he joined another line it would grind to a halt and the one he left would accelerate. Baggage claim, thank heavens for hand luggage, and then through the ominous and slightly intimidating but, seemingly always deserted, green channel and out into the real world again politely turning down all the offers of a squirt of this or that scent from the trade stands situated along the walk way. Why did people buy huge sticks of Toblerone at the airport anyway? At each point he had tried to phone Norman who, Wil knew, was an early riser but he got no response. Nothing. He was getting more and more worried. That had been a couple of days when Norman had not answered. It was not like him.

Out of the airport buildings and onto the railway platform he waited and waited, pacing nervously and impatiently frequently checking the destination board mounted high above the platform and then his watch, until the long dirty train crawled into the station. Late as usual. Normally he mentally checked the numbers of competitors for seats standing on the platform but on this day he would not have cared if he stood for the hour's journey to Eastbourne. He waited and waited some more, then thankful to have beaten the rest of the swarm he flopped into an empty seat. The train loitered its way to the coast seemingly stopping at every group of five or more houses just in case someone wanted to get on or off. Eventually it pulled into Eastbourne station and Wil dashed for the taxi rank. One waiting. Miracle. Wil jumped in.

As the cab neared eighty six Wil looked at the plain blue van parked outside the house and the bicycle leaning against it. He did not recognise it and it did not have any markings on the sides. It must have had something to do with the house because there was nothing else around and he could not see any people on the ground near to the van.

Lewis and Harvey looked at each other when they heard the key slide into the lock and the front door swing open.

"Who the heck is that?" asked Harvey rather pointlessly but hoping it was not the management coming to check up on them. Lewis shrugged his shoulders and Lottie kept on looking through the books at the seemingly incomprehensible figures. Norman looked on as well but no-one saw him.

Wil called out "Norman. Norman are you about? It's me, Wil. I've been calling you. Where are you?"

Harvey looked over the hand rail down into the hallway.

Seeing a face through a small gap in the papers and hearing footsteps on the wooden floor Wil called up "who the hell are you? What are you doing here? Where is Norman?"

"I'm sorry but who are you?" countered Harvey.

"Never mind who I am, who are you", this was not getting very far "where's Norman?"

Harvey came down the stairs and reached into his pocket for his identity card. He showed it to Wil.

"I work for the council. Did you know Mr Bay?"

"What do you mean did I know Mr Bay? Of course I know him. Where is he?"

"Well I am afraid I have some bad news for you. Mr Bay was found dead the other day and we have been called in by the council to check the place for information about Mr Bay and then, if needs be, to clear the place out".

"What happened?"

"I am not really sure but I think he was found in the kitchen after having a heart attack".

"Oh my God," said Wil clamping his hand over his forehead and then scraping it back across his head flattening his hair as it went to the back of his neck. He knew he shouldn't be so shocked after all Norman was getting on a bit but as well was being shocked he was angry that he had not been there for Norman when he needed him. The trip to Greece suddenly seemed such a waste of time. He quickly started worrying about the future as well.

"So what are you doing here then?"

By now Lewis had joined Harvey in the hallway. "Like I said we are here to check up on any relatives or friends that can sort out the estate and arrange a burial. If there are none then we take an inventory of everything that is here and arrange for the house to be cleared and everything to be disposed of or sold. Although we are a bit stuck identifying some of the things Mr Bay had here. Are you a relative?"

"No, no I am not a blood relative but I guess I was the closest to Norman. We used to work together quite a lot. There is probably a will around somewhere and you will probably find that I am named as executor and sole beneficiary if that is any help. He didn't have any family".

"Yes, that would certainly help if you know where it might be. What did you work as?" asked Lewis hoping it might throw some light on the back room.

"We did some investigation work," Wil said deliberately being a bit vague. He looked around a bit more, looking into the front room seeing all the boxes still piled up. Nothing looked as though it had been disturbed. He looked upstairs.

"Have you cleared anything from upstairs yet?" Will asked.

"No sir we haven't. We haven't cleared anything yet. To be honest we were a bit flummoxed about what we found".

"Have you been in the rooms upstairs?"

"Yes we have. One of our team is up there now. It's all a bit," he hesitated, "a bit queer isn't it. Do you know what it is all about?"

"I do," and Wil, not looking at them pushed past and headed up the stairs not offering any more information. Harvey and Lewis followed.

As he went into the back room Lottie looked up.

"What are you doing in here?" asked Wil with a little more impatience and urgency in his voice.

Lottie looked startled and past Wil to see if Lewis and Harvey were following

"Look, I'm sorry I don't know your name," started Lewis.

"It's Kingdon, Wil Kingdon," as he moved over to the desk.

"So Mr Kingdon, as I said Harvey and I were called into the house and we got here a few hours ago. We looked around downstairs and only found loads of boxes of papers and documents except in the dining room where there was just the table. Then we came up here assuming it was just a normal old house with a load of clutter only to find this." He gestured sweeping an arm in a semi-circle in front of him. "This is not a normal old room is it?"

"Well you're right there," acknowledged Wil.

"Because we did not know what it was all about we called in Lottie here," pointing to where she was standing still with an old book in her hand. "She works for the local museum and we thought she might be able to explain some of this".

"But I don't think I can," chipped in Lottie. "Can you?"

Wil ignored her and looked around the room seemingly checking things that he expected to be there were there. It all seemed to be in order. "So that's your van and bike outside the house is it?"

"Yes", replied Harvey.

"You haven't moved anything or thrown anything out have you?" he asked Harvey and Lewis.

"No, nothing has been moved. It is all where we found it except a few files of dust. Because we did not know what it was we thought we had better leave it until we found out more about it. We haven't reported it to the council yet because they, like as not, would just tell us to clear it whatever it is. We are more used to old sofas and televisions. Not this".

The attempt at humour was lost on Wil but he did feel grateful that nothing had been lost.

"Can you explain what it is all about?"

"I can, but I doubt that you would believe me. What we really need to do is sort out the council issues and, from my point of view, keep the house going as it is so I can carry on with Norman's work. What can we do?" he asked Lewis.

"Ideally what we want is a will. If we can see one and it states that Norman left everything to you and you can prove who you are then we can just write the job off as completed with no action required and leave it to the legal bods to formalise everything. While they are doing that we can leave everything as it is now. Do you know if he had one, a will that is?"

"I am pretty sure he did. I do know that he regarded me as the next of kin, if you like, perhaps next in line might be a better term and that I was to continue with the work and to do that I would need all the kit that is here in the house. Have you tried looking in the office upstairs?"

Nobody had so they all trooped into the back room and started looking through drawers and folders looking for the will. More than once Lewis hoped to himself that the will, if there was one, was not hidden amongst the papers stored along the walls or hidden in a safe or something behind the piles. If it was they would be there for days.

It did not take long to search all the obvious places in the room but no will was found. The only other place they might consider was the downstairs room and the big round table. Single file they went downstairs again and stood around the table but there did not seem to be any drawers that might contain any paper work.

Wil felt all around the edge of the table looking for anything that might resemble a handle to a secret drawer but after three circuits he had found nothing.

Lottie started prodding the top not really knowing why but just trying to seem as though she was helping. In the centre of the table top there was a small circle of mahogany veneer with what looked like an ivory banding around the edge and some intricate marquetry work inside. She ran her finger around the edge and then lent gently on the centre. It acted as a button and instantly released four drawers from around the edge of the table. They all jumped back as the drawers revealed themselves. Suddenly it all seemed a bit like a scene from the Indiana Jones movies.

Everyone took a drawer each and eagerly rummaged through the paper work and bit and pieces in them. Pens, pencils, paper clips, bits of string, scissors, small boxes of playing cards that came in Christmas crackers all sorts of things that might have come in useful at some time but never did. Bills, letters, scribbled notes, some yellowing with age and some with more scribbles and diagrams, more bills. Small wooden boxes, small bottles, tape measures, rubber bands, drawing pins. Seemingly everything except a will.

"Yes"! Exclaimed Wil eventually. "Here it is, the last will and testament of Norman Bay".

He opened the envelope and took out the single sheet of paper. Unfolding it he quickly scanned the single sided sheet of paper. Sure enough it simply stated that the house and all its contents would be left to Wil. It was properly signed and dated and, to Lewis, looked quite legitimate.

"Great, then we need do no more. We can nip back to the office and say that everything is in order and needs no interference from us".

Harvey looked up and asked "but I would like to know what is going on and maybe even try to understand what mister Bay was doing," he looked at Wil hopefully.

"Me too", chimed in Lottie.

"Not quite sure why but me too", added Lewis.

Wil looked at each of them and thought deeply. He could perhaps do with some help at the very least to get the house sorted out and then maybe, just maybe, they could help him with his other work. "Ok then what about if we meet up here again in, say a week or two and we can discuss what we have found, I can give you some back ground information and we can plot a way forward. What do you think?"

Everyone agreed and they arranged to meet the following week.

TWELVE

Town was never going to win any civic or architectural prizes. It was not a pretty town. It was an industrial town through and through. Even in the pale, soft morning light that should have made anywhere look pretty it was ugly. Hard, grey and ugly even for a far eastern European town. The fact that it was a large town squeezed tightly into a space suitable only for a small town did not help. The hills that towered over the town meant that the space into which new buildings could be shoe horned was strictly limited. The steepness of the sides meant building only took place on the valley floor except for the desperate or crazy who perched unsubstantial buildings on even less substantial legs trying to get a foot hold in the steep hill sides. Inside the houses they hoped for no landslips and that the concrete and steel in the legs would resist the corrosive atmosphere but even that gamble was limited. This meant that the buildings in the valley itself were almost Victorian in their overcrowding. Back to back, side by side two up and two down with small back yards and steep pitched rooves with tall chimneys trying to take the black sooty smoke away from the windows. There were no attractive wooden houses or wooden beams and carcasses. No brick or plastered houses. No detached houses or gardens just cobbled or hard compacted earth yards. No pretty windows or doors, little greenery and what foliage there was struggled to be seen was permanently covered in a thin film of grey ash. No trees except small withered looking stumps with occasional weak looking branches not strong enough to hold the smallest of birds even if there were birds to hold and little colour except for the discarded coloured paper and packaging blowing along the streets. The roads were straight and pot holed with rusting, abandoned cars dotted along the length. Even the cars that were still being used looked like rusting, abandoned cars. All their windows were smeared with the same ash as the bushes. It was all concrete and rusting iron and steel. All grey with splashes of grime and dirt. Grubby windows and grey building blocks with dirty air.

But what it did have was coal and plenty of it or, at least it sat on plenty of coal. The hills seemed to be made almost entirely of coal and everywhere you dug into the ground there were coal seams and where there was coal there was money and as ugly as the town was it was still a rich town. Or, at least some of the folk in the town were rich. Rich enough not to have to stay in the town and spend their money. The money and their time was spent in towns and cities that were attractive and clean.

The rest of the country needed coal and coal at the lowest possible prices and Town was able to provide it and at the right price. To satisfy the demand hundreds of miners and their families had moved to Town over the years and they were prepared to live in its drabness and dig in its tunnels. It was worth putting up with the terrible weather, the overcrowding and the ugliness for the money they could earn. Even mining cheap coal brought higher wages than working in the factories powered by the coal and was definitely better than working the soil that covered the coal on the farms. The working days were long and life expectancy was short but most of the miners considered they would only work there for five years, earn their money and then move on. But five years often became ten and ten became twenty and before they knew it the life expectancy caught up with them and they never moved on ending up being buried between the soil and the coal layers.

Not only was Town ugly but it was also polluted. It was frequently named in the top three polluted towns in the country. The hills, as well as being rich in coal, meant that the smoke from the coal fires and factories that supported the mining stayed in the town frequently creating thick, yellow smogs that burned the eyes, choked the throat and reduced visibility to a few yards. The winds that swept across the rest of the country steadfastly avoided Town and refused to clear the smog so it stayed and choked people protected by the high mountains. It was considered a perfect example of the pollution that would affect the rest of the globe that burned Town's coal by the hundred tons unless something was done but nothing was being done in Town except to make matters worse every year.

On the morning of a mid-February day the breath of the miners squeezed out of their mouths and tried to part the yellow cloud of smog as they trudged wearily towards the pit entrance. It was the end of their night shift and they had been hauled hundreds of feet away from the pit face by small, uncomfortable and noisy trains to small, uncomfortable and noisy lifts taking them up towards the pit entrance. There they spilled out laughing and joking, lighting cigarettes forming a procession taking them out through the tepid showers into the changing rooms and out from the coal ladened, black air of the pit into the yellow pollution ladened smog of the town. The fact that the pit was warmer than the icy street just made everything worse. The few flakes of snow even seemed to be having difficulty falling through the air and those that did seemed to be yellow by the time they hit the ground.

They emerged from pit site onto the top of hill 17 where they had been working a few hundred feet below ground. Hard, calloused hands carried smooth, worn picks and shovels. Walking briskly the sweat and dust still present created the uncomfortable layer between skin and rough clothing that no amount of showering could remove and it was accentuated by the coldness of the air. The men stopped at the gates of the site and screwed their eyes at the weak sunlight. Most lit up more cigarettes and pipes adding to the pollution in the air and their lungs. But that simple task expressly forbidden below ground signified the end of the shift and a bit of cigarette smoke was the last of their lung's worries. They were out of the pit and safe again. Safe, at least from the pit but not from the pollution. Below them, further down the hill there was a layer of pollution that seemed almost thick enough to walk on. The sunlight could hardly penetrate it and the rays that bounced off of it were a dirty, yellow, contaminated colour. Nothing moved below them and all that could be seen were the upper storeys of the higher buildings and a couple of church spires looking as though the town had been swamped by a yellow sea.

Tomos had worked in the pits in Town for nine years. His five year anniversary had come and gone just as the money that he had earned had come and gone and he expected the tenth would do the same. He had actually been born in Town and had first gone down the mine at sixteen. Now he looked fifty. Even asleep he looked old. The lines in his face were deep and were highlighted by the ingrained coal dust that could never be completely washed out. His body was covered in scars but not scars as deep as those in his mind caused after being trapped below ground twice in his nine years. Safety was not a strong issue in the pits and, so it transpired, neither were the wooden pit props that had twice buckled and trapped him in the hot, black, confined pit face. But twice he had been rescued by his comrades who knew what it was to be trapped and knew the danger they were putting themselves in trying to dig out their colleagues. Twice he had vowed never to go back down the pit and twice he had gone back trusting fate could not be so cruel to him again.

He should have known better as his father and grandfather had both worked down in the pits and both were still there buried under tons of earth that had collapsed on them. Tomos remembered the twelve days that rescuers had tried to reach his father and his mates who had been trapped when a roof collapsed along dozens of metres of the mine but they could not rescue anyone. The rescue teams had barely got out themselves when further collapse after collapse put them in more and more danger. But life in Town was cheap, cheap as the coal, and no sooner had the rescue teams come out of the mine and the shaft being declared a burial site than the mine owners started up another excavation and the men started going back down into the ground.

As he sucked the smoke from the cheap cigarettes deep into his lungs he could almost feel it combined with the coal dust and the smoke eating away at his lungs. He coughed and coughed some more joining in with others all coughing around him. He always had an acid taste in his mouth that seemed to be eating away at the tissues and his lungs. Every day it was getting more difficult to breathe and this lungs felt as though they were dissolving. But that was not the only thing that was wearing away in Town on that day.

As she lay on the uncomfortable bed under the surprisingly clean blankets Tomos's wife did not stir. Normally she would have been up and awake by five getting ready for Tomos to come home back from the night shift under hill 17. The breakfast would be being prepared with a hot bath ready and a warm fire in the grate. Showers were fine but a good hot bath could really get to more of the ingrained dust as well as soothing exhausted muscles. But today it was already well past five. The bath was empty and the embers from yesterday's fire laid cold and dead in the grate. There was no breakfast on the table. She did not stir and nor did the three children in their beds along the short corridor.

The night shift had been into their hut to drop off their lamps, punch their work cards and hang up their helmets and they were surprised to see no-one there to meet them. The morning shift should be there, yawning, joking and complaining. Well rested after a good night's sleep ready as they ever would be to dive into the earth. But no-one was there. The hut was empty. Their equipment still hanging on the pegs instead of off their belts. Outside the gate there was no-one there. It would not be like the owners to let the night shift out early so the day shift must be late. But why?

Back in the ugly houses wrapped in yellow, thick smog no-one moved. No-one was moving because they were all dead. Every last one of them. Tomos's wife was dead. His children were dead. The wives and children of all the miners were dead. It was as though a sudden, fatal black death, a plague had swept through the town taking everyone it touched.

The baker was not at his ovens, the policemen were not on their beats. Shops were not opening, traffic was not moving, papers and milk were not being delivered. Families and neighbours died in their beds. The only ones left alive in the town were the coal miners coming off their underground night shift.

THIRTEEN

It was a typical early autumn afternoon in Eastbourne. When the sun was out it was acceptably warm and comfortable but when it went behind the heavy, slow moving clouds the wind whipped up and the rain started making the temperature drop by double digits. The rain drops falling on the window panes sounded as though they were as heavy as small stones being thrown against the glass. Then in a blink the sun was out again, the clouds melted and the rain stopped and she could sit in the cosy office feeling the warm sun on her face. With the brightness of the sun and the fact that the central heating was pouring heat out at a furious rate it almost felt like summer in the small office she was pleased to call her second home.

One of her pleasures was to sit back with a cup of tea in the comfortable office and stare out of the tall windows that covered two sides of the room. To all intents and purposes and to any impartial observer she was day dreaming but she preferred to think of it as planning, considering, weighing up options and deciding on important courses of action that would definitely be taken, eventually, maybe.

To one side of the building there were public gardens with large swathes of lawns criss-crossed by paths disappearing into banks of brightly coloured bushes. Dogs scampered about chasing invisible rabbits and actual squirrels sniffing where other dogs had been and looking round occasionally to see if their owner was following. In the middle of one of the lawns was a perfect circle of rough-hewn stones. Inside of the circle of stones the ground was covered with a thick layer of shingle and small pebbles. Standing planted, driven into the shingle was a sculpture arranged in another circle consisting of a group of blackened tree trunks over ten feet tall stripped of all branches. It reminded her of the twelve apostles standing round in a circle representing a local legend about twelve yew trees planted by monks from the Abbey of Grestein in Normandy who had been living in the Old Chapel in Ratton. The legend had it that if anyone cut down any of the trees they would die soon after. No-one took much notice until, on three occasions, someone cut down one of the trees and, sure enough, each person died suddenly soon after. After the third time no-one went near the trees and they were preserved. Seemed they were slow learners.

On this day though Lottie was staring out of the other grimy windows looking at the golfers in the distance struggling with the weather and changing into and out of weather proof clothing. Some were holding onto their golf bags as the wind tried to blow them down the course. They could be seen hacking through the long, wet grass looking for the ball that would have been counted as a fantastic shot if it had not, once again, been blown off course and off the otherwise perfect line through which it had been hit. Some golfers had resigned themselves to getting wet or were already so wet through they didn't bother to put on their water proofs and, instead, put on a face reflecting their suffering and stoicism. Others struggled against the wind. Try as she might she could not understand why people wanted to hit a small ball around a huge field with a bent stick trying to get it into a small hole while taking fewer strokes than the next person or, at best, trying not to lose it all in British weather and at huge cost.

On this afternoon she was paying particular attention to one golfer in eye achingly bright colours that she presumed passed for fashion in the club house who was searching through thigh length grass swishing at it with his club presumably looking for a ball that they both knew was never going to be found. Her attention was switched back into the office when Wil suddenly sat forward in his chair straightened his back and looked to be concentrating.

Since their meeting at number eighty six Wil had taken to popping into the museum office to meet Lottie and to use the extensive research facilities that she, as a member of the council team, could access. But then again he would also often just pop in for a cup of tea and a chat.

Without looking away from the window she asked "what is it?"

"Shh, just a minute." He kept very still seeming to be listening for something.

Lottie turned away from the window as the golfer slipped another ball out of his pocket and let it drop to the ground.

"There's a problem. Looks like it might be a biggish one."

"How do you know?" she asked as she moved over to where he was sitting.

"Just a feeling. I think there must have been a fracture somewhere. A bad fracture by the sound of it. Want to come?"

Will had gone over to the desk by the door and rummaged around in his battered shoulder bag. He grabbed the wooden box that Lottie had first seen in Norman's house all that time ago and placed it in an empty spot on the desk. Carefully he undid the wooden box and took the brass one out and lifted its lid. Shaking some of the particles onto the black surface he bent over putting his face closer to the surface as he tried to determine the message. Eventually he looked up. He knew the site of old and had been there several times before. It seemed to be a particular point of weakness between the current Royal Sussex County hospital site and the sea front. After having been to the location before Wil had formulated a theory that the hospital had unconsciously been built where it was because it was close to a weak spot.

"Let's go". Lottie, slammed down her only half drunk cup of tea, grabbed her coat and bag and was half way down the stairs before she realised Wil was not following. She dashed back up the stairs, "What are you waiting for?"

"Come on lets go", he shouted as he made for the door grabbing his bags and pushing the box into it on the way. Feeling a touch of déjà vu she followed him out of the office.

Wil and Lottie hopped into their car and set off for Brighton only twenty odd miles away.

"So what's the problem in Brighton then?" asked Lottie

"It seems there has been a tear in the partition. The other side are worried that unless it is repaired quickly it will continue to get bigger. It's very weak at the best of times down here but it does seem to be getting worse."

"Why is it so weak down here?"

"It's like everything else. It is stronger is some parts and weaker in others. Bit like a sea mist. Sometimes it is thick and sometimes barely there although overall it does seem getting thinner and thinner".

"Any ideas why it is so weak?"

"Well, the partition is generally getting thinner, maybe we think, because of pollution, same as everywhere else, but areas like Brighton are weak anyway and we think there may be several reasons why it is weak and getting weaker but we are not certain. It's quite bad up in some parts of Yorkshire too. When I was up there we had loads of tears because they also had weak partitions".

"And there is a thinning in Brighton then?"

"Yes, I think so. Around this part of Sussex and, like I said, around places like Penzance and in parts of Yorkshire like Whitby and Guisborough there is something odd. To make it even worse, down here, in Sussex, there were a lot of associations with the devil and evil and the underworld which is a good link to activity because back in the day people would relate problems they had to devilish activity. It was all part of the heaven and hell thing and what happens if you are good or bad in life. They were very big on spirits and the after-life down here and pretty wary of old Nick".

"Devils' Dyke for example," chipped in Lottie. She was also thinking of the stone Celtic cross that was in St Mary's churchyard after having been brought up from Cornwall for some reason that is now unknown.

"Yes, that's one example. Do you know the story of Devil's Dyke?"

"Yes I think I do. The people held that the devil wanted to drown the people of Sussex for some reason, probably because they had built a lot of churches" offered Lottie

"That's right. Possibly he wanted them gone because of their strong links to the partition. Norman was not the first Sussex person to be heavily involved in trying to explain it all and I gather he did a lot of research about all of it. Anyway the devil was supposed to have, overnight, started digging a hole to flood the area with sea water and hence it was called Devil's Dyke. The only reason he stopped was that he was supposed to have seen a light and thought morning was coming but not before the clods of earth he was digging and throwing over his shoulder formed the Isle of Wight and Chanctonbury."

"Must have been a pretty big spade," observed Lottie.

"Anyway, apparently Saint Cuthman who used to wheel his mother about in a wheel barrow. Um, that had nothing to do with the story. But he had over-heard the devil plotting with himself about the flooding of all the churches and Cuthman told Sister Ursula who lived in a small chapel in Saddlescombe. They created a plan and it was Ursula who lit the candle and made her cockerel crow making the devil think it was morning".

"Must have been a pretty big candle," more Lottie observation. "Didn't know the devil was so thick." "Light," continued Wil "especially candle light is very important to the people in this part of the world. Partly because of the devil but also because it is believed that people see a bright light as they die. Incidentally, another story about Cuthman, did you know that he was supposed to have been a shepherd and one day he wanted to leave his flock so he drew an invisible line around the flock with his staff and cleared off, to get his lunch or post his pools coupon or something. Anyway when he came back all the sheep were still inside the circle he had drawn starting the myth that sheep all huddle together when they are in danger."

"Down here one of the famous lights of course is the Beachy Head light". Wil mentioned it as they passed the area in the car. "Back in the early seventeen hundreds there was a curate of St Michael's in Litlington called Jonathan Darby whose duty was to bury the bodies of ship wrecked sailors. He was supposed to have built a tunnel called Parsons Darby Hole down to the beach from Birling Gap where he hung a light to guide shipwrecked sailors. The Seven Sisters which make up Beachy Head were quite a sight for the ships sailing close round the coast and there were many ship wrecks, but not all of them accidental because of the smuggling that was supposed to be going on."

"So that's why there is a lighthouse here."

"Yes, there was the Belle Tout originally and that was the Lloyds optical station. That was built on the cliff but now there is the famous red and white light house in the sea that everyone knows about".

Getting hooked on the telling of local folk tales Lottie continued "I remember the tale of the moon-rakers who hid their barrels of smuggled spirits in the pond at Alfriston. One night, as they tried to fish them out some customs officers walked by and asked them what they were doing. Thinking quickly the smugglers said they were trying to rake the moon out of the pond because it was made of cheese. The customs men thought they were idiots and walked on".

"So all round here is a bit of a spooky area," concluded Lottie.

"Sure is, there is definitely something different down here and that might be why so many people come from all over the world to throw themselves off Beachy Head".

"Is there anything else that is a bit odd round here?" Lottie had always lived in and around Eastbourne but had never heard some of the stories that Wil was telling.

"Oh yes there are loads. There's the Pinette gate for example."

"I've heard of them. They are gates that are set on a central spindle instead of having hinges on one side. They are supposedly only found in Sussex".

"Yes. They are normally only found in churches. The church in Friston has a good example of one. It is thought they symbolise the passing in and out of the spiritual world and I expect a lot more churches round here had them. Problem is that they were not very user friendly so I expect a lot were replaced with ordinary gates".

"And?" Lottie questioned eager to hear more.

"Well there's loads more. For instance the Chanctonbury Ring".

"Go on".

Will drew a deep breath "well it is an earth work looking out over the Sussex Weald and dates back to around the Bronze age, around seventh century BC. It was built just north of a ridgeway or pathway probably so it was easy to get into. Later on it was a fort but it was thought to be originally built to be a religious place and, curiously, when the Romans occupied it centuries later they built temples there so there must be something about it for people to recognise it as being a religious area".

"What else was it used for?"

"Well no-one really knows but it could have been a religious area, close to a pathway so people could evacuate from their village into it in times of distress either from other tribes or from the devil himself".

"There he goes again".

"Yes, it is said you can summon him by walking round in six or seven circles, ideally backwards and he will appear and give you a bowl of soup".

"That doesn't seem very devilish".

"No, but they also say that you can see fairies dancing in the ring on Midsummers Eve, or that it is haunted and that is why there are no birds on the hill. Take your pick".

A bit further on Wil pointed over towards St Dunstan's hospital in Ovingdean. "There's another thing. St Dunstan who became the patron saint of the blind with the hospital down here in Sussex was once a blacksmith although he eventually became arch bishop of Canterbury, anyway he was supposed to have tweaked the devil's nose with a pair of red hot pincers".

"And then, of course is the Long man in Wilmington. He obviously features because Norman had him marked up on his maps in his house".

A few minutes later and they had driven a little bit further into Brighton, on Marine Parade Wil stopped the car and looked down the street. They had arrived at their destination.

"I can't see anything unusual," observed Lottie peering down the promenade.

"No, there's probably nothing to see at the minute. But there possibly may be in a bit".

They both climbed out of the car and as Wil went to the boot Lottie involuntarily started to lick her tingling lips as she walked to the back of the car.

As she stood next to Wil he was removing a black box which was slightly smaller than the brass one she had seen earlier. Putting it on the parcel shelf he opened the lid and allowed a flap to drop down and secure itself along the top front edge of the box. The result looked like a square black screen set on a matching black box with no obvious pattern or markings. Slowly a mist seemed to appear on the front surface of the top and it started to form numbers. It formed the number 237.

"What does that mean?" asked Lottie.

"The number gives me an idea of how big the tear is".

"So what sort of size is the tear? Is it a big one?"

"No, this is not very large."

"So how large is large then?"

"Well it is usually quite small, maybe a dozen or two but it can range to thousands, even tens of thousands in theory and that is really big and can be disastrous in local areas. Mind you it is exceedingly unusual to have something that big. I have never seen one myself but there are accounts in some of the older texts. The real problem is that there might not be a single tear but there might be multiple tears and it can be really difficult to restore them. The fear everyone always has is that, sooner or later, there will be a really significant tear and if it cannot be repaired God only knows what will happen. There have been a couple of single tears that have been pretty big and caused lots of damage but they have been kept quiet so as not to disturb and panic people. One of the worst was in a truly God forsaken place called Town where the whole village was wiped out. Luckily it was in a very authoritarian country who squashed all the reports of it although, obviously we got to hear about it but we are not going to spread the news. In a way it is quite useful that the powers that be do not really know what is really happening and they try to explain it away with reasons they think will satisfy people."

"You mean this happens all the time and no-one knows about it?"

"Well, yes and no. It does happen all the time and has happened from the beginning of time, and I don't just mean our time, and people do know about it especially the big ones but, like I said it does not become general knowledge. Problem is that some of the occurrences will be getting so big that they will not be able to be hushed up and they will be happening more often. Eventually there will be a really big one that will cause significant damage and that will be difficult to explain away".

"Might I have seen anything happening?"

"Almost certainly. But you would not have known what it all meant. For example you might have caught a breath for some reason or felt your lips tingling".

"I just did".

"Well that is your rather prehistoric sensory system letting you know that there is a transient about".

Lottie felt something between disgust and fear that transients had been so close and she had known nothing about it. In fact she was not sure what a transient even was. As far as she was aware a transient was a person always on the move, otherwise known as a tramp. She had seen plenty of them sleeping rough in the huts along the promenade at home but was pretty sure her lips had never tingled when she went past them. Maybe her nose screwed up at the smell but her lips did nothing.

Wil opened up the map he had brought and consulted a post-it note on which he had noted the co-ordinates he had jotted down from the box in the office.

FOURTEEN

He looked up from the map and peered down the road. In the distance were a large number of individual and distinct shapes, almost invisible to the ordinary human eye but quite distinct to Wil. They were mostly around eight feet tall and did not really seem to reach the ground. It was almost like they were hovering. They were milling about standing close together, looking lost and doing nothing. It almost reminded him of a coach load of tourists being disgorged onto an unfamiliar pavement with no-one knowing where to go or what to do and wanting someone to take the lead so they could follow. He sensed discomfort and the need for help.

Wil sensed Lottie looking at him knowing that she could not see what he was seeing.

"What are you looking at? " She asked him.

"There they are, down the road, a couple of hundred at least. I have to help them to get back where they belong".

Lottie looked down the road again trying to follow Wil's eye line but she could still not see anything.

"Are they causing any trouble?"

"No, they are just waiting looking a bit bewildered. They don't want to be here but don't know how to get back."

"So what are you going to do to get them back then?"

"Well, there are two things. First there is an incantation that we use that guides them back through the partition gap. It's a sort of way of giving them directions which they can follow. With what we say and the marshals on the other side helping we can get them back then, when they are all back, we try to repair the tear or, at least, those on the other side can repair the tear".

With that he stepped away from the car and started walking away from Lottie and the car with his arms outstretched speaking words that were unintelligible to Lottie. She thought he looked faintly ridiculous walking with outstretched arms and speaking mumbo jumbo. Could have been a drunk on a Saturday night out. Not such an uncommon a sight in Brighton. She followed him.

As Wil walked towards the group he began to feel them turning towards him and focussing on him and what he was saying. As he got closer he could see that they were now turning away from him and pointing towards the crossing point through the partition. Slowly the numbers seemed to be going down as they obeyed the incanted instructions and returned from whence they had come. By the time he had reached them there were just the last one or two making their way back until, when he stopped walking and lowered his arms, there were no more shapes. They had all gone home with no damage done.

With that he turned and returned to the car and consulted the box in the boot of the car. This time the number read zero. All had been returned.

"Great. They have all got back. Now they can get on and repair the tear."

FIFTEEN

"And now some breaking news. We are just getting reports of an accident on the London underground". The newsreader was calmness personified as she glanced between the autocue and the pieces of paper being thrust in front of her. To make matters worse she was being spoken to through her ear piece by at least three people and was also trying to see what was being shown on her monitors. Breaking news pretty nearly broke newsreaders especially when it looked as dramatic as this seemed. Trying not to break eye contact with the camera for too long she cast around for information to impart to the audience.

Almost as if her voice and brain were separate entities she carried on speaking while all the other information was being processed. "It seems as though emergency services and police terrorist teams are racing to the scene of a major incident that is unfolding on the London underground where it is feared there have been very many fatalities. It appears that around eight twenty four this morning there was an incident on an under-ground train on the Jubilee line travelling between Westminster and Waterloo."

As she spoke the roads which were already packed with morning commuter traffic were being swamped by emergency service vehicles from all over London. Cyclists on cycle lanes scattered as cars moved to allow blue lights to go past. Buses just stopped at bus stops and didn't try to move with their controllers telling them that progress was going to be impossible. Black cab drivers suddenly had to put their knowledge to the test and swerve off the primary routes and take back ways that only they really knew to get their customers to their destinations. Other hire cars with less local knowledge had to re-programme their sat-navs and hope they were going in the right direction.

All the major hospitals were being put on high alert. Dusting off their major incident protocols clearing accident and emergency departments, assembling crisis teams and waiting for news about numbers and potential types of casualties. Covert security forces mingled with the crowds looking and listening for any suspicious communications, watching people, looking for signs of weaponry. Cordons were thrown around a wide area surrounding the two major stations involved. Police tape by the mile was being unfurled and strung between lamp posts. Drivers of cars caught on the wrong side were told to get out, leave their cars and get onto the right side of the tape. Police officers started shepherding people away from the scenes not knowing quite what had happened. Pedestrians bumped into each other as most were holding their phones aloft trying to film whatever it was that was going on and not looking where they were going. Offices, cafes and coffee bars inside the cordons emptied pouring their occupants onto the streets.

Helicopters from the police, rescue services and the press circled overhead. Drones quickly deployed by journalists and rescue services vied for space over the area and outside broadcast vans were being deployed wherever there was space with reporters chasing anyone who looked to be in authority for information and then broadcasting to the twenty four hour rolling new channels. Windows of buildings all along the approach roads were thrown open so people could see what was happening. Chaos reigned but no-one above ground knew why.

The alarm had started as soon as red lights started to blaze on the giant track monitoring board in the London Underground control room.

Gill Dredge was the morning supervisor in the huge operations room overseeing the network of trains bringing hundreds of thousands of people into the city on just another ordinary day. Usually dozens of people sat quietly at their desks arranged in three ranks all with their own computer screens and phones but all facing the giant boards. They almost uniformly had head phones over their ears and a variety of china and plastic cups to their lips. On any normal day they would monitor their sections of the under-ground and ensure that trains were running smoothly and watching screens showing hundreds of thousands of commuters dashing about the city with phones to their ears and coffee cups to their lips. Later in the day they would be replaced by thousands of visitors to the city wandering about consulting maps and trying to work out where they were and how to get where they wanted to be. Problems usually only amounted to broken down trains, failed signals, idiots on the lines or power failures and they could be problem enough but this was different. As soon as the klaxon sounded and the red lights came on Gill put her coffee mug down and pulled her rather comfortable chair closer to the desk and the array of screens in front of her. One screen had a flashing red border and a graphic indicating the two stations closest station to the incident. Somewhere a train had stopped where it should not have stopped. She flipped a switch and all the screens on her desk started showing her scenes shot from the CCTV cameras in that location. Some were fixed showing a still picture and others swept side to side showing panoramas. Apart from the crowds of people milling around the platforms and concourses not knowing where to go or what to do there seemed to be nothing out of the ordinary. Knowing there was a problem somewhere the station staff were seen implementing their major incident procedures ushering the people away from the stations, down the tunnels and up the now stationary escalators towards ground level.

She had seen many incidents on the underground in her time covering fires and terrorist attacks and even bombs but there was nothing on her screens that seemed to suggest either one of those. Both types of incidents usually generated lots of smoke and often fire. With fires in particular there was often a rushing wind as air was sucked into the fire pulling scraps of waste paper and other detritus with it and there was always fire and smoke alarms going off especially if the fire was inside a tunnel. But now they were all silent. Either there was no fire or all the electrics had been disabled. But all the emergency lights were on and the cameras were working so there was power down there. There was also often a recognisable focal point from which people would be running but there was nothing like that. People were all running but in the directions the staff were telling them to run and that was out. Gill briefly hoped the staff were actually pointing them in the right direction. They could not know what the incident was or where it was. But up and out was safe, usually. Hopefully. It was all very surreal. Something had obviously happened but from where she was she could not tell what. But despite this she activated all the appropriate actions. Better to be safe than sorry. All trains on that line were told to stop at the next station. Any between occupied stations were stopped in tunnels and the doors temporarily sealed to stop people getting onto the lines. As soon as practical all the power to the lines was cut and passengers told to exit at whatever station they were at. Gill felt bad that the system had ground to a halt with thousands of people being inconvenienced without an apparent reason or explanation but that would have to come later.

In case the incident was going to spread all the trains on other lines that passed through or close to the affected stations were halted in the same way effectively shutting down most of the London underground system. At each one staff guided passengers to the surface batting back all the questions and complaints as best they could without knowing why the system had come to a halt. With a huge chunk of the underground closed down, buses and taxis banned from main thoroughfares across the city today would not be a good day to try to get to work.

As soon as her coffee cup hit the bench the phones started ringing with reports of what had happened coming in. The telemetry from the affected train started to appear on her monitors and she focused her CCTVs onto the train and more local units. One train, it appeared had stopped inside a tunnel in between stations for no apparent reason. The train had been working just fine from its early morning start. On screen against the engine identification information came the service details and its recent history. It was all just fine, no reports of any failures or previous breakdowns. Next to the train information came the profile of Jev, the train driver, and he seemed to be an exemplary employee with no disciplinary or reliability issues. From what she could see a train had just come to a sudden halt inside one of the longest tunnels on the network. It was by no means a rare occurrence, trains broke down all the time, sometimes they were stopped because there was something or someone on the line, occasionally there was a power failure but usually these were reported by the driver or were noted by other monitoring devices but today there was no warning or alerts. There was power. The train did not seem to have de-railed or left the tracks. Monitors would have detected if it had. There was no communication from the driver or security guards or transport police that often travelled on the trains but maybe there were none on this one. It surely must be a million to one that the train breaks down and all communications break down as well and, anyway, the customers evacuating the platforms seemed to be using their mobile phones.

In Waterloo and Westminster stations the security and rescue teams quickly assembled pulling on their bright orange coveralls and white helmets switching on the high intensity head lamps. Ready packed kits for first aid, engineering and firefighting were slung onto backs and once given the all clear the teams gathered at the Westminster platform edge waiting for the specialist inspection teams to come down and inspect the areas before they could jump down onto the lines and race along the tunnels towards the trains. The team monitoring the incident put their well-practised routines into effect but it soon became apparent this was no ordinary incident and they were soon floundering. Risk assessments had been written, contingency plans plotted but this was not fitting anything they had tried to foresee. This was going to be seat of the pants territory. Was this the big event that

London had been waiting for ever since nine eleven or seven eleven? Had there been a terrorist strike and if there had been why on this train and this time? And why could they not raise Jev on the phones? Just maybe there had been a problem with him and he had stopped the train or maybe there was just a problem with the comms as well as with the train. But the mobile phone providers had already been able to confirm that the handsets of people on the train were working. It was just that nobody was using them. Everyone was hoping for a simple reason but everyone feared it was a far from simple reason.

On the TV screens the face of a reporter popped up being jostled by hundreds of people either trying to get away from the area or by rescue teams trying to get in. Everyone tried to overhear what he was saying to try to learn the causes of the chaos.

The on screen TV newsreader announced "We can now go over, live to Piers who is at Westminster. Piers what can you tell us about what is happening down there this morning". Rosie Lands looked hopefully into the screen waiting for Piers to appear and take the pressure off for a couple of minutes. Long enough for her to get a grip of the situation and calm down a bit. The few seconds it took for Piers to appear on screen seemed like hours and her face started to feel numb as she tried to hold her calm expression.

"Thank you Rosie. I am outside Westminster station in the City of London this morning", Piers started looking about him and trying to make sense of what was happening. "Scenes here are pretty frantic with emergency services of all sorts racing into the area and down into the station. At the minute we do not know what has actually happened down there apart from the fact that a train had stopped in the tunnel and, as a result, all other traffic has been shut down and a major incident called. The Jubilee line tunnel between Westminster and Waterloo, which is where we think the incident has happened, opened around 1999 and is only about half a mile long but is one of the busiest on the network with around 100 million passengers going into Waterloo from the four lines that serve it every year and trains running every two to six minutes depending on the time of day. It is 39 metres underground with Westminster station being close to the Houses of Parliament and the Elizabeth Tower. In fact there was a lot of concern at the time of construction that this was not deep enough and that the tower would be in jeopardy when the line was being dug. Of course it is also below Portcullis house, where many of the members of Parliament have offices and close to Westminster Bridge which has been the site of previous terrorist attacks. There is some concern that the incident involves the seat of government but no-one is sure". Google had been consulted hoping to find something to say to the cameras. Something, anything until they could actually find some real news to broadcast.

As he looked around towards the entrance to the station a fleet of ambulances and police cars swept passed with blue lights flashing and sirens blazing.

Confusingly police motor bikes and fire engines rushed back in the other direction. To anyone watching the television it was quite apparent that the reporter had not the slightest idea what was happening. Nevertheless he continued.

"It is still unclear what has actually happened. There does not appear to have been a fire or explosion. Fire officers have been down there, at least to the platforms, and reported no smoke or flames on them or coming from the tunnels. There appears to have been no explosions as witnesses have not reported any loud bangs and there doesn't look to be any damage. There also does not appear to have been a crash, derailment or collision as the first rescuers albeit viewing from a safe distance have been able to report back that the train is just stopped on the rails with no apparent damage. At the moment it is still a mystery especially as there have been no reports of anyone escaping from the train and coming back down the line and into the station nor does there appear to have been any mobile phone communication from anyone on the train. Because there is so much uncertainty the rescue parties on the platforms have been told to stand down until specialist search and rescue teams can get to the site."

As he was speaking the military were busy erecting tents for triage points and decontamination areas to clean the yellow hazmat suits the soldiers were pulling on. Police were continuing to shepherd spectators away from the area clearing out and closing shops, evacuating people from their homes and diverting traffic. Gradually the area become clear of everyone except the rescue services. Even the journalists were being forced further and further away from the scene, still talking, and their drones were being shot down.

Mat Combe had spent many hours in the gym, partly to get out of the house, partly because he was as vain as hell but mainly because he knew he had to be fit for the job. Even though the exercises he did seemed to have little benefit for what was actually required for the job he persisted hoping it was all better than nothing. In his mind it as always a bit of a toss-up. Is all the work in the gym making him fit for work or is all the exercise he gets at work making him fit for the gym? Bitter experience had shown him that although he thought he was fit if he took up another sport he always found muscles that he never knew he had and found movements that he just could not make. The only thing he did find was that he could never improve the mind numbing boredom of the gym and the fact that if he could run ten kilometres today he would have to run twelve tomorrow or lift fifty kilos today and fifty five tomorrow to get the same feeling of achievement.

He had always wanted to be a fire fighter and still thoroughly enjoyed the excitement of a shout, the anticipation as he pulled on his protective gear and the mental planning as they raced to a fire or emergency. But when the opportunity came along to also be a specialist in hazardous chemical and radiation rescue work he had jumped at it. Perversely the amount of time they spent in fire prevention and the stricter and stricter rules around building and fire safety meant they had fewer and fewer calls on their services as fire fighters and sitting around twiddling his thumbs was not one of his favoured non activities. Since volunteering for the new speciality he had lost count of the numbers of hours he had spent in the huge yellow suit sweating buckets as he lugged the heavy breathing apparatus about and the curses he had used trying to manipulate fiddly little tools wearing the thick red gloves. But now all the practice was coming to the fore and he was attending his first real emergency situation.

Trudging down the road from the hastily erected white and blue tents to the opening of the tube station was the first time he had actually worn the suit in a real life situation and he was feeling apprehensive about what he was going to find. Concentrating hard he walked down the suddenly very narrow steps into the darkness. His headlights fixed to the sides of his helmet shone only where he looked and everything else was black. The only sounds to be heard were his heavy breathing inside the suit and the occasional muffled sounds of his suit fabric rubbing against itself. Sweat formed on his forehead and started soaking into the thick towelling head band round his head and just over his eye brows. The large, clear face panel in the suit started to mist up around the edges so he turned on the miniature fans located at the top corners letting them blow air over the screen gradually clearing it. He tried not to think too much about what he might find down in the tunnels and he half hoped that there was nothing too challenging for him to deal with. On the other hand he was booted and suited ready to deal with emergencies so it would be a great challenge if there was something. Maybe he should not have watched all those horror movies about monsters or aliens who emerged from dark holes or tunnels.

Behind him a bright light threw his bulky shadow onto the walls. He looked around having to shuffle his whole body through a hundred and eighty degrees and saw Mead trundling towards him. The robot reconnaissance crews had arrived and had unloaded their robot vehicles and sent them down after Mat as soon as possible. Mat had seen the motorised or was it mechanical exploration and assessment devices being made on one of his training days. Walking through the factory he had eventually come across a little line of completed MEADS waiting for deployment and now one was following him into the tunnel.

About three feet square and standing two feet high the vehicle was moving along on four inch wide tracks with rubber pads that made it quiet but also meant it could easily climb and descend stairs. On board were high resolution day and night vision cameras that could move through three hundred and sixty degrees and project 3D images to the handlers. It carried varieties of pneumatic tools, grabbers and pincers, gas cutters and saws on hydraulic arms that were stowed along the body but could be made to reach out far from the machine itself. It also carried a small chemistry laboratory that could sample air, liquids and solids and give accurate analyses within minutes. It had all been modelled on instruments sent into space and was highly sensitive and manoeuvrable. It was a robotic Swiss army knife plus. Mat stepped aside as Mead trundled on determinedly ahead and into the darkness. He was pleased to see Mead but knew that whatever Mead found he would still have to go in after him.

SIXTEEN

The trailer they were sitting in was the exact opposite of Doctor Who's Tardis. It looked big on the outside but when you got inside it was so small. Not only was it small but it was cramped with dozens of computers and small screens lining the walls. Reflected in the light from the screens was the four man crew of the van. To maximise the limited space available two of the men faced one way and two faced the other way but they sat shoulder to shoulder in one line down the middle of the van perched on stools that were just a bit too low, a bit too small and a bit too uncomfortable to be sat on for any length of time. Unfortunately they knew that they would be sitting there for a considerable length of time and that their discomfort was the last thing anyone was going to worry about. The numbers, size and electrical activity of the kit also made it very hot in the van with precious little fresh air getting in through the woefully small ventilation slots but at least it meant the coffee did not go cold too quickly. Well, that was if they had been given any coffee and if anyone had brought egg sandwiches for lunch there was going to be trouble. But none of that seemed important as they watched the pictures Mead was sending back.

"Ok clever dick but this is a freaking nightmare. What the hell is going on down there?"

Phil Ching had been steering Mead along the long tunnels and down the stationary escalators watching as it passed Mat and occasionally stopping to sample the air or to look around for anything that might be suspicious or give them a clue as to what was going on. Mat followed a few meters behind the machine watching what it was doing and listening to the commentary from the non-Tardis. Slowly they passed through all the public areas eventually reaching the platform. Mead had trundled determinedly along and down the slope at the end of the platform and fearlessly bowled into the dark tunnel. Mat bowled slightly less fearlessly in after it. Mead followed its lights moving easily over the track sleepers. Mat, grateful for the superior lights on Mead followed less elegantly and sure footedly and with the odd expletive as his cumbersome suit made life difficult. Eventually they reached the train. Now they could see it just ahead absolutely still and snuggled into the close fitting tunnel.

"Nothing. Absolutely nothing. Right lets go into the tunnel". Mat gave a commentary that the four men in a van had already surmised.

Phil slowly inched the robot along the track towards the lights of the train leaning forward on his stool and peering at the small screen in front of him. Stopping the robot close enough to be able to see the graffiti on the front of the cab Mead went through the testing routines for any gases that might be present. It tried to detect the presence of any explosives or any radio activity but everything came back to Phil and to Mat as negative. The video camera on Mead rose up on a long, slender arm and looked into the cab window. The sounds of the lens focussing was all that could be heard. As it rose on its pneumatic struts looking like a grounded submarine raising its periscope it looked into the cab and there it saw Jev, the driver, slumped over his controls his inhaler in his open hand.

Mat watched on his hand held screen seeing everything as the men in the non-Tardis and the operational managers saw it. It went through their minds that the simple solution was that he must have had a heart attack or something and collapsed at the controls with the train stopping automatically when he released the inappropriately named, dead man's handle. But why were there no sounds coming from the rest of the packed commuter train? Surely, even if the phones were not working, people would be banging on the doors and windows. Surely they would be shouting and calling for help? Why were there not people trying to get down the line away from the train? Mead had super sensitive sound detection. He could pick up the smallest sounds and had heard the rats scuttling about the tracks further down the lines as he approached the train but now there was nothing. Not even a rat.

The laboratory on board the robot sprang into life again sucking air into its sensors looking for gases maybe sarin, maybe chlorine something to explain what had happened but there was nothing. Displays showed 'Negative' to everything tested for. There was no gas of any sort there apart from oxygen.

Another sensor went out and Mat could hear the slow click of the Geiger counter trying to detect any radio-activity but there was nothing more than would be expected as back ground activity.

Mat looked up as best he could as a small drone flew over his head navigating a narrow gap between the roof of the train and tunnel. Red and blue lights flashed on it as it hovered slowly inching its way down the tunnel and a bright white laser light shone down onto the train. Mat was impressed by the skill of whoever was flying the thing, presumably somewhere up top, but the camera pictures sent back to Mat and the operators were of little assistance. Clever and manoeuvrable as it was it could not see down the sides of the train or into the carriages. Eventually it slipped back down the tunnel towards the station. It quickly became apparent to Mat that neither the drone nor Mead was going to be able to get down the side of the train or into the carriages. That was going to be down to him and him alone.

"This is all bloody ridiculous. There is nothing there".

"But that's a good thing isn't it?" offered one of the non-Tardis staff.

"It's like the bloody Marie Celeste!"

"I think you will find the Marie Celeste was a ship and that is was found completely empty. This is a train. And it was full!"

Ching leaned back in his chair and rubbed his face with his hands. He slowly exhaled blowing a raspberry with his lips in frustration. On the one hand it was good there was no gas or radioactivity and there was obviously no fire or explosion damage but there was still no explanation. He called Mat and told him the results which relieved him as he carried on following Mead into the scene but he, too, was puzzled.

"Guess it is. No gas, no poison, no explosives, no bombs, no derailment, no crash, no sound, no nothing. Guess that's good but it sure as hell does not help to explain what has happened".

He called down to Mat again. "It's OK, you can go on in. It seems safe. Mead can't get down the side of the train cos it's too close to the tunnel walls. At least there is nothing we can see but take care something weird has happened here."

SEVENTEEN

Mat was relieved that there seemed to be no hazards ahead of him but he carried on in his bulky suit just to make sure. Better to be safe than sorry until the situation was resolved.

He carried on walking down the tunnel towards the train that was still illuminated by Mead's powerful headlights even though it was making its way back to the tunnel opening and the platform.

Eventually Mat got to the train and climbing up onto the bumpers he looked into the cab to see Jev's body slumped over the controls.

"Well that could explain why the train had stopped", he thought completely dispassionately. But he could not help but wonder why there was no noise from the carriages. Why were people not walking down the line or at least banging on the walls and windows trying to get out or attract attention?

He climbed inelegantly down from the bumper and onto the track and then tried to squeeze his bulky suit between the train and the tunnel wall. No easy task even though most of the suit was air. It did occur to him that if there were no harmful agents in the area he could take the suit off and be safe. But then again maybe there was something harmful that could not be detected. Better to be safe than sorry. He consoled himself that there were no known gases involved so even if the suit ripped on the numerous projections from the tunnel wall at least he would be safe but the bulky oxygen tanks were difficult to squeeze through the gap and he would be getting no medals for gymnastics wearing the inflexible suit.

With a struggle he made it along the side of the train to the door of the first carriage. Reaching into his back pack he pulled out a small set of extending ladders. Shaking them to extend he leaned them against the train and started to climb them up to the level of the windows. As soon as he looked into the first carriage he could see why there was no-one on the tracks or banging on the walls. They were all sat in their seats or lying on the floor and all seemed to be quite motionless. No-one was moving. No-one was standing. The ones lucky enough to have got a seat on the crowded train were slumped to the right or left in their seats. Some had their faces resting on their knees. Many still had ear plugs in and phones or tablets in their hands. A few had an open book or newspaper in their laps as if they had dozed off and let the book go. The ones that had been standing and strap hanging were all lying scattered across the floor and seats. They were lying over each other and on the laps of the seated. A couple had obviously collapsed but their hands had been caught in the straps and they were hanging one handed from them looking down at the floor. Some seemed to have been trying to escape with half smashed windows or forced doors. Were they all unconscious or were they all dead? Suddenly he felt pleased that he had kept his suit on. Even though he had been told there was nothing dangerous down here something had killed or, at least, incapacitated, all these people and he did not know what it was. Maybe it was something new that Mead was not able to detect or identify.

Satisfied he was going to have to get into the carriages he reached into his pack again and pulled out a set of mechanical jaws. Using the sharp point he smashed them through the rubber seals on the doors and started to pump them gradually forcing open the carriage door. Eventually after much effort and sweat the gap was large enough for him to gain entry to the carriage. He stood looking at all the bodies around him assuming there was nothing he could do for them. He used a small hand held scanner and ran it over a couple of the closest bodies. It detected no life in any of them. They were not unconscious. They were dead. After a couple of minutes looking up and down the length of the carriage trying to assess the numbers affected he started to make his way along the eight carriages only to find the scene was the same in each one. Some carriages were more chaotic than others with the central carriages being more packed with bodies than the end ones. Wherever he looked there more bodies in piles over the floor, bags and cases scattered everywhere but no-one outside the carriages. Five maybe six hundred bodies. He had radioed back but the body cameras he was wearing had already sent back the pictures that he had been seeing. The men in the van looked at the pictures Mat was sending back but none said a word. This was beyond understanding.

Slowly he edged back to the front of the train and stepped back onto the track in front of the driver's cab. Not being able to do anything more and with no apparent urgency to effect a rescue he started to trudge back to the platform only to be passed by other rescue workers dressed in their white suits with hoods tied tightly round their faces which were covered in thick white respirators and Perspex goggles. Some had large red crosses on the front and back of their suits all had their names in thick marker pen and some had number which must have meant something to someone. Behind them came more tracked vehicles carrying tools, lighting gantries, first aid packs and water.

Mat retraced his steps back along the platforms and down the seemingly interminable tunnels up into the bright morning air. After he had been through the wash tent to scrub his suit he reported to the controller's office to find everyone arguing amongst themselves about what had happened and how they should proceed.

Outside spokes people who had been hastily briefed with what little was known were facing a barrage of reporters and TV cameras bombarding them with questions about what had happened. Defensively they were reporting what they knew and that was only that they had found the train with what looked like several hundred dead bodies and no explanation. They desperately tried to down-play what was obviously going to be a massive incident to try to stop any mass panic. People were going to want an explanation soon and reassurance that they were safe. Two things the site managers could not give.

Below ground a battery powered loco had been brought into the tunnels and was being attached to the stricken train with the intention to pull it down to the next platform where more people would be able to investigate what had happened and remove the bodies. Above ground, now that the details of the incident were becoming known, if not the cause, barriers were being erected between the entrance to the station and the lines of ambulances that were ready to collect the bodies ready for examination and identification.

Just inside the concourse just out of the view of the public and the cameras were queues of trollies each with a black body bag waiting for the occupants of the train. Slowly each body was carefully carried out of the carriages and placed with what was presumed to be their belongings inside a bag which was then wheeled up between the screens to the waiting ambulances. One by one they peeled off with their blue lights turned off to one of the several identified receiving mortuaries only to be replaced by another ready for its new cargo. Once empty scientists and technicians of all descriptions descended on the train itself taking samples of all the seating, rubbish and even dust and air samples putting them into labelled plastic bags for transport to the forensic laboratories all over the country.

Somehow the scale of the incident was going to have to be shielded until some rational and believable explanation could be created.

EIGHTEEN

"This bloke must be going mental!" Holly Wells threw down the report she had been reading for the third time and walked away from her desk wringing her hands. She strode across to the office and thrusting her hands deep into her pockets she looked out across the square. Everything looked quite normal out there. Cars went past, pedestrians went past a little bit quicker than the cars, and pigeons strutted up and down the pavement in between the pedestrian's feet expertly dodging the electric scooters that weaved and whizzed their way down the pavements. All was as it should be. As she tossed her thoughts around in her head her colleague, Gail Sham, picked up the report and started thumbing through the pages once more half hoping that she had mis-read the report or that, somehow, it had changed to make more comprehensible reading.

Suffocation.

Holly started mumbling more to herself than anyone else in the room "how in hell can six hundred and sixty five people all suffocate at the same time? On one train? It's ridiculous, that cannot be the reason for this".

"But there were no traces of any toxins, poisons or gases. Three robots had eventually been sent down and nothing was detected. Even when the rescue services went down they could not detect anything. When Mat first went down there they didn't see any rats but after a bit, when the other rescue teams went down and saw the rats running back, they took off their helmets they were fine. Miners had canaries and we have rats. Nothing was there".

"If it was okay for the rats to come back it was alright for the folk down there", chipped in a voice from the back of the room.

"Yes, but did the rats just run away because they sensed something wrong? There didn't seem to be any dead rats in the area so whatever did for the people did not do for the rats".

It was only after the post mortem reports started to come in that the cause of death for virtually all of the deceased was deemed to be suffocation. A couple had had heart attacks but that was put down to the situation they found themselves in and their deaths were not attributed to the actual cause.

"There was nothing found in the bodies either. All the bloods came back normal. Nothing in the lungs or tissues. No damage to the bodies other than those that were caused in the scramble. They did just suffocate", came another voice.

The report documented that once the bodies had been extracted from the carriages they had been taken to the local mortuaries to be examined by teams of hospital and Home Office pathologists. They took innumerable blood and tissue samples from each body which were sent off to laboratories for examination hoping to find some sort of clue as to what happened. All sorts of abnormal results had come back but they were all put down to the person's physical condition at the time. None of them could be related to their deaths.

"Yes, thank you", chimed in Holly sarcastically and not without a bit of anger "I can read, I just can't believe it. What do we know of the area, are there any mines or geological faults or anything in the area? There must be something we are not seeing."

"No. Nothing. The whole area was extensively surveyed before the tunnel was built. Any signs of instability or mine works would have meant the tunnel could not have been built or would have had to be significantly strengthened. Anyway the surveyors have been down since the incident and found nothing unusual".

"What about gas pockets? Were there any of those?"

"No, Holly, nothing was found. They did sample drillings out to each side of the tunnel as they dug specifically to look for gas accumulations but none were found. They even repeated that all along the length of the tunnel after the incident just to see if there was anything that had been missed before. But they didn't find anything".

"Well it's a blood mystery then. At least if it had been a terrorist attack we would have had something to go on but this". Her voice tailed off in frustration at not being able to understand.

After a few minutes one of the voices in the back of the room spoke again. "The only thing about that tunnel was interesting was that it was driven through an old plague pit. Thousands of skeletons had to be removed and re-interred. In Sussex I think".

NINETEEN

The Grand hotel was not exactly one of the best hotels in Westminster and its name was a rather an exaggeration of its quality but then the budget did not stretch to one of the best ones and, in any case, luxury was not top of the list of requirements. It was more important to get close to the source, or potential source of the problem quickly so Helen and Wes Lawns had booked in on the Thursday morning and immediately set up their equipment in their room. They had been monitoring the partition around London as usual for a couple of days before and had come to the conclusion that there was potential for an incident somewhere in the vicinity of Westminster. The problem was that they could not determine when it might occur so they decided to take a room in a local hotel just in case something happened. At least they would be closer than they would otherwise be and might even be able to stop anything happening.

Moments before the morning sky was lit up with blue emergency vehicle lights Helen and Wes had picked up the problem in the tunnel as it was developing and before it had actually happened. They rushed out of their room trying to get to the source as quickly as possible. Prevention would be infinitely preferable to repair. Keeping an eye on their detection equipment they quickly arrived at the platform that Jev should have been stopping at but they quickly realised they were too late to stop the partition tearing. Indeed before they could have done anything the disaster had happened but, at least, they were on hand to help usher the spirits back as quickly as possible and to help with the repair.

They had just finished their work when the alarms went off and they were swept with the rest of the passengers away from the platform and up the stairs to pavement level. It had not been easy getting back to the hotel with the police busy setting up cordons and keeping people out. Crossing the roads was a danger in itself as emergency vehicles rushed back and forth not expecting to see people inside the cordon. Eventually they made it back to their room and settled down recording the events and watching the commotion outside.

Helen and Wes had met over ten years ago on one of the occasional meetings, organised by Norman Bay, which were held to pass information about. It was important that all areas of the country were being covered and that the keepers were able to get to know each other and compare experiences. Since then they had barely ever been apart and in recent years had spent more and more time monitoring and repairing the partition. Today was no exception. At the beginning of the week they had detected the unusual and unexpected change in the partition. A weakening that was initially difficult to explain. At least it had been difficult to explain until the announcement that a huge data warehouse had been turned on in central London. Massive increases in the use of the internet for communications, commerce and entertainment had meant that all over the world huge data centres that drew everything together, stored all the data and serviced all the interactions were being built all over the world and it was noticeable that they were having an effect on the partition.

Here in Westminster Helen and Wes had seen the effect for themselves and they had been monitoring the flux being caused. They knew that the partition could react very rapidly if stressed, although it could equally be rapidly healed. It was a bit like a drop of soap, the data centre, being dropped onto an oil film, the partition. As soon as they came in contact a huge hole could be blown in the oil slick by the soap drop but it could soon reform. Here the data centre was the soap and the partition the oil slick.

This particular day had started quite quietly. The partition came and went but seemed to be holding firm. Slightly worrying was the activity on the other side. There was an unusual amount and it appeared the equilibrium was being disturbed almost as if it was tipping on one side and everything was being thrown to one side. This could mean the worst of both worlds. High levels of activity, concentrated in a small area putting large stresses on a thinning and weakening partition.

Eventually and predictably the partition gave way just as Jev pulled out of the station and into the tunnel. As the last carriage left the platform behind the spirits from the victims buried in the plague pit poured across the partition and merged into the same confined space of the tunnel. The train usually pushed the air in front of it along the tunnel and out into the station pulling air in behind it but the presence of the spirits had the effect of displacing the air in the tunnel and the train carriages which rapidly became a virtual vacuum.

Helen and Wes had worked frantically putting into action familiar routines although attempting to cope on a scale they had never seen before. It was only a matter of minutes before they had restored order guiding the spirits back onto their side of the partition and giving enough time for it to be repaired and preventing a reoccurrence but it was all too late for the train in the tunnel between Westminster and Waterloo.

TWENTY

International Working Party for the Provision of Intensive Electromagnetic Radiation based Communication and Control Systems.

Summary Report

Chairs: **Professor Sir Hugh de Beachy**

Doctor Lady Alice Park

Aim:

The aim of this ambitious and ground breaking international project is to engage governments and governing bodies on a national and international level to participate in the design, funding, construction, deployment and maintenance of a network of low orbit and geo-stationary satellites interconnected with high intensity and broad range base stations and data storage and handling complexes. This development and deployment is designed to support current requirements for electromagnetic communication and control systems and facilitate the expected future expansion and development of communication systems supporting twenty first century and future transport, commercial, financial, social, health and intellectual systems.

Background:

Since the early 20th century communications have been based on two different technologies: cable transmission or radio wave technologies. Initially this was used for the provision of non-irradiating electromagnetic radiation in the form of radio waves supporting systems such as national radio broadcasting systems, RADAR and television broadcasting. Originally this was centred round single, central sources transmitting a single signal one way to receivers. Telephonic communication was solely based on point to point cable technology transmitting audio signals in two directions either through copper wires or, later through fibre cables.

The basis of the non-cable systems that were to replace the cable systems was Electromagnetic Radiation (EMR) which is a low energy, low frequency form of non-ionizing radiation and is considered safe and non-injurious to the human being. The **Frequency** of EMR is defined as the number of cycles of a wave that pass a point per second and is measured in the System International (SI) units of Hertz (Hz). Frequencies range from 30 kHz to 300 Giga Hz with the range of 300-900 MHz being the most common. The range of frequency used is known as the **Band Width**.

Electromagnetic radiation can be found in the forms of Ionising (IEMR) and Non ionising radiations (NIEMR). IEMR is a high energy form of radiation and has the ability to cause human and animal DNA damage and, hence, in high levels is incompatible with health and life. However, although unrestricted use of NIEMR is potentially damaging when it is used, for example, in high doses for the generation of LASER radiation or in the production of microwaves for cooking it is generally used at energy levels low enough to be considered not to be harmful to life if used with appropriate precaution.

The development of mobile phone and internet communications based on NIEMR in the late 20th and early 21st centuries drove a very significant increase in the use and demand for connectivity, transmission speeds and carrying capacity both in terms of numbers of communication events and the volumes and types of data being transmitted. The principle of the technology was based on the ability to communicate between two or more people who may not be in fixed positions. Cable based systems became obsolete not providing the same flexibility of service or the capacity and speed that were demanded and necessary so were considered unable to cope and were gradually phased out. Communications were therefore entirely based on NIEMR systems.

To serve increased demands for electrical power overhead and subterranean transmission lines proliferated and they increased in capacity from the early and mid-21st century. Also as fossil fuel based power generators were gradually closed down from the early two thousands in response to climate change pressure, renewable power generators such as solar, wind and wave sources were initiated. However installations, generally, were of low output compared with nuclear or oil powered stations which required there to be multiple sites of generation, far more than was required from power stations requiring thousands of extra miles of transmission cables. They also consumed large areas of land or, the ocean based generators, proved hazardous to shipping movements. However these sources eventually proved to be too unreliable for a nation to depend on as sole suppliers of electrical power and they failed to provide consistent, sustainable and sufficient levels of energy despite sophisticated battery storage systems and there were issues with short half-lives of the machines and the inability to recycle them. This was exacerbated by the world-wide adoption of electrically powered transport systems, all personal transportation as well as trains and commercial vehicles had to be powered by electricity by the mid twenty first century, together with the abolition of gas based household services such as cooking and heating.

The most reliable provider, albeit with its own health and safety issues, was nuclear based generators which kept supplies in line with demands. Large installations were replaced by multiple, small scale generators which still required a greatly increased cabling and distribution grid.

Despite the inexorable direction of travel there was some early medical and scientific resistance to the provision and scale of NIEMR as far back as the 1970s. There were claims that the radiation, despite being non-ionising, was having negative health effects causing cancers and other forms of tissue damage. Sources of the radiation was identified as coming from above ground electricity transmission cables which were said to generate electrical fields and corona (small charged ions). This was repeated as the levels of grid infrastructure increased to accommodate the extra power generators. Although, eventually, it was accepted by providers and medical representatives that magnetic fields could potentially stimulate nerves and muscles this could only happen at levels much higher than those found around power lines. The girds were therefore considered safe.

There was also initial concern that mobile phones, which were the first major development and implementation of NIETR for the general population, could cause brain damage or cerebral or facial cancers due to the proximity of the radiation source to the body's tissues. However many studies by the mobile phone companies showed that although the amount of radiation generated by a mobile phone was higher on initial contact than initially thought the duration of the interaction meant that the average level of radiation exposure fell. Significantly they were able to show that the total amount of radiation emitted from a mobile phone was significantly less than the levels required to cause tissue damage and it was concluded that they were therefore safe to use.

Initially mobile phone coverage, which at its inception was quoted in Generation Levels (1G, 2G 3G eventually to the last so named level 15G), in the early stages were analogue and it was not until 3G that digital technology took over which has been the case ever since.

The early development of the mobile phone meant it was used almost exclusively for transmission of the spoken word but by the early part of the 21st century the instrument had developed into a hand held multi-functional computer with terabyte capacity. The increased functionality and high speed processing power led to the development of devices that became more integrated into life styles such that day to day activities were not possible without a hand held "smart" device. The telephony aspect became a decreasingly important component.

In more recent years the standard computer based systems of communication and entertainment have themselves been usurped by the fundamental life management systems such as tech to tech communication, autonomous transport and delivery systems. The advent of the quantum computing systems raised the role of the mobile computing devices from desirable to essential and the speed and capability of the systems put these systems on a hitherto unexpected level. However such dependence on a high capacity, multifunctional information technology based life support system made life very fragile. Power, function and rogue state and ideology based terrorist activity caused outages of functionality which caused severe disruption on frequent occasions. The result of such activity caused many national emergencies as failures of communication and the back office tasks maintaining finance and banking, commerce and national safety became compromised due to ransomware attacks and malware installations by rogue states and terrorist organisations. Review of systems suggested that the systems at the time were counter-intuitively insufficiently grounded in everyday life and were inadequately supported in terms of volume and reliability. Much more investment in terms of finance and technical intervention was required to support and develop systems to incorporate increasing functionality but also to protect and supply reliability of service.

THE FUTURE

The transformation from a uni-functional mobile telephone capable of only making and receiving telephone calls to a multi-functional personal societal integration device (PSID) required significant technological improvement. In addition the development of many other computer led facilities such as drone delivery, autonomous transport, crypto coin mining and transactions and personal surveillance meant that there became an urgent need for increased band widths, data transfer rates and transfer speeds. This was required to facilitate and accommodate increased audio and video communication together with addressing latency or delays in downloads which have advanced significantly. These developments have been enhanced and made possible by the support of international co-operation and standardisation of all system elements.

There are considerable risks associated with this high level, highly expensive development of new and comprehensive communication systems. For the world to be able to adopt the potential for exponential growth and development outlined in this plan will require the involvement of national governments across the globe. Opting out of large countries with high GDPs and therefore the ability to commit significant funding to the project would cause the project to fail. Similarly the opting out of geographically significant countries which might house base stations and terrestrial assets would also handicap the project. Of course multi-national dependence on a single system could have the potential of countries using the systems to monitor activities across unfriendly countries for espionage purposes or to disrupt national systems with the introduction of malware. There would therefore be required mechanisms for monitoring participation and ranges of sanctions to ensure that the systems were not abused.

However, early progress and development has proceeded exponentially. In 2015 there were only 7.4 billion people on the planet with around 5 billion mobile phone users. As the availability of equipment grew so the number of phone calls increased and so did the duration of the phone calls. Alongside this there were massive increases in personal messaging and, facilitating this, the numbers of social networking interactions also soared. Eventually these sites became discredited through misuse of personal data and fake data and the numbers of subscribers fell dramatically resulting in many ceasing to be viable organisations. However the development and growth of new, more secure and trusted multi-functional applications that were more capacity hungry has outstripped the loss of networking sites and created huge, increased demand for functionality. In addition there has been an explosion in the numbers of, primarily, entertainment and leisure based industries providing streaming services for products such as music, film and gaming.

The simple use of a mobile phone has developed in to the need to support:

- Knowledge and entertainment based resources
- Driverless transport and navigation system for:
    - Cars
    - Buses
    - Trains

- Motorcycles, scooters, bicycles and other individual forms of transport
- Ships both commercial and leisure craft
- Airplanes, commercial, leisure and military.
- Aerial taxis
- Satellite and out of atmosphere craft.
* Fixed wing and rotary drones for
  - Geographic reconnaissance for water resources etc.
  - Population surveillance in general but particularly in high concentration scenarios such as concerts, sporting fixtures or social gatherings such as Mardi Gras.
  - Delivery systems such as the Scuttle Bugs small volume computerised delivery robots replacing high street commerce and food deliveries.
  - Delivery systems for medical purposes such as samples and drugs.
  - Traffic monitoring and speed control for management purposes.
  - Wildlife surveillance for protection against poachers and to monitor protected species and reintegration programmes
  - Policing of illegal activity such as logging, illegal plantations, drug cultivation and water abstractions.

- o Migration routes and the movement of large numbers of people away from areas of desertification, conflict or rising water levels to ensure target countries are not overwhelmed.
- o Military applications which are classified.
- o Agricultural crop planting and surveys
- o Submersible drones for sea surveys
- o Monitoring waste collections, large scale fly tipping, accumulations of such items as tyres.
- Three D Printing from centrally held, patent protected patterns.
- Potential for teleportation of inanimate and later animate objects
- Facial recognition technology throughout the world so that population movements in general can be monitored and specific monitoring for criminals, terrorists or other people of interest can be maintained 24/7 and universally.
- Vehicle tracking and monitoring to ensure taxation on mileage of personal transports and commercial carriers can be monitored and charges raised as well as population monitoring.
- Health monitoring and constant telemetry to ensure patients with heart pacemakers, diabetic and blood pressure monitoring can

be constantly monitored for timely health interventions.
- Supporting the now cashless society. Since money in the form of coin and note has been abolished all transactions of whatever size or value are conducted electronically for convenience, security of a cashless society, health and disease transmission reduction, population monitoring and spending trends.
- Ocean cleansing systems such as the gargantuan waste dumping craft, the small surface dredging systems delivery waste to the central ships and the submersible systems trawling below the surface and delivering to the central ships.

FORWARD PLAN

A plan to support the developments and inevitable expansion of system based on NIEMR on a global basis and to ensure uniformity, standardisation and quality control of multiple inter-related and pan continental systems is required. In addition to supporting significant increases in volumes of local traffic the committee proposes an international project to cover the globe with ultra-fast, immediate response, high volume microwave communication based communication systems produced by a dense network of geostationary low orbit satellites that are economic to launch, maintain and replace. They would also be future proofed with significant capacity for expansion.

In preliminary discussions fifteen countries have offered to be the first launch sites with manufacturing spread across eight countries. These have been selected on criteria such as their financial ability, their scientific and technological support structures and their geography. They are:

USA	Australia	India
Russia	Egypt	Japan
Canada	South Africa	Brazil
South Korea	United Kingdom	Spain
China	Sweden	Nigeria

English will be the universal language.

Initial deployment will be 1500 satellites with positions relevant to the numbers of transactions and population number. First adopter countries will be served in the first wave and their geographical location will determine many satellite positions ensuring maximum connectivity. This will also serve to inform future deployment sites and their space/ terrestrial locations. It is anticipated that within ten years there will be over 50,000 satellites within the network.

Control and maintenance of communication will be supported across all satellites from all land based stations with a central overall command and control centre in New York administered by a rotating governance committee with members drawn from all participating countries. This will be located in the now defunct United Nations building but will connected via the networks to individual countries. Future developments and plans will be formulated, discussed and implemented from this location.

It is anticipated that applications and volumes for all known functionality will increase which will undoubtedly require an increase in the numbers of satellites. The initial deployment will serve a limited number of countries with further countries coming on line as satellites are launched and base stations constructed. The final numbers of satellites in the network will depend on the total numbers of countries involved, the current applications and work-loads and the yet to be agreed future proofing for as yet undetermined expansions.

For example, there is currently little activity in the polar-regions but with the increase in mining activity and population growth as the ice caps recede and temperatures rise satellite coverage will need to increase in these locations. Conversely as ocean levels rise and desertification progresses other hitherto heavily populated areas will become devoid of population and therefore electronic activity will reduce. The satellite network will be flexible enough to permit the addition of unlimited numbers of satellites, a variety of sizes of satellites and allow the relocation of satellites already in orbit.

This will also be the case for hitherto desert areas such as the Sahara and central Australia which will support increasing numbers of people as land is reclaimed through irrigation and cultivation. These, amongst other sites will be able to support significant volumes approaching thousands of square kilometres of solar panels feeding into grids supporting the need to increase electricity supplies supporting, primarily, transportation but also the need to have continuous, uninterrupted activity of all personal and strategic devices.

Although not in the initial plans it has been considered possible that manned support stations held in slightly higher orbits may be a more cost effective and speed sensitive support facility recognising the fact that the system would be critical to the functioning of society. For example, the infrastructure required to maintain low altitude aircraft activity control for drone movements could not be allowed to fail. Emerging "return to base" facilities for drones would help prevent catastrophic failure but with hundreds of thousands of delivery and personal transport drones in the air at any one time a failure of the air traffic control system would cause massive public chaos and undoubted loss of life.

Future developments will include the integration of all systems with bases on the Moon and, potentially, Mars.

EXPECTED COSTS

1500 satellites at $3,000,000 each

37 support stations at $150,000,000 each

Running costs $100,000,000 per year

Anticipated overall cost $57 billion

Full breakdown of set up costs, support, maintenance, development as percentages of GDPs of participating countries are published in Appendices F1-27 of the full report.

RISK ASSESSMENT

Satellite loss

This could occur in a number of ways:

Collision: Mitigated by computer guidance systems detecting units and using individual drives to prevent collision.

Falling to Earth: Loss of orbit might cause satellites to fall to Earth due to gravitational pulls although impact damage would be reduced by burn up of units as they fell through the Earth's atmosphere with little likely to impact the surface.

Failure in communication: Loss of individual satellite communication would be compensated by close support of units in close orbit and the ability to launch repair or replacement units at short notice from local maintenance bases.

Increased volumes of non-ionising radiation: All communications for all purposes will be through the medium of non-ionising radiation: Early studies showed that the amount of ambient radiation the population will be exposed to will be non-harmful to both the individual and the environment.

CONCLUSION

The committee commends this proposal to all national governments and nations and proposes that all parties indicate their commitment to the global communication project by committing financial funding, human resources, relevant intellectual property and territorial and energy sources to ensure the new communication revolution can impact the global population ensuring the impact is greater than any previous revolution.

TWENTY ONE

Things had changed quite a bit at number eighty six since Wil had moved in and he felt ready for his first meeting. It was a few weeks after Lewis, Harvey, Lottie and Wil had met for the first time at the house and although they had all kept in touch with each other this was the first time they had all met again at the house. Mainly because the discussions they had had when they first met were quite interesting they had all agreed that they would like to learn more and if Wil was willing they wanted to meet again and maybe help him if he needed any. Wil, looking to the future, and having concerns about the state of play decided it would be a good idea to strengthen the team. So one summer's evening they all piled in through the newly decorated front door for the first meeting immediately noticing they were not met with piles of newspapers.

Looking to the right the front room had also been cleared out although there was still only the one chair in it but at least the walls could be seen and light was getting through the newly washed curtains more easily. The almost virtual carpet had been discarded and the bare boards, although not polished, did look clean. With a little imagination the different colours of wall paper caused by some being exposed to the light and others being covered by layers of newspapers could be seen as a pattern. Without imagination the whole could do with replacing.

At the back of the house the kitchen surfaces were clear although it looked as though Wil had the same appetite and culinary skills as Norman with the exception of chocolate biscuits as there seemed to be even more packets and especially empty wrappers. The cooker could actually be seen and the kettle looked to be the most used piece of kit in the room.

The table room at the back of the house still had the table in the centre although there were now some chairs around it and the curtains at the clean window were equally clean. Everyone was eagerly looking forward to seeing the upstairs room so they went up the uncluttered stairs no longer fearing for life or limb.

"Well you have certainly been busy up here!" exclaimed Harvey looking into the still immaculate but very different room.

"Yes, I have made a few changes".

"You can say that again", said Harvey looking enviously at the bank of computer screens now balanced rather precariously on the small desk. Around the house every surface had been swept of dust presumably making thousands of insects homeless at a stroke or a wipe but the shelves in this room remained immaculate. Some of the older files had been moved to the floor being replaced by small USB sticks hung from the shelf above and all with small plastic labels with date ranges. The top shelf still held all the impressively bound reference books but now they were neatly arranged left to right in height order.

Wil started to explain what he had done. "First thing was to go through a lot of the newspapers. I didn't go through all of them 'cos there were thousands but I sampled a few piles to see if there was anything of interest. Eventually I decided that Norman had been a bit of a hoarder and there was nothing much in the papers that would be of any help".

"Even if there was what was the chance of finding it?" said Lottie

"Quite. I presume Norman must have been able to remember a lot of what was in them but he couldn't have remembered it all so what were the chances of any of it being helpful? Anyway he seemed to have clipped out all the relevant stuff and put it in the files. So out it all went".

Reverting to type Harvey suggested that the recycling places must have been delighted or horrified when tons of paper turned up on their door step.

"Not too pleased, but it did mean I had a bit more space to move around in".

"Bit more space," repeated Lottie in surprise "but you soon filled it up again," waving to the screens.

"Yes. I had a lot of trouble trying to get Norman to embrace technology and I never did quite manage it but I thought it was going to be necessary in the future if what I think is going to happen happens".

"So what do you think is going to happen?" Asked Harvey "and what exactly is this partition you kept mentioning?"

They all went back downstairs into the table room and each pulled out a chair and sat down ready for an explanation and all feeling a bit like they had just returned to school. Wil sat down, leaned forward resting his elbows on the table and inter-lacing his fingers. Looking down at them he drew in a deep breath. He knew this was going to take some time and some believing but he cast his mind back to the day he was sitting, expectantly at the table and Norman started explaining what was going on.

"Right, so Norman and now I were, are, guardians, monitors, not sure what is the right word is but whatever it is we look over what we call the partition. What is the partition? Well, a pretty fundamental question. The partition is effectively a barrier between two worlds. Our world and the spirit world".

He paused and looked up at the faces of the other three to see if they had already given him up as a nutter. They hadn't. Yet.

"So the partition is a kind of wall that stops the electrically slightly negatively charged spirits of the deceased coming back into our world. The thing is that the partition has historically been a fairly fragile structure at the best of times and occasionally it fails. It could be just that it becomes too thin and breaks or, maybe, there are stressors that impact the partition and cause it to break and they could be any number of things. When there is a break it means that the spirits on the other side come across and into our world and they have to be sent back. Sometimes it is small numbers, maybe one or two, maybe none come across and it is just a tear but sometimes larger numbers come across and they have to be sent back and the tear or fracture in the partition repaired".

"A wall?" Harvey asked sceptically. "A wall like a brick wall?"

"Hang on", chipped in Lewis "let's go back a bit. Are you saying that when we die we go over this partition into some other world? Are you crazy?"

Wil was almost relieved that Lewis had challenged the notion so quickly. It was a natural reaction to those that did not believe in, what they liked to call the afterlife, and Wil now had to convince him of its reality.

"Just going back to the wall thing, no it is not as fixed like a brick wall might be it is much more fluid and fragile. If you think of it as more like a layer of oil on a lake separating the water and the air. It is thin but viscous. It moves constantly sometimes being thinner and sometimes thicker. Sometimes there is no layer there at all until it flows back together again. If you think of a layer of oil on a pond. If a feather floats down it will rest on the oil and not go into the water but if the oil layer breaks the feather will go into the water. All the spirits are encompassed by the partition but they are not held in one place like they would be if it was a brick wall".

"So all the spirits, feathers, are held in place by the wall, oil, and if that breaks they come into our world, the water. And do they stay in one place on the other side of the wall?"

"No, not all of them. Like I said the partition moves. Sometimes it might circle, say, one round Eastbourne and another round Hailsham. Sometimes the partition encompasses both together and spirits can move across between the towns. Sometimes a single partition can encompass the whole country but then it starts getting very thin and fragile. One thing it cannot do is exist over water so all the spirits are held over land."

"So it's the spirits that are held back by the partition and not us?"

"No it's not us, and this gets a bit complicated. We can move through it without disturbing it. It's a bit like in the movies where they show ghost walking through walls. Actually it is the other way round with the partition. We can walk through it because it just flexes as we go through and reseals itself. Like swimming through water. It is there but if we come in contact with it, which obviously isn't very often, we can pass through it. We do it all the time but the spirits cannot move through the partition itself and we think that is something to do with their slight negative electrical charge. A bit like fish cannot pass out of the water. They can only move through it when it breaks".

"But why would they want to come back across the partition?" asked Lottie.

"They don't want to come back. It is not as though they try to break down the partition or have any choice about where they are. Go back to the shepherd Cuthman, remember him? He drew a line or partition between his sheep and the outside world and the sheep stayed on one side of the line and did not cross it. Usually the spirits stay on their side and do not cross it. If they appear here it I because they fell out of their side not because they consciously moved out".

"So what do you know about the other side?" Asked Lottie drawing on her degree in religious studies and thinking her tutors would have had a ball if they had been aware of any of this. If any of this was actually true.

"Well, we don't know a lot about it and there is no way of communicating with the other side so, truthfully, we know nothing about it at all. It appears that they just do not have the same type of feeling or sensations that we do. They don't fight. They have no competition. They don't have to eat or drink. They don't have to work so there is nothing like money. They all just seem to exist in peace and harmony if you can believe that. But what is their purpose is not known. A bit like when we ask ourselves why we are here. No-one really knows he answer".

"So it is really difficult to understand what life, if you can call it that, is like over there but I suppose it must be there for some reason", added Lottie.

"Difficult to imagine all that peace over there, everyone argues here all the time," chipped in Lewis well aware he was extremely argumentative.

"True, but if you take away all the things that people argue about, things like religion, the partition has no place for religion, take away politics, take away greed and hate, take away competition and it is all just like a giant Woodstock concert or Glastonbury but without the mud. The last thing they want to do is to come back. They may also be from generations long ago so they have no role here and we wonder if they do come across whether it actually distresses them. You can imagine what a Victorian would think of the world today let alone a Tudor or Anglo-Saxon".

"So they can't help it, coming back into our world. Is that what you are saying?"

"No they can't and they work very hard to make sure that they do not. Just like we work very hard to make sure they cannot."

"How do you know if they have come across or if the partition is broken"?

"Well, those on this side with the responsibility do have a second sight, a sixth sense if you like but we also have some tools and, of course, training".

"You say you look after it on this side, so there are guardians of the partition on both sides of it?"

"Yes, not surprisingly we on this side die and we just carry on when we go over to the other side. Norman's probably there right now learning the ropes".

"And you are one of them?"

"Yes, I am. Norman trained me but there are lots of us about. It is a great shame that we cannot learn from those on the other side. It would be so useful to understand their side but it just may be that we could not understand it. It seems so very different over there".

He looked up to the ceiling and smiled as if acknowledging Norman in the room. Quite why they did they did not know but the others all looked around half expecting to see Norman in the room maybe nodding his head in agreement.

"Ok, so two questions. How do you put them back and how do you repair the partition?"

"Well, putting them back is quite easy bearing in mind they do not want to be here so with only a few rare exceptions they are happy to go back and co-operate completely. Of course there are a few exceptions and they are the basis of all the horror films that you might see. The so called evil spirits that want to do harm and damage things. Maybe spirits that did not want to die and want to be back in our world. I hesitate to say the real world because who is to say ours is the real world".

"Just a minute, are you saying this is not the real world?"

"Well it is our world but is it the real world? What is the real world anyway?" he said stressing the word real. "The dinosaurs might have thought theirs was the real world. If they could think. Whatever came before them probably thought theirs was the real world and whatever comes after us when we are all long gone will think theirs is the real word. But maybe the real world is the constant emptiness of an empty planet. Maybe we are just blips of infestations on a planet and the real world is just millions of empty planets that might, once upon a time have had life or may have life in the future long after we are gone. Maybe the other side of the partition is the real world".

"Well that sounds a load of old nonsense. So what about repairing the partition. How do you do that?" Lewis was not being convinced.

"Well usually, if it is small enough, it just repairs itself. If you think of water. If you drop a stone into water the surface breaks to let the stone through and as it sinks the water parts to allow it to sink but as it passes through the surface of the water comes back together again. The partition is much like that. It can break and then reseal itself as if nothing has happened. Of course in many instances there are no spirits near the partition when it tears so nothing can leak through. Going back in time, of course, there were many, many fewer people so fewer deaths so fewer spirits on the other side. We assume the space on the other side of the partition has remained the same, just as the size of the Earth has not changed, so there was never a lot of crowding. Now, of course, with billions of people and the population growing all the time it must be getting more crowded on the other side. I think they have calculated that there have been something like a hundred billion people living on Earth since day 1. The problems start if there is a big tear and either it is too much for the partition to reseal or if too many spirits pour across because they are in the vicinity of the tear. Then the partition definitely cannot repair itself and needs our help".

"Does that ever happen?"

"It does and it is happening more frequently with bigger tears."

"Why?"

"It could be a number of things. One is that it appears the partition is becoming more fragile which is a problem because there are more pressures on it from more transients, that's what we actually call them rather than spirits, being on the other side which is another issue and the other is external pressures on it."

"Well why is it more fragile now?"
"We think one of the reasons is pollution. One of the thoughts is that there is so much atmospheric pollution that it is softening the partition and dissolving it away. The problem too is that the areas where there is most pollution, look at some of the huge cities, are the areas where there are the most people at risk because there are the most transients on the other side. The other thought we have is that the partition is made of something brought to the Earth on inter-stellar winds. We don't know what it is actually made of, we have never been able to sample it for testing so we assume we cannot make it because it is not made of something on this planet. The issue may be that the pollution in the atmosphere is preventing whatever it is that makes up the partition getting to it and reinforcing it. On the opposite tack we know some of the weaknesses correlate with times of high solar wind activity so maybe there is something out there that we do not know about that can dissolve the partition and also something that can be used to fabricate the partitions".

TWENTY TWO

"But, so what? A few spooks leak out of their cage and flit about on a day out until they get chased back. Why should that bother me? What harm does it actually do?"

"Well my friend, your few spooks might seem harmless and they, essentially, are safe and don't intend to cause any harm. Of course there is the odd exceptional poltergeist or malevolent spirit and that can happen when there is a problem with transitioning but they are really mainly only in films and people's imaginations. They are different cases and can really be ignored although I will grant you there are the odd exceptions. But the presence of real spooks, as you call them, transients as I call them, can cause several problems for us and by us I mean everyone, everywhere. They can affect anyone and everyone, everywhere and, of course, everyone will eventually become one".

"That can't be right. We've all read about the ghost in the house shifting things around and slamming doors – big deal but you are saying we all become one. We all turn into ghosts."

"That's right although I wouldn't say that we all turned into ghosts. Ghosts is not a great term to use and I really don't care for spooks either. You have read about malevolent spirits and, like I have said, you have seen it in the films but let's pretend that, actually, they do not exist except in books and films. But that doesn't mean that spooks as you call them do not exist."

"Ok, ok so poltergeists do not exist but people are always seeing the lady in whatever colour dress wafting up or down the stairs how can she threaten us?"

"Let me give you a couple of examples of the problem. The average spirit, if there is such a thing, is not just a shadowy mist that resembles a person. Well, it is a shadowy mist sometimes but it is more than that. Spirits actually carry a small negative electrical charge. Almost everything carries a charge. That's how the EEG or ECG at the hospital works and you know you can light a light bulb using a potato".

Harvey looked quizzically at Lewis with an expression suggesting that Wil was either having a laugh at their expense or was going nuts.

Wil continued. "Anyway, they have a negative electrical charge. Some have a bigger charge and some have a smaller one. No-one really knows how they pick up the charge but it is thought that they pick it up as they pass through the partition between the worlds a bit like you picking up a static charge by rubbing against something. Anyway, however they pick up the charge there has been plenty of investigative work done to suggest there is a negative charge in the vicinity of spirit activity. Norman was actually one of the main investigators that proved this. Now, normally this is not a problem but recently it has become more of a problem. Have you noticed there are more people with asthma?"

Lewis and Lottie were taken a bit off guard by the question. It was not quite what they were expecting.

"What the hell has asthma got to do with it?" asked Lewis

"Have either of you got asthma?"

"No, but my sister's kids have both got it," chipped in Lottie.

"Does anyone know how they got it?"

"No, it was put down to the old house they lived in and the damp in it. The drafts can be like the north wind in the winter and it does always smell a bit on the damp side".

"Good, so there has been a massive increase in the number of asthma cases over the last number of decades and no-one knows why. In fact they say there was no such thing as hay fever back before Victorian times and that it is actually a new thing that never existed before. Some people say asthma is down to atmospheric pollution from things like car exhausts or from chemical pollution. Some say it might be down to all the electromagnetic pollution from phones, Wi-Fi and the like and that might actually be the cause of more than just the asthma but no-one will actually commit to a reason."

"Ok so what is happening, and like I said before what the hell has an increase in the number of asthmatic wheezers got to do with ghosts?"

"Yes, spirits" stated Wil correcting Harvey as if conclusively making a point. He settled back into his chair. "Spirits," he repeated.

"You have got to be out of your mind. Ghosts, I mean spirits, give us asthma. Ridiculous. We have never seen hide nor hair of a ghost, spirit, in my sister's house and the kids still have asthma", Lottie was becoming less convinced and was still having problems with what Wil was saying compared with what her tutors had been saying at university.

"Just because you have not seen a spirit does not mean they are not there," stated Will.

Lottie looked at him not knowing if he was joking or not but he did not look as though he was joking. She suddenly felt a bit scared. She was never quite sure what she would have done if she had seen a spirit but the thought of them being there all the time without you knowing was not a comfortable thought.

"What is the main thing people say when they say they have seen a spirit?" asked Will.

"I don't know. They float about. Appear and disappear".

"Yes, they appear and disappear. And how do they disappear? Where do they disappear to?"

"They just vanish or walk through doors or walls".

"Exactly if they come across the partition they can pass through solid objects. Everyone believes spirits pass through walls. It's been in the films for years. Solid objects mean nothing to spirts, they pass right through them. Door, walls," he paused and looked at the trio continuing "you and me".

"But not the partition?"

"No, not the partition. Seemingly everything else but not the partition".

"What, spirits pass through us!" That was more than enough for Lottie. "Not only can spirits be about all the time, unseen, but they also pass through us."

"Why not? You're solid. Some of us are a bit more solid than others" shooting a glance at Lewis.

"That's disgusting. I don't want things passing through me. How can they?"

"Things pass through you all the time and you don't notice. Solar winds, neutrinos, electromagnetic radiation. Ever feel any of it?"

"Well no I guess not."

"And nor will you. Just like a spirit passing through you. Never feel it – maybe."

"What do you mean maybe?"

"Well, you might actually feel it and some might feel it more than others. Of course the vast majority of time there will be no spirits about because they will be safely on the other side of the partition. Ever shivered for no particular reason?"

"Yes."

"Ever heard someone say they felt as though someone had walked over their grave?"

"Yes."

"So just suppose they are references to a spirit passing through someone. Do you know what sharks do as they go into the attack?"

"No thank goodness and I am guessing they do not go through you. Well not like that anyway".

"When they get really close to their prey they roll back their eyes to protect them which means they cannot see where they are going. Instead they rely on the electrical activity in their prey being detected by sensors around their mouths."

"And what has that got to do with anything?"

"Ever felt a tingle in your lips when you are about to kiss someone?"
"Can't say I ever noticed," said Lewis

"I have," said Lottie looking a bit bashful.

"Well notice next time. The lips are very sensitive to electrical energy just like the shark. When you go in for a kiss they will tingle just before you make contact. Alternatively, sometimes you might feel you want to lick your lips sometimes for no real reason. Granted they may be dry or covered in doughnut sugar but other times there may seem to be no reason. Now that tingling might be a sign that a spirit has just passed through you or is in the close vicinity and you are picking up the electrical energy".

"Yeah, right and next thing you'll say is that your lips will tingle when the shark is attacking. Well I've got news for you there might be a lot more going on than just my lips tingling if a shark attacks. There could be a whole lot of pollution problems at the very least".

"So I might detect them even if I could not see them," summed up Lottie.

"Correct".

"But people often see spirits," she continued.

"Sure but only because spirits have been made visible perhaps because of atmospheric conditions or perhaps because the person seeing them is sensitive to them but it is actually very, very rare and not all the sightings are genuine anyway. Have you ever seen anything out of the corner of your eye that was not actually there? I am pretty sure that people who say they have seen spirits are actually concocting the vision in their brains to explain what they think they might or might not have seen".

Harvey was not being convinced. "So spirits or ghosts are about all the time but people do not always see them?"

"Right, they are about, but of course they should not be and even if they are it is pretty rare. They are here because they have moved from the other side of the partition where they should stay"

Will saw Harvey's look of disbelief. He was not convincing him.

"How many times have you ever seen someone out of the corner of your eye only for there to be no-one there?"

"So, Wil, is it possible that you can see people who you knew who have died? There are times when I feel that my dear old grandma and grandpa are around me. Is that possible?" interrupted Lottie.

"It is possible, yes." answered Wil

"How?"

"Well like I said the spirits stay in roughly the same area where they crossed but they do move about. Sometimes your grandparents may be closer to you but much of the time they may not be very close. If they are close and that coincides with a particularly thin partition you might feel their presence quite closely".

Lottie wished that she could have actually spoken with the spirits or at least seen them but she was pleased that there was the possibility that her grandparents were still about and maybe saw what she was doing.

"So just going back to what you were saying about seeing things out the corner of your eye. That happens. So are you saying that every time it is a spirit?"

"Quite possibly. As with all this there is a lot of theorising but it could be that you might see a spirit if they are there are the atmospheric conditions are right. Think about your breath on a cold day."

"On a cold day I see my breath."

"And on a warm day?"

"Ok so on a warm day I do not see my breath."

"Quite it is all down to atmospheric conditions and it is the same with spirits. If the conditions are right, for example the electrical conditions, you might see them."

"But how can there be different electrical conditions in the atmosphere?"

"Well the obvious one is electrical storms. It's not actually a coincidence that the film makers associate storms with monsters and spirits. Well, actually it is probably a coincidence but they are actually right. Lots of electrical charges in the air when lightning is about. Look at doctor Frankenstein's lab, top of the castle right in line of all the lightening. Problem now is the amount of electrical activity in the air is much higher than ever before. Ever walked under high energy electric cables?"

"Yes," said Lottie, "where we used to go horse riding we had to ride under gantries with high powered electric cables".

"And what did it feel like?"

"Well you could hear the buzzing and it did give you a bit of a head ache as you rode under it. Even the horses did not like it. They would shake their heads as if there were flies buzzing around them".

"So the microwave goes off and a spirit might appear but how come some spirits are supposedly seen in the same place over again and how come they are spirits for years ago?"

"Right, ever heard of ley lines?" asked Wil.

"Yes I have," said Lottie.

"Good, ley lines were discovered, invented or described however you want to put it by a bloke called Alfred Watkins around 1920. He reckoned that significant things like churches, stone circles, burial mounds and anything with some sort of religious significance were all connected by lines of energy and the things built on them were built on them for that reason. They were not just plonked down at random. There was a reason".

"And the reason was?"

"Depends on who you talk to. Some say they were significant places for the people and they were built on straight lines for easy access. Seems reasonable. Others say they were actually lines of energy and places were built at intersections where the energy was at its greatest."

"And the point is?"

"That there are lines of energy all over the world and where they intersect they can interact with spirits in the area and cause them to appear to the naked eye. That is why some spirits appear in the same place, because they are trapped in the lines. There is a strong line that goes through Beachy Head and up through Jevington, Alfriston and, of course, the Long Man in Wilmington".

"Ok so ghosts or spirits can be around all the time, we might only see them if they hit a high energy area and we might tingle if they pass through us. What the hell has it all got to do with asthma?"

"Yes, sorry, we drifted off topic a bit. If a spirit, negatively charged, passes through a person that charge could, if it was high enough, or the person was sensitive enough to it, could affect the tissues as it passes though. Now it just so happens that the lungs are the most sensitive organs to negative.electrical charges. The electrical activity then seems to make the lungs even more sensitive and that is shown by the person becoming prone to asthma. It is particularly so in kids whose lungs are not fully developed and are more sensitive so spirits passing through kids sensitise lungs and cause asthma".

Wil continued "It also just so happens that the numbers of cases of asthma are increasing most in the more densely populated parts of the world. More people, more deaths. More dead people then the chances of spirits being about increase. The more electrical energy there is about the greater the chance of spirits being about".

"So what can be done about it? Does it just continue until everyone gets asthma?"

"Oh no the future could be much, much more serious than that. The situation is getting much worse and Norman was one of the foremost authorities on it. He will be greatly missed".

"Missed by who exactly?" asked Harvey.

"People like me for one. He trained me over the years and many others but he was the expert and even he was tested on occasions. That is what all this paraphernalia is all about," he gestured at the bits and pieces around the room.

"Hugely increasing populations, massive increases in electrical and magnetic activities. Atmospheric pollution. Increased numbers of coffee shops – well maybe not that one. It is not good. Of course it is the numbers of spirits or ghosts that will increase as the increased populations die off. Did you know that for twelve thousand years there were no more than four million people on the planet? Now there are knocking on for seven or eight billion. With no major wars or diseases like we used to have the population is going to keep rising. People are healthier now, give or take, and are living longer. Okay so people are tending to have smaller families in some parts of the world but in others they still have huge families and the numbers keep going up and there is one certain thing and that is that all the living people will eventually become dead people. Like I said before it is reckoned that from the beginning of human habitation there have been over 100 billion people living on the planet. The second probable thing is that if the presence of a spirit can cause asthma in certain circumstances and there are more spirits then the numbers of asthma cases must therefore rise".

"So everyone who lives, dies and becomes a spirit. The spirit world numbers increase in direct proportion to the numbers of people living and dying".

"Right, but that's not the end of it unfortunately".

TWENTY THREE

The soft autumn mist swirled gently over the lightly dew dampened fields of harvested corn. The birds busied themselves flying between the fields and their nests singing as they flew high into the trees of the numerous small copses in the pretty area of Picardy. Their busy, excited chatter filled the air competing with the burbling of the river making its way to the ancient city of Amiens.

Corporal Albert Praed lifted his eyes to the clear blue sky and watched two butterflies wheeling and fluttering in the warm air. It was a perfect, perfect morning.

It was all so different to the last time he had been there. That was October 15th 1916. A day that lived in his memory forever. The place was very far from being perfect on that day. There were no birds, no butterflies and no copse. The only thing that was the same was the name. Somme. Back then it was a ghastly, grisly area of God forsaken ground. Earth churned and blasted to kingdom come. Crater upon crater created by thousands of rounds of high explosive lobbed from behind German and Allied lines all filled with pools of stagnant water, stinking, still. Wooden stakes joined by mile upon mile of rusting and twisted barbed wire. Every now and then there would be a patch of material torn from a soldier's uniform as he tried to clamber over the infernal stuff blowing in the gentle breeze. Not a tree was to be seen, not a green leaf, even the sky was leaden grey. The air was thick with the smell of cordite, despair and hopelessness. The only relief was the smell of strong cigarettes and thick tea wafting from the deep trenches.

Not so many years ago, but many lifetimes ago, he had been standing outside the enlistment offices in his home town joking and laughing with his friends who were all keen to join up and fight the Germans. It was all going to be a great adventure and they did not want to miss out. They all said the war was going to be over by Christmas and they all wanted to be part of it. The enlistment process was very efficient and the queue moved quickly. Forms were filled in, personal details noted, ages lied about, next of kin worryingly listed and dates for attending the nearest military base were distributed. It would not be long now. Albert, who had never been more than a few miles from his home town would be off to jolly old France.

In the blink of an eye he was standing in line wearing his new and rather uncomfortable uniform, shiny black boots that, although desperately uncomfortable now, he was told would wear in and become comfortable after a few hundred miles of marching. In his hand was an unloaded rifle, they were not to be trusted with live ammunition yet. Wait until they are facing the Hun for that. On his back a pack that, he was told, contained everything he would need overseas. So it was that he set off marching through the town to the cheers of the population and the sounds of the brass band. The streets were decorated and it was almost a street party. How it all was to change.

The trains were full of laughing and chatting freshly trained soldiers all heading for the channel ports. They smoked and looked out of the windows seeing the steam billowing out of the engine up front and down the length of the train. New friendships were made and plans for the future determined. Stories and photographs were exchanged. Cigarettes and sandwiches were shared. After a quick boat journey and then a quick trip on rather uncomfortable French trains they were in another world. This was the world of war. The action at the front, or more accurately the inaction, had lasted for months now. The one big, decisive battle that was charted on maps back at head-quarters had descended into hundreds of small ones as small groups of soldiers would fire at each other as and when anyone was foolish enough to give away their position. Albert had arrived at the front only two days after the start of the campaign and aside from the movement of a few yards forward and then a few yards back he was where he had started surviving on a diet of unidentifiable meals being brought up from the rear, cigarettes and adrenalin. The smart, clean and uncomfortable uniform was now filthy dirty, creased and uncomfortable. The shiny black boots were covered in a permanent layer of mud that had to be chiselled off with the bayonet permanently slung from his waist and they were also still uncomfortable. Some of the bits and pieces in the back pack were useful but the chocolate and the cigarettes were the most appreciated items.

The majority of shells that constantly whistled overhead and were initially terrifying were now usually ignored unless finely tuned brains calculated ones falling in the near vicinity. Occasionally a shower of mud and water would rain into the trench if the shell exploded close to them but otherwise they had been as much a nuisance of wasps on a summer picnic. Other trenches had not been so lucky. Many of the friends he had made in the queue at the enlistment office had travelled over with him would not be travelling back. New friends were made as they arrived as replacements in the trench but very often they too disappeared into the mud or were carried back to the field hospitals with terrible injuries.

This morning they had been called to breakfast earlier than usual which alarmed them. Routine was comfortable and boredom was safe. Any changes to it could be worrisome. As sure as eggs were powdered eggs that meant something was happening. Rumours started to spread along the trench that today was going to be a big push. Today would be the start of the end of the war just like it had been umpteen times up to Christmas 1914 when they had been promised the war would be over by. Sure enough straight after breakfast the orders started to come through, guns were loaded and bayonets fixed. Uniforms straightened and mud brushed off as much as was possible in such a mud pit.

The British army had to be smart as it went over the top. Cigarettes, many being last cigarettes, were lit and ashen faces were deep in thought. The brass bands that saw them off on their adventure were a distant memory and all they waited for was the sound of a whistle above the sound of thousands of shells that they were to march to today.

They did not have to wait long which was just as well. Standing in a trench waiting to face the guns of the enemy was not a good place to think in. They all knew they were there to do their duty but they all knew that today could be the end of their war if not the end of everyone's war. Bravery was not the word.

Suddenly the artillery behind them stopped and the whistles blew. Over the top mate and keep your head down. Almost at once the demented wood peckers a hundred yards away started to tap their bullets out in a continuous, murderous stream and Albert heard them streaming past him. Corporal Praed kept his head down not needing to look where he was going but out of the corner of his eyes he could see his mates falling either side of him. His rifle felt heavy and useless in his hands as he tried to clamber across the muddy pits and wire. Occasionally he would raise the rifle and point it towards the enemy trenches and let a bullet off. He knew it was not going to kill anyone but it made him feel better. As he was plunging down the side of one crater he felt a hard slap on his chest. He looked down and was relieved to see nothing. But the blood was already pouring from his chest underneath his uniform. He looked to each side not really knowing what he was looking for and he tried to carry on walking but it was becoming very difficult. The rifle suddenly felt very heavy and he felt cold. The sounds of battle seemed to diminish and he heard the brass band from home. As he struggled on a pain started in his chest and he dropped his rifle in the mud. Suddenly he knew what was happening. It was the last thing he ever did know as he fell, shot dead, into the mud.

It was all so different now. As Albert moved across the field he heard the incantations coming from close by. The voices were loud enough to drown out the bird song but were not being shouted. They sounded comforting, something that he wanted to hear and he headed towards the sound. Suddenly he became aware he was not alone in the field. He could see hundreds of people all in what looked like uniform, although it was difficult to make it out, moving towards the sounds of the voices. But there seemed to be German uniforms as well as British and other uniforms he did not recognise. They all looked calm and unperturbed as they moved slowly in the same direction.

It had been over a hundred years since he and all the others had ran across these fields towards the machine guns and now he was walking them again with his comrades from all that time ago and he felt content that he was being guided back home and he was happy to go.

TWENTY FOUR

"So spirits can get out of the partition and if they don't get sent back then they could cause asthma?"

"That is a possibility but it could be much worse than that if they can get across in significant numbers and in the wrong place. Let me ask you what you think happened to the dinosaurs?"

"Right so we have ghosts and spirits and then you go off on asthma and now you are onto dinosaurs. Are you having a laugh or something?" Lewis was not convinced that this was a sensible discussion.

"No, it is all linked, just go with me. What happened to the dinosaurs?"

"They died out millions of years ago".

"How did they die out?"

"Wasn't it said that a meteor hit the Earth and sent up clouds of dust that blocked out the sun for years reducing the temperatures and making all the vegetation that the dinosaurs ate die off so they died off as well and all the non-veggie dinosaurs died off as well because they couldn't eat the veggie ones".

"Correct, that is one explanation but I can give you another one".

"Don't tell me they all got asthma and died off".

"Not quite but there are some links. But first another question – how long has man been on Earth?"

"What is this some sort of pub quiz?"

"Just tell me. How long has man been on Earth?"

"I don't know. A couple of million years," Lewis stabbed in the dark not knowing where the argument was going.

"It depends on which argument you believe so let's say that in some form or another humans have been around for two million years or so but it is really in the last two thousand years that numbers have really been rising. Now your starter for ten is how long did dinosaurs last?"

"Blimey, I don't know. Millions of years. Tens of millions of years".

"Yep, millions of years. Let's say a conservative estimate of hundred and fifty million years. Now how long did a dinosaur live?"

"Like I am going to know that".

"Well, let's say twenty to thirty years. Now for some maths. If one dinosaur lived for twenty years and then another came along when it died over a hundred and fifty million years that would mean there would be seven and a half million dinosaurs living and dying if they did it one at a time. If there were a thousand dinosaurs to start with then after that time there would be seven and a half billion dinosaurs. Same as the numbers of people now."

Wil looked at the other three who were all looking blank and more than a bit puzzled. He continued.

"So we can safely assume that because the dinosaurs did not live one at a time there were hundreds of billions if not trillions of them of all shapes and sizes over those millions of years. Admittedly not all of them as big as the fancy ones that get all our attention. But assuming their spirits acted the same way as ours do then there were billions maybe trillions on the other side of the partition. Again, assuming they worked the same way ours does then there must have been occasions when the partition broke down and they came across. A big difference though was that there seems to be no electrical pollution of the Earth or any pollution for that matter as far as we know. And there was no way of repairing the partition."

No, they still looked blank. This was going to take a while.

"So they did not have a Norman or me or the rest of us to repair any fractures if they did happen. Fortunately it is a bit different now. We have been able to work out some facts at least about the partition and found ways to maintain it and get spirits back across it if it does break down. In fact this was being worked out hundreds of years ago. We are just the latest to learn about things. Dinosaurs never quite managed that. Another crucial thing is that the land mass was very different then. There was very much a single land mass and not loads of smaller masses separated by water".

"What has that got to do with it?"

"Ah, like I said before spirits seem not to be able to cope with water. Although they seem to be weightless they cannot exist over water so any bodies of water act as boundaries, similarly the partition does not seem to exist on water. Really we do not know the real reason but those are the two most favoured observations."

"Just a minute" started up Lottie "are you saying that animals have spirits the same as we do?"

"Of course they would. Why wouldn't they?"

"But I thought it was a religious thing. You know you behave and your spirit goes to heaven, misbehave and you go the other way. There was no mention of animals having spirits".

"Religion has nothing to do with it. The partition existed way before any religion was dreamt up. After all dinosaurs, arguably, had spirits and they were not conspicuous church goers. Religion hijacked the ideas of spirits for their own ends. All religions use their own version of life after death because they wanted the power over the people. If they could scare them enough about heaven and hell then the ignorant population would believe them and do everything they could to make sure they went up not down. To make sure they were acceptable to religious leaders they would enrich the churches and as a consequence religious leaders and give them huge power. Irrespective of religion all humans live and die but so do all animals. What is the difference apart from the fact that animals do not have religion? Just because we choose to believe in something higher does that mean we are more likely to have a spirit world. To answer myself – no. Animals and we are all the same. We all live and die the same way. Here today and gone tomorrow and we all have spirits. Dinosaurs included."

He paused a minute.

"Everyone wants to think they are not going to die but when they do then they hope there is somewhere else to go after we die. Maybe somewhere better after all for centuries life down here was pretty horrible. It was all disease, hunger and war with short ugly life spans and tough times. Although listening to some now it has not got any better. Anyway, belief in a glorious hereafter or paradise perhaps made the tribulations down here more acceptable. Nothing the religious leaders could do about it, in fact they often made it ten times worse, so why not offer paradise on the other side if you behaved yourself. Did prehistoric man believe in God?"

"Well there are plenty of things that suggest man did believe in something that they would pray to and ask for help from. There are heaps of historic buildings that we think were linked to religious practices".

"Quite, religion hooked onto that idea and used it for its own purposes refining it as it went. If you prayed to the god they represented – whoever it was and obeyed their rules, whatever they were and gave them your money or goods then the chances of you going to heaven would increase. If you did not and misbehaved or didn't give them your money you went the other way. Nice little earner if you can convince people of it. Of course nowadays some religions are in decline because people do not believe but others do and they have a really strong hold on their followers. It really doesn't matter what they believe they all live and they all die and trip across the partition and there is no belief in any gods over there".

"But you are saying it doesn't matter if you believe or pray or whatever you will still die and will still go to the spirit world?"

"Yes"

"Why?" It was getting beyond Harvey. "Why go to the other side. What's the point? What's there? What do the spirits do? Are they there for eternity?"

"Good questions. I wish I had the answers. You might as well say what is the point of life itself? We hang around the planet for seventy or eighty years trying to stay alive, procreating so there are even more people trying to stay alive and then we die and soon it was as if we never existed so what is the point of life? Is it just a crack at perpetual motion? Once life has started it just goes on and on until one day it is all wiped out and it starts all over again? It doesn't seem to bother any other planets. Nothing is there so what is the point of them. What is the point of millions of stars, planets and galaxies swilling round in a great open space that, presumably, goes on forever? Bit too deep so maybe I can have a go at answering the last question. It is not thought that the spirits last for eternity. There is no evidence, for instance, that the dinosaur's spirits still inhabit the other side. Somehow they seem to have gone. I certainly have never seen any and there are no human time records of them ever coming across the partition."

"So, like I said. What is the point?"

"Yes, and how do we know people do go across to this place anyway?"

"There are no eye witnesses of course. No-one has been able to report on the journey and come back as it were but there are clues. I presume you have heard of out of body experiences?"

They all agreed. "Lewis has had a few of those, especially on a Saturday night haven't you Lewis?"

Lewis ignored the comment and feigned deep interest in the discussion.

"You might have heard of people saying that as they thought they were dying they saw a tunnel or corridor which they had to walk down. Sometimes people on the verge of passing will sit up and look into the distance seeing something that we cannot see".

"Yes, and if it is not their time then they come back from the light and carry on living."

"Exactly. Heard them talk about the Pearly Gates. When you die you pass through the Pearly Gates?"

"Yes we have all heard that one. So the Pearly gates open to let dead people through into the next level?"

"Well Pearly Gates is a bit of an embellishment but there are no actual gates and there are no actual pearls but there are at least openings in the partition that you pass through to the other side. Now these openings, doors, gateways whatever you want to call them are planned and regulated. Sometimes they are marked but usually they are only apparent on passing maybe at the end of the corridor at by the white light. Of course the snag is that it is only a one way gate. Once through it there is no voluntary coming back into our world. But tears and fractures of the partition can happen and spirits can come the other way even if only involuntarily."

"Anyone seen any of these gates?" Wil continued with a question.

They looked at each other and all shook their heads.

"You have. Think more."

They thought more and still shook their heads. This was getting all too difficult and crazy and thinking was just making it worse.

Wil got up and walked over to the map and jabbed his finger onto it.

"Long Man mean anything to you?"

"Well it was supposed to represent the gates of hell," suggested Lottie.

"Exactly. East Sussex must have been a centre of expertise of sensitivity or something because they could identify where there were Pearly Gates. Where people passed between the levels and they marked it with the Long Man".

"But you said animals could go across as well".

"Why shouldn't they? Just because we think they do not believe in gods like we do. Anyway we are only animals the same as them only we are not very clever ones because we bugger things up as we go along and at a very rapid pace. Other animals don't do that and dinosaurs lasted for millions of years. We won't."

"So on the other side are animals and humans," Lottie started to try to clarify the issue.

"Yes."

"And do they occupy the same space. Can we see them on the other side?"

"Well, we think they do not occupy the same space as they have different levels of electrical charge. We do not know how the levels are determined but it might be down to things like brain size or rather the electrical activity of brains."

"Bit worried about you, Lewis, you might end up in the wrong bit if you haven't got enough brain activity", chipped in Harvey.

"So if they are both on one side can they both come back onto this side?" continued Lottie ignoring Harvey.

"Yes they can but we think there is a different sort of partition that divides the animals from the humans. We don't know why there is or should be but if there is a different one it might be that it is stronger than the human partition. Of course if both of them broke and spilled all the spirits onto the Earth then we would be in trouble. Just imagine the numbers of animals that have lived, the numbers that are slaughtered every year to feed us. If they all came across as well as the humans there would be a disaster. But generally, if they do come across we cannot see them. But other animals can."

"How?"

"There are plenty of stories about animals being spooked by ghosts if you pardon the expression. A friend of mine had a dog that would not walk past a particular bench in the park. It turned out that there was an old lady who sat with her dog for hours on end on the bench almost every day just watching the world go by. One day she died as she sat on the bench. Her dog sensed this and after giving a long howl promptly died of grief himself. It was said that the spirit of the dog would sit by the bench waiting for his mistress to come back. My dog could see the spirit of the dog and would detour right around it. Did you have a dog?"

"Used to," said Lewis.

"Ever see it looking at something that was not there?"

"Yes, sometimes he would look, cock his head on one side as if he was listening."

"He may well have been listening but it was more likely he was seeing. Seeing animals from the spirit world. Maybe, sometimes he was scared by them. Did he ever raise his hackles or growl and then run away?"

"Sometimes."

"Then he had probably seen something that had frightened him and he cleared off."

"So you are saying that there are spirits of everything including the dinosaurs swilling about on the other side with the potential for coming back into our side?"

"We might see a ghost of a dinosaur?" chipped in Harvey rather hoping that he could. It would certainly help in putting the bones the archaeologists dug up easier.

"No you won't see a dinosaur ghost or a woolly mammoth or, in case you ask, a blue whale. Interestingly we do not know what happens to sea creatures. We have never had a case of a whale or anything else like it so we assume they do not share our side of the partition but we do not know where they go. But that brings us back to the point you asked about earlier. What is the point?"

"Yes, what is the point?" Harvey repeated remembering what he had said what seemed to be days ago.

"So let's agree that millions of years ago and for millions of years there were many, many billions of dinosaurs living and dying with their spirits going over to the other side".

"Agreed".

"Occasionally one comes back across the partition but generally everything stays in place. There is nothing to disrupt the partition and it holds".

"Agreed".

"So to be rather simplistic about it all the world was a natural world. There was no Man about to fiddle with it. Everything had slowly developed or evolved to live together with no unnatural influences. But one day the partition fails catastrophically. It effectively disappears and all the spirits pour out into the living world. Billions and billions of them. What happens next?"

"All the others get asthma?" Harvey chipped in hoping to be helpful but not banking on it.

"Not sure you are taking this seriously now. No they did not all get asthma. They all died."

Will paused to let it sink in. The others were quiet.

"They died. All the living dinosaurs died out and it was due to the partition failing and all the spirits of the dead dinosaurs falling into the real world?" queried Lottie.

"Correct."

"Okay but first how did the partition break down and why did it cause the living dinosaurs to die?"

"First things first. How did the partition break down? Well there are numbers of reasons why things happen. A wall might fall down because the foundations move, because something crashed into it, because someone knocks it down, because a bomb drops on it. Loads of reasons and that is the same for the partition. In the dinosaur case we think it is down to something like atmospheric pollution or global warming."

"What!" exclaimed Harvey. "They had global warming and that caused them to die out. But we have global warming now, allegedly, and it is supposed to be because of human activity. Car engines, home fires and burning fossil fuels and that. Didn't think the dinosaurs had cars and power stations. So if global warming killed them all out does that mean we are all going to die out because we have global warming?"

"Global warming has always happened just like global cooling. We have always had ice ages and hot spells but they are usually spread out over thousands or millions of years. It happens naturally but now we are told it is happening in tens of years because of the build-up of carbon dioxide and other gases in the atmosphere. But we are told this by scientists who do not know their Bunsen burner from their slide rule."

"True, but like I said I am pretty sure dinosaurs did not have cars or factories or power stations pumping out carbon dioxide and the others into the atmosphere".

"No, no cars and no carbon dioxide but there was plenty of methane".

"Methane?"

"Yes methane. Global warming, such as it is, is not all down to carbon dioxide. There is a lot of methane now and that is more polluting than carbon dioxide and, back then, there was a lot. So where does it all come from?"

"Cows. Today it all comes from cows. And Harvey," chipped in Lewis trying to get his own back on Harvey.

"Yes, definitely cows and possibly Harvey. Why does it come from cows?"

"Because they eat a lot of grass and that produces methane. But Harvey doesn't eat grass".

"Okay so cows produce methane and fart a lot. Cows are farting us to death."

"Well not quite", Wil smirked a bit and continued "cows eat vegetation and fart and belch a lot and it probably doesn't help but that is not what I am getting at. So what about vegetarian dinosaurs?"

"So they are huge compared to cows. They eat huge amounts of grass or greenery. They produce huge amounts of methane. They fart for Gondwanaland or Pangaea or the super continent and fill the atmosphere with methane. Billions of dinosaurs each producing more methane than a herd of cows."

"That's disgusting" said Lottie as she screwed up her nose. "Gigantic dinosaur farts. Wouldn't want to be standing behind one." She thought back to her horse riding days riding across the downs behind a horse who would suspiciously flick their tail to one side and then spend the next five minutes farting in her face as she followed it.

"Gigantic dinosaur farts from billions of dinosaurs over millions of years and they get the same polluting effect we have produced in a couple of hundred years, if that. Clever aren't we?"

"So you are saying the increase in the gases in the air raised the temperature of the Earth and that had an effect on the partition and it broke and the spirits came across and killed off the dinosaurs?"

"Yep. And it is not quite so different from today. Methane is made up of carbon and hydrogen and lasts for around seven and a half years before it is broken down to carbon dioxide and water and there we are with an atmosphere packed with methane and carbon dioxide."

"So it was an accident that it happened wiping them out. If it had not happened then the dinosaurs might have been around today".

"It's possible. Of course if the dinosaurs were still here then we probably would not be. It might also mean that the creatures that were on the Earth before the dinosaurs appeared might still have been there and the dinosaurs may not have existed. The planet has been around for around 4 billion years and the dinosaurs stared something like 250 million years ago so what is to say that there was another huge form of life on the planet millions of years before the dinosaurs and if there was what happened to it and if nothing had happened and it was still in existence what would it look like and would we or the dinosaurs ever have existed? It might also be that after we have all gone, which might not be too far in the future that another form of life will appear on Earth as different from us as we were from the dinosaurs and as different from them as they were to what came before them. It might be that the clearing of the Earth through the breaking of the partition is not accidental or, at least, it is not a bad thing. It might be a way of clearing one population and letting another start."

TWENTY FIVE

"Hang on a minute. Are you saying that the loss of the partition is a natural occurrence and happens to clear the Earth to let it start again?"

"Yes, that is a distinct possibility, and it might already have happened several times and will probably happen to us. May even be happening to us right now. Will probably happen more times in the millions of years to come with whatever forms of life appear on the planet assuming we leave anything that could support life. Whether it is a deliberate plan or just a consequence of what happens on Earth is another thing. Depends whether you believe in a grand planner or maybe just a natural order of things. A rhythm that repeats itself every few million years".

"Whatever might follow us will depend on whether they could live on bits of plastic, old bicycles and shopping carts," added Harvey drawing on his years of house clearance experience.

"Whoa, just a minute. Are you saying that global warming is our dinosaur farts and it might destroy the partition and allow all the spirits to flood the Earth and kill humans off?"

"Not just humans. Everything. And it might not be a determined act of clearance it might just happen by accident."

"Crap. Just sci-fi nonsense. Where would that all have come from?"

"Ever read the bible?"

"Well, no, can't say I have. I was waiting for the film," admitted Lewis. Harvey and Lottie both nodded their heads in agreement.

"You know the story of Noah though don't you?"

"Of course. Everyone knows that one. God said there was going to be a great flood that would wash away all evil and Noah had to build an ark to save his family and all the animals of the world".

"That's right. Good old Genesis. Ever heard of Deucalian?"

"Duke who?"

"No not Duke who, Deucalian. He was the son of Prometheus and husband of Pyrrha."

"Oh that Deucalian" said Harvey with gusto. "No, never heard of him".

"OK stop me if this sounds familiar. Prometheus, one of the Titans in Greek mythology warns Deucalian that Zeus is fed up with all the evil in the world and he is going to send nine days of rain to kill off all the evil in the world. Deucalian, who was the king of Thessaly, and his wife were the only ones to be spared".

"What about the animals?"

"No, no animals. That has to be the problem with the Genesis story. Along with all the other problems. How do you collect examples of all the animals in the world and how do you stop them eating each other? And if you are going to leave one out why would you miss out the unicorn? Save poisonous snakes, wart hogs and insects but lose the unicorn?"

"So the point is, again?"

"The point is that the same story comes up all over the place. There is some catastrophe that wipes the world out. They give you a glimmer of hope like Noah and his family being saved or Deucalian and his wife being saved but it's hardly likely they are going to repopulate the world between them. But maybe in real life there are no survivors. Might not be very acceptable to all those who are lost so it must just keep them on the straight and narrow."

"Seems the odds of winning the lottery are better than being a Noah or Deucalian", observed Lewis reflecting on his inability to win the lottery.

"On the other hand if there is the slightest chance of being washed to Kingdom come we might as well enjoy ourselves now and to hell with the ten commandments".

The three did not look impressed so Wil continued. "So what if there was no flood of water. What if there was a flood of spirits? Suppose there was a tear in the partition? Suppose it disintegrated completely like it did for the dinosaurs? What would the effect be?"

"Everyone gets asthma and we see ghosts all over the place?" it seemed the logical conclusion to a crazy discussion for Harvey who was getting a bit bored with the notions.

"No much worse than that. Remember that I said spirits can materialise where electrical energy co-ordinates are favourable and that they can penetrate tears in the partition. They can pass through solid objects and they have a negative charge."

"Yes we got all that. Not sure we believe it all. Any of it actually but for the sake of argument carry on".

"The main and most important point is that the spirits actually also occupy space. They may seem ethereal, floaty, of no substance but they do actually occupy space. They displace air".

"What, you mean they come back like their body was. In a shape."

"Everyone who has seen a ghost, or claimed to have seen a ghost, has described a human shape. The shape is usually proportional to a human body, if a little bit bigger, and might have some recognisable characteristics but the idea of them wearing particular sorts of clothes or uniforms are a bit of artistic licence on the behalf of the teller of the story. They do not have clothes but what they mostly have is volume. They occupy space".

"So they occupy space. What is significant about that?"

"What if, at the end of the dinosaur period, the partition ruptured because of the high levels of methane and the billions of space occupying spirits of deceased dinosaurs poured onto a finite area of land surrounded by water but where all the living dinosaurs lived?"

"Beats me."

"So billions of spirits each occupying a space and being able to pass through the living so they overlap, if you like the living. What happens if you are crushed in a crowd of people?"

"You cannot breathe. You suffocate"

"What happens if you are in a confined space? Trapped underground for instance?"

"Same thing."

"So what happens if there are space occupying objects not only crowding you but passing through you and enveloping you?"

"Same thing again I suppose. You suffocate."

"Exactly and that was what happened to the dinosaurs", Wil stated triumphantly slapping his hand on the table as if he had conclusively proved his point.

"You are saying that the spirits of dead dinosaurs broke through the partition because of the living dinosaur farts and it suffocated the whole lot of them?"

"Yes. Well maybe not the whole lot of them but enough to put an end to reproduction leading to dramatic falls in numbers and eventual extinction."

"You're barking", Harvey looked at Lewis for back up and saw him nod but just a little. Lottie showed no reaction. It all seem too fantastic to be believed. But then, just maybe it made sense and right now she couldn't think of any counter arguments.

"Hang on a bit. You are saying that if the partition breaks everyone, everything on the planet dies and the Earth starts all over again."

"Yes. Well it could happen like that and maybe not overnight. Of course it could be that human numbers would fall so much that they could not recover even with the spirits still present. They may not be able to farm or get enough to eat. How would you get on if there was no supermarket at the end of the road? How long would you last living on the land? It happened with the dinosaurs. It might have happened to whatever was living millions of years before them. It might have happened on any number of planets in the universe. Everyone thinks there might be life on the other planets. Well there may well have been but they may have gone the way of the dinosaurs and the planets are just waiting for life to start again. Like it did here ending up with us".

"And we are going to go the same way? It might be worth stocking up on the essentials before the corner shop goes pop. You know stuff like toilet rolls and chocolate biscuits."

There was much nodding at the mention of chocolate biscuits.

"Certainly is possible although we are much more inventive. Yes we have global warming and Lord knows we have been battered by the eco-mentalists enough over the years. One stressor is that because of the huge and increasing population numbers we have millions of cows, millions more than we used to have and they all produce methane not to mention the pigs, sheep and the rest. We also have huge demands for electricity which had been generated using fossil fuels, we have millions and millions of cars, usually stuck in traffic jams, pouring out gases so we seem to be talking about carbon dioxide and methane being parts of the problem this time. But, and it is a gigantic but, we also have massive amounts of electrical energy and radiation. And to cap it off we also have nuclear bombs, potential starvation, possible droughts, viruses, antibiotic resistant bacteria and all sorts of other ways of killing ourselves off either directly or indirectly without affecting the partition. Brilliant aren't we".

"So on one end we have the possibility of getting asthma and on the other end we have total wipe out."

"Well there is a third way" said Wil trying not to sound too dramatic.

"And that might be that we do not believe any of it and just get on and hope for the best."

"That might be a fourth way but let's look at the third way. What if there was a bit but not a catastrophic and total tear in the partition. Suppose a lot of spirits came across but not all of them? What might happen then?"

"Presumably it would be like the flood story but not on such a large scale?"
"Exactly and this has happened time and again over history but it is only when it happens on a really large scale does anyone take any notice. The last thing Norman did was to go to Tunbridge Wells to see the guy that died in a climbing accident."

"Yes, we heard about that on the TV."

"Well that guy was trapped in the same place where a tear occurred and a small number of spirits poured out. They occupied the space all around him and he suffocated. Norman had to get the tear repaired and get the spirits back to the other side. No-one took much notice of it at the time because it was such small scale and easily explainable even if not correctly but if it happens on a large scale, as it has done, it tends to pass into folk lore. Examples like the TW one happen quite often but it is quite rare for larger ones to happen. Thank goodness."

"You can say that again. But the news said the bloke had a heart attack".

"Thank you. Heart attack is a good excuse for an unexplainable death and it keeps everyone quiet. A fracture, leak and consequent death is rare and the latter day Noahs and Deucalians, that is Norman and me, do not broadcast the happenings. We just get on and repair it and record it. But soon there may be a deluge of spirits rather than water of biblical proportions."

The room went quiet. It all sounded stupid but what if it was true. What if there was going to be a deluge. Lewis couldn't help but think his association with this house had started off so simply. Just go and sort out a house, clear it out and come back for tea and biscuits and now here we are listening to fantastic tales about dinosaurs, the end of the world and spirits. Maybe he was still asleep it will be like the character Bobby Ewing in the TV series Dallas all this would be a dream and unreal, he would wake up and be back on the cleaning job. On the other hand.

Eventually Wil started talking again.

"You have heard about Atlantis". It was not so much a question as a statement.

They all agreed it had been a rather agreeable nightclub at the end of Eastbourne pier. Lottie recalled staggering down the pier at chucking out time trying not to get her high heels caught in between the pier board walk and looking forward to a kebab to eat as she made her way through the town to the taxi stand.

"So Atlantis was a lost civilisation – not a night club. A magnificent city swept away by the sea but what if it wasn't engulfed by water. What if it was engulfed by spirits and then got washed away."

"No don't like that one. I prefer the thought that a giant tidal wave or something swept the city away and drowned everyone. In water." Lottie shook her head disbelievingly.

"What about Pompeii. That was overwhelmed by volcanic ash which rained down and suffocated most of the population so there are examples of places being wiped out by space occupying phenomena."

"And you say this has happened before" continued Lewis.

"Well you could be right about Atlantis but there are hundreds of cities out there lost for centuries. Built up and developed over long periods of time and then they suddenly lose the whole population leaving the buildings to be claimed back by vegetation. There are examples all over the world and they are the ones that have been discovered there are probably hundreds more that have been completely lost where the populations and the cities have vanished forever never to be found again. We have lots of buildings and evidence of civilisations that have been lost but we have very little evidence of dinosaurs considering the numbers there must have been and no evidence at all, at least that we recognise, of what came before the dinosaurs but they all came and went just like the ancient civilisations."

"Again, you say that these are examples of where partitions have torn and spirits came and suffocated the populations but you don't have any proof of what you are saying".

"Not easy to prove what happened to the dinosaurs and for millions of years nothing did happen to them. They just carried on evolving and producing large quantities of methane. And going back in our history there were not as many people in those times. So not so many people, not so many spirits. There had not been the time to build up any natural pollutants, shall we say, like methane and carbon dioxide so there was unlikely to be any strain on the partition. Not so many spirits came across but they were probably concentrated in small areas maybe surrounded by water. Like Atlantis. And maybe there were no people about who could or needed to repair the partition or who even understood what was going on. If you look at some of the books upstairs though you can see that Norman had catalogued thousands of incidents that he recognised but, perhaps, others did not. As well as the ones he got involved in he had gone back through the history books to look for potential instances and did find some. The key thing is that the numbers have been increasing in recent years and that increase is becoming exponential. I have scanned them all onto the USBs and created a cross referencing system so we can easily scan what has been happening".

"But anything like a big issue would cause a bit of a panic."

"Certainly would. It would be a bit like the plague hitting London and people dying all over the place with no explanation except this would be must faster and there would be nothing like the symptoms they got with plague".

"So maybe it was more like Pompeii" Lottie chipped in helpfully. "That was a sudden cloud of ash that choked the population in a matter of hours".

"Exactly. It is a good example. One difference being that the ash covered the whole city and everyone could see what happened. With spirits there is no damage. Nothing left to see".

"It can also be repaired and perhaps reinforced so it does not tear in the first place" added Lottie optimistically

TWENTY SIX

"But even if they did all come back, there's plenty of room isn't there? They don't need houses and stuff. Surely they could just spread out."

"They could and they do to a certain extent but they are a bit like the living in some respects. Although they do not need houses or food or that kind of thing they cannot exist in areas where they could not exist if they were living. For example they cannot exist in deserts, tops of mountains or over water. They are pretty much restricted to areas where we live and that is something less than fifteen percent of the surface of the Earth so not a lot of space really".

"Even so there must be a massive amount of space to fill".

"True, but like I said they tend to congregate where they lived and passed through. So areas with high populations have high density spirit populations. There are no trains or cars on the other side no way of moving even relatively small distances so they just hang around where they passed over. If you could imagine a brick on a table. How would it move around? It cannot so it stays put. If another turns up then space has to be made. Bit like the tube. It might be packed to the gunnels but if someone is determined to get on then everyone squeezes under everyone else's armpit to let them it. Until there really is no room left and then there is a problem".

"What about wind?"

"Wind. Are we talking wind wind or are we talking dinosaur fart wind?"

"Wind, wind. Can't they be moved around by wind wind?"

"Well I know I can be moved by fart wind especially if it is in a closed space and after a kebab," added Lewis unhelpfully.

"Well they do move a little with the atmosphere but it is not a conscious move. They cannot say that they want to hang around London today and the Lakes tomorrow. They move a bit with eddies and currents in the atmosphere but their world is not affected by weather like ours is. There is no hot or cold. Nor rain or snow. No seasons. No measured time. It is very different to ours. At least we think it is".

"So what you are saying is that where they peg it is where they stay".

"Yes, that's the main reason. But there are other reasons like ley lines, lines of electrical charges which act a bit like fields of cows hemmed in with electric fences. But mainly it is just that they cannot move anywhere else. That's why sightings of the same thing are reported in the same place. Why, for example on Culloden moors there have been repeated reports of the dead soldiers being present. It is not because they want to stay in Culloden it is just that they cannot move anywhere else".

"Okay, so if they died in Eastbourne they stayed in Eastbourne?"

"Bit like those that have moved to Eastbourne and now refuse to move on, shall we say"?

"Yep although in really populated areas they might eventually fill the available spaces and start spilling out onto the boundaries".

"Except across the sea."

"Except across the sea. But they might start to merge with spirits from Brighton, Hastings and so on. The partition is also quite fluid. It can, in theory at least, extend, for example, all round the coast line of Britain so there is a lot of space for spirits to move about it. Alternatively it can cover many very small areas like just around Eastbourne or even, perhaps, just around Meads. It can ebb and flow joining up and splitting apart. It is not a solid entity like a biscuit tin and we are not sure why it seems to drift abut as it does. We don't know why, today, it is just around Eastbourne and tomorrow it is around Eastbourne and Hastings".

"So what's the problem?"

"One problem is not so much the space they have to exist in for one thing, as far as we can tell there is no limit to the amount of space on the other side, not like there is on this side. Our rules of physics do not seem to apply over there. The problem is if the partition between their space and our space breaks down particularly because we, on Earth, do have limited amounts of space. The other problem is that the whole partition thing seems to be thinning. So if, for example, it spread around the coastline it would be much thinner than it would have been if it spread around the coast a century ago. There is just less of it to go round. It also seems to be a bit less flexible. Once upon a time it would merge or demerge easily but now it is a bit creaky and less flexible".

"The partition?"

"Yes, the partition".

"And what would happen if it did break down?"

"Well, like I said it actually breaks down all the time naturally and when it does spirits can pass from their world into ours if there are any in the vicinity. If it is a small break and only one or two spirits come across it is not a problem it might mean, for example, a candle that was burning might go out for no apparent reason. Someone might get tingling lips. But because it is small they can be returned easily and the partition repaired. There might be no spirits in the area of the fracture at all so there is no problem there. The real problems arise if it were to be a big break or a complete disappearance. Then all the transients would flood into our space and then there would be a massive problem not only in getting them back but also in repairing the partition so they stay on the other side."

"Sorry, not really getting this but what would the problem be?"

"Well I said that although the spirits have no real form they do occupy space. You cannot see them but they occupy space. So in a way there would become a vacuum."

"So?"

"You're not really getting this are you? What would happen if I was to stick your head in a vacuum and believe me I am beginning to wish I could?"

"I wouldn't be able to breathe".

"Quite. It would be a bit like putting your face in water. There is no air because the space that would contain the air is occupied by the water. In this case the space that should contain air to breathe is occupied by spirits".

"But surely if people saw it coming they would get away. If they saw a giant wave coming towards them, like a tsunami, they would run away".

"If they saw it coming and that is the clue. But you cannot see a rupture in the partition coming. You cannot see the partition at all. It just happens and spirits would instantly pour over and there could be one of there could be millions, hundreds of millions of them in an instant. It would be more like the ash cloud that covered Pompeii. It would just suddenly happen. There would be no warning and little chance of escape."

"But surely there would be time?"

"It wouldn't be like a snow fall where it happens slowly over a period of time. Nor like a hurricane or tornado where you can see it coming. It would be more like someone coming up behind you and throwing a blanket over your head. It could be that localised and that quick."

He paused to see if it was sinking in.

"Just imagine London. Eight million people and a blanket is thrown over them all. Where do they go? Suddenly all the air is gone and they need more in a matter of a couple of minutes and it doesn't come".

He paused again hoping his explanation was becoming clearer.

"So they all suffocate and die. Check out the latest USB on the shelf and look for an incident on an underground train in London. That was a big one that was hushed up by the authorities and blamed on terrorists even though they could not find any evidence like gases or poisons or explosions".

Wil pointed to the ceiling and Harvey went upstairs to the back office and collected the USB Wil was talking about. He loaded it onto the laptop and they looked at Norman's report.

"Yep, so if it's like the tube incident and there is a big rupture then all the people affected die and then there are millions more going over to an already crowded other world putting even more pressure on the partition which breaks more often and kills more people and so on until there are no more people", Lewis tried to sum it up more for his own understanding than anyone else's.

"Just like there were no dinosaurs and possibly no more whatever there was on the planet before the dinosaurs," added Lottie trying to show she was getting it.

"Exactly although it could be a number of small tears or a large number of huge tears or a complete dissolution of the whole lot. A lot depends on whether there are areas of extreme stress on the partition and whether they join up and whether the partition has become weakened all over and less resistant to fracture".

"Surely it also depends on whatever it is that is weakening it. If that continues then the dangers continue," observed Lewis.

"Quite. And what is weakening it then?"

TWENTY SEVEN

It was early evening in New York, the spring sun was just setting and the city was as warm as ever under a darkening blue sky. If you looked up between the glass, concrete and brick cliff edges that were the skyscrapers and through the light pollution you could just imagine the fleets of satellites taking station all across the globe with pulses of communication waves flying between them and the tens of billions of ground receivers. For months commercial and national rockets had been launched at almost daily intervals. Russia, America, India, China, Europe, Japan and Canada had sent rocket after rocket skywards each carrying up to a hundred satellites and each on a pre-programmed course to deliver its payload into the exact position. On the ground the satellites had been assembled in high tech factories all over the world. Robot after robot polished and painted as if they were the old Victorian steam engines that drove the first industrial revolution. All factories across the world, uniquely, worked in collaboration using exactly the same plans to produce identical units. From the spotlessly clean and air purified factories where they were built they were shipped, trucked and flown with great care to the closest launch station and placed in equally spotless storage units waiting their turn to be sent aloft.

On the ground the base stations and data centres had been designed and built from, mainly prefabricated, raw materials in double quick time. Each roof was covered in solar energy cells to supplement the huge power demands of the servers. Air conditioning units all along the side walls kept the temperatures down to operational levels. Inside the buildings row after row of power hungry computers blinked, clicked and whirred into life storing information, controlling, monitoring, driving, entertaining and watching.

Once the initial proposal documents had been published there had been constant pressure placed on all nations to sign up to participate in the biggest communication project ever attempted. Through combinations of promises, threats, carrots and sticks almost every country signed up and started directing resources towards the end goal. The powers that be in charge of the project had not wanted to chance any of the participants backing out at the last moment, especially the richer ones. Once agreement had been reached the already laid plans swung into action and the project was quickly pushed to the point of no return. Even when that had passed the pace of the project did not slow down and hence this point had arrived in double quick time and to the chagrin of the investors almost on budget rather than wildly over the budget which they had hoped for. Never mind the impacts on society and the noble notion of a great revolution it was really all a great opportunity to make obscene amounts of money. This was to be the greatest communication project the world had ever known and it would have an enormous impact on the world and the bank balances of the few. Unfortunately the powers that be did not realise it would have a much bigger impact than even they had planned.

Today was the day when everything was going to be officially connected. Everything was working. After the success of the first wave of implementation the massive upscaling had swung into action with manufacturing geared to pour more units into the system until everything was in place.

Across the world every base station was up and working. Thousands of operatives had been trained and were in place. Thousands upon thousands of hours had been spent testing and retesting, modifying, tweaking and re-engineering until everything worked. Area by area had been wound up and tested. Risk assessments had been written and tested, disasters simulated, profits gathered. The power generators had been warned that today was the day when their systems would be challenged by the biggest surge in demand they had ever experienced. Nuclear stations were working to capacity, batteries charged by wind turbines were at capacity, and prayers were being said that winds across the world would continue to provide the required power. Wave, hydro-electric and thermal sources were on line and being monitored. The time was fast approaching when the symbolic green light would be pressed by the president of the United States inside the old and now defunct United Nations building on East 42nd street. Today the first global, international communication system that would enable so much would fire up and be accessed by billions of people eager to be part of the revolution.

As the natural sun light dimmed powerful arc lights popped on and focussed on the balcony specially built into the side of eighty sixth floor of the sky scraper especially for this occasion. The walls on all sides and below the balcony were illuminated with the flags of the world and the proprietary symbols of the major industrial companies that had built the connecting network. Music blared out from massive speakers set alongside the building. Coloured laser beams shone from dozens of drones that had been pre-programmed to perform intricate aerial dances while shining their lights into the sky and onto adjacent buildings. Behind the front wall of the balcony were the neatly arranged microphones waiting for the President's address and high above his head the huge red light that would turn green as he pressed the more accessible start button by his dais. In New York itself and across thousands of miles the huge numbers of data centres that would store all the data generated by the new systems would be stored hummed gently as they consumed vast quantities of electricity.

This day was truly to be the start of the Information and Communication revolution and it would make the Industrial and Technological revolutions look like minor blips in human development.

Eventually the president took his place on the balcony to huge cheers from the masses assembled below. His face appeared on TV and huge display screens across the world. He smiled and waved not entirely unaware that behind the scenes there were more than a few grumbles about him seeming to take all the credit for something that was planned long before he had even become president and what involved tens of thousands of people all working on the same project to very tight time schedules.

"People of the world, fellow citizens" he started looking out at the crowds from between his autocue screens "evolution has seen many great, significant changes that have revolutionised the way we live. The Industrial Revolution changed us from farmers to manufacturers and inventors, the technology revolution changed us from hardware users to information users and inventors and now the communication revolution is enabling us to step back and allow intelligent machines to act as our servants. The new super-digital revolution will enable us to keep in touch and informed as never before, to transport us and our goods and to monitor and clean the world and its seas. This truly is the start of the third and greatest revolution. The exciting prospect is that this is only the start. This development is the equivalent of the leap made from the cotton gin to the computer. From the wheel to flight. Developments will continue, more applications will continue to come on stream improving the lives of every one of us wherever they are on the planet. We will be able to look back in the future as this day being the start not the end of tremendous things to come. So on behalf of all the countries participating, all the people who have worked for this moment, all those who will be keeping this immensely complex systems running and, of course, all of you, I declare this project open".

With that he pressed the green button turning to look upwards. The light above his head turned from red to green and cannons fired ticker tape, gold and silver paper strings into the air. Everywhere fireworks lit the skies around the world, champagne corks popped and laser lights swept across the skies. Crowds around the world cheered and the new age began.

Populations around the world went wild. It was midnight on New Year's Eve all at the same time. For years they had read about the project and listened to all the benefits it was promised to bring. People already drunk on electronic devices of all sorts were going to be allowed to access so much more than they had even dreamt of and everyone wanted to be the first to start.

Fleets of drone taxis and autonomous vehicles that had been seen about in small numbers as they were being tested became available. For months they had always returned to their giant parks but now they could suddenly be put into use. They flowed out in constant streams obeying the demands of sensation hungry trippers. Drones that were designed for deliveries took to the air and buzzed about in their hundreds of thousands all over the world all seemingly narrowly missing each other as their GPS followed routes and detected other drones avoiding collisions. Robot delivery carts did the same on the ground rumbling along packed pavements at a maximum six miles an hour weaving their way to their destinations. Centrally computers guided every thing. Plotting the routes, avoiding collisions, returning to base. Communications went stratospheric even though people had had decades of electronic communication. But this was different and everyone had to talk to everyone one to one and in huge group chats as if it were a million New Years all rolled into one all with pictures and video. And the systems facilitated and recorded every last interaction. New tech fascinated and mesmerised people and they believed it made their lives so much better but data was the new currency and it was powerful and had to be collected. Nudge power based on the data was a very powerful method of population control and coercion and there was money to be made from it and the chance was not going to be lost. Everyone could now also be watched, followed, identified. Almost everything they did from spending to travelling to meeting others could be monitored and logged.

The surge in power demands meant all power stations across the globe were stretched to the limit. Every source was fed into national grids. Batteries were quickly drained, solar cells were sucked dry. Every wind turbine, hydroelectric plant and wave generator was brought on stream. But it worked and it worked brilliantly.

Wil, Harvey, Lewis and Lottie looked on in consternation. This was not going to end well.

In the days, weeks and years that followed the launch more and more applications came on line. All the road and rail systems moved over seamlessly to computer guidance and control. Punctuality of public transportation systems surged to levels unheard of outside of Japan. Ticketing was computerised and access denied ruthlessly to those without tickets. All journeys made and who were making them was recorded and stored. Everywhere was monitored by CCTV and stored.

Road traffic police almost became redundant as the autonomous fleets of cars replaced personally driven vehicles which meant there was no speeding nor accidents and collisions. Blind people, handicapped people, old people and young who had previously been unable to drive or use private transport could now order a car and tell it where they wanted to go and it would take them. Conversely millions of people around the world who used to commute to central offices no longer did so. They worked from home linked by virtual meetings. Air pollution levels fell as electric cars took over from petrol cars as did noise levels. Traffic jams disappeared, traffic lights became redundant as finely computer controlled cars were able to manoeuver around each other without stopping at junctions.

Delivery drones filled the air buzzing between depots and delivery points. Empty ones raced back to base to collect more. Samples were ferried between hospitals, lunches were delivered to people sunning themselves in parks guided to the exact spot by their mobile phone signal, more elaborate take-out meals were delivered to homes, dogs were walked by drone that could even collect their waste, and litter was collected by drones patrolling along busy roads where humans dared not venture. Above them at slightly higher levels passenger drones ferried people directly between spots being much faster, but more expensive, than road based transport. Complex mapping far in advance of the major commercial air traffic control and management systems ensured there were no collisions and the 'as the crow flies' routes adhered to. 360 degree sensors scanned all around the drones keeping them clear of power lines, tall buildings and other drones.

At sea commercial and passenger shipping carried on their majestic ways guided by computers that plotted routes taking into account weather systems and other ships. But a new generation of huge ships twice the size of the largest container vessels and almost completely unmanned scoured the seas day and night acting as bases for sea cleaning drones. They were powered by vast solar energy units arrayed across the huge desk powering the silent and emission free engines. Speed was not the primary requirement but ecological operation was. Working from them were drones that scanned the oceans identifying pockets of flotsam and jetsam that they scooped from the surfaces of the sea and ferried back to the home ship. When they returned to the base the decks would temporarily open up allowing the drones to dump their rubbish before heading back out to sea. If necessary the drones would land on wireless charging points to replenish their power sources ensuring they worked for maximum periods of time. Beneath the decks machines would sort the flotsam compacting what it could and storing what could be recycled. Beneath the sea large submarine drones combed the depths for rubbish collecting it in their huge gaping 'mouths' much like basking sharks collected plankton. They would sort the rubbish and fish allowing the fish to escape through channels along the sides of the mouth enabling the compacting of the rubbish further back into the submarine. They, too, would rendezvous with the mother ship when full docking in huge pods underneath the ship allowing water tight seals to open and cranes to unload the packed rubbish for recycling.

Drones in their millions took to the skies. As well as the delivery drones they were used for myriads of uses as various as monitoring shore lines for swimmers or boats in trouble, for oil spills or for sharks to monitoring farms looking to see which ready for crop harvesting, monitored ploughing being undertaken by autonomous tractors guided by GPS, fed back to the farmer the soil quality and dryness, monitored the sky for cloud cover and potential rainfall. Across the massive million and more acre farms of Australia outback drones could pinpoint individual animals and they could launch micro drones to herd the cattle to places where they needed to be. They were being used to monitor water sources, snow lines, potential avalanche risks, volcanic activity, and massive locust swarm activity – anything that people needed to monitor remotely and continuously. Remote areas were now accessible and could be photographed, monitored or have supplies delivered to remote populations. Wildlife wardens could easily track their charges, if necessary dropping food to them or even herding them to water or safety. They could quickly intercept poachers and some had military grade firearms to attack any groups of them. Wars could be pursued using drones to deliver larger and larger explosive devices, to spot and plot the movements of any and all kit and fighters. Displaced populations could be identified and tracked and supplies ferried quickly to them. They could be used to attack ground based ordnance and even attack each other. The human soldier was becoming redundant.

It was all based on communication and the storage of the data generated by the communication. Everything was closely monitored but the one thing they could not monitor was the effect all the radiation based traffic was having on the partition.

TWENTY EIGHT

Many years before the president had made his momentous speech. "Have you read this crap?" Will had asked waving the International Working Party for the Provision of Intensive Electromagnetic Radiation based Communication and Control Systems report in his hand over his head. "Have you? Have you?" He could barely contain his fury as he slapped the report down on the table exhaling loudly overwhelmed by frustration and in the absence of any suitable swear words. Some years before the president opened the new digital and comms age with such fanfare Wil had read and re-read the launch documents for the project and could not believe what he was reading. The others, intrigued but not quite realising the implications had also ploughed through it.

"I can't believe they are actually going to go through with this".

Since Norman had died and Wil had moved into number eighty six and the four of them had met regularly to learn more about the partition and what was required to maintain it. The first job Wil had had was to try to explain all the fundamentals to the group and get them to understand what he was all about. Since then they had met many times discussing and re-discussing what Wil had said and he felt they had gradually come on board.

Now all the papers that Norman had accumulated over the years had gone navigating round the house was much easier not to mention safer. The kitchen was no longer a health risk and the layers of dust had been consigned to other, outside locations. The place actually looked like a house now with the exception of the round table room and the upstairs office. A couple more computers appeared and Lottie and Harvey had loaded the contents of the paper files so that they could be easily cross referenced in the future. Norman had been very good at collating the information he had gathered over the years but the technology he was comfortable with extended only as far as the corded telephone they eventually found in the hall and it did not include computers.

"Yes I have, or rather, we have read it", answered Lottie slightly more calmly waving her arm to encompass the others in the room. Lewis had stayed and remained part of the group although he still carried a baggage load of cynicism. He rather felt it was his role to shoot down all the fanciful ideas that were brought up. In fact all four of them had all read the paper but had all come to different conclusions.

"Surely it's a great thing. All round the world things will work the same. All the manufacturers like the car makers will have electric cars with the same management systems, the same navigational systems and the same autonomous driving systems, the same charging plugs. Wherever you go you can whip out your PSID and off you go". Lewis was thoroughly in favour of progress and was always banging on about the new apps he had found which although very clever seemed to others, especially Harvey, as pointless solutions to non-existent questions or problems. Although not quite as Luddite as Norman, Harvey was happy with his mobile phone, with the emphasis on the word phone, which was so old it was bordering on obsolete and had long ago been abandoned by the manufacturers as not worth supporting or updating.

"So everything is going to look the same, do the same and be the same everywhere? Uniformity is going to be the key and everything is going to be driven by a few massive corporations all working for the good of the people", Lewis's cynicism knew no bounds.

"No, not necessarily. Just to take one example, you say about cars all being the same well at a simple level different car manufacturers, for example, can make different styles and even different classes of cars. Cheap cars for the likes of you and me or ones that cost a bit more and have more luxurious additions but underneath they will all be the same. You know how you like going to McDonalds and the like when you are abroad because it is familiar well you will be able to hire any car anywhere in the world because they will all, essentially, be the same, inside at least".

"Everyone likes to see what they have in the shops abroad when they are on holiday so I suppose you could be right," Lewis almost accepted the argument.

Putting her religious studies hat on Lottie said "I think that is why a lot of people like going to churches when they go abroad. They are all pretty much the same and people feel comfortable with that".

"The cars are practically the same now or at least were and the churches always have been. They all had internal combustion engines or diesel ones, cars not churches, when they were allowed and they all worked in roughly the same way but there were still lots of differences. Well that all goes. Engines might be a little bit different like they are now but look at the chargers. Petrol pumps were pretty much the same they all fitted all cars but when electric cars first came out manufacturers could not agree on one style so they all made different ones. Now everything will have to be standard and you can charge up anywhere."

"Ok so maybe standardisation or cars might make things easier but that isn't the question as far as I can see," said Will.

"Cars are only one thing. There are thousands of examples of other standardisations and that may be a good thing so what is the problem then, it still all looks good to me. Just think you could go anywhere in the world, automatically have translation services to order transport you are familiar with, order it to go anywhere you want without you having to navigate or know the local rules of the road, order it to stop at the nearest coffee shop or hotel, order a drone with food or whatever to meet you at a certain point and it will communicate with the car to meet up. Terrific, who would not want that?" continued Lewis.

"The problem isn't the things, forget about the things themselves and think about how the things will work. Not so much the cars power units but about the cars themselves especially the autonomous ones and even more especially the millions of drones that the network will enable and support. Look at the huge increase in radiation that is going to be generated controlling these things and making them work. Think back to the early days when there were cancer scares because of the potential of radiation from mobile phones. No-one was able to live within a few metres of a base station and as they became more functional they had smaller operating radii so there were more and they were closer together. And now there are going to be so many more, so enormous and so powerful. Everything will be driven by IT. Standardisation is really irrelevant. The key thing is that everything will be driven by IT, monitored by the satellite networks bouncing signals off millions of base stations, connecting billions of bits of electronic kit that we will demand more and more of. Massive increases in electronic radiation. "

"But researchers said they were all safe".

"Yeah, and who did the research? Once they said smoking was safe and it turned out to be anything but safe. Diesel was safe but it wasn't and had to go, plastic was safe but it wasn't and now every living thing on the planet has micro-particles of plastic in their bodies just because people wanted to carry little plastic bottles of water around with them. And don't even get me started on all the chemicals that were poured into us by one means or another with next to no thought about the effects they might have on us. So can you really believe what they tell us about all this radiation?"

"But things like plastics have been used for years and there have been no real issues about health and we tip tons of drugs into us every year".

"Depends what you mean by health issues. Everywhere on Earth is up to their ears in plastic pollution. It might not affect our health directly but it certainly does indirectly. Yes, and I might take issue with you over the safety of chemicals. Many of the chemicals that were in everyday items have been withdrawn over the years and there have been issues with the safety of drugs that cause more harm than good. Look at the great opiate issue in the States where millions of people were hooked on drugs and died of them because of the opiates they were safely prescribed, using the term safely loosely. And who said they were safe? The people making and selling them. For many years there were no real antibiotics because all the bugs had developed immunity to them all. Because of that thousands, hundreds of thousands died of innocuous things like simple infections caused after operations or from even getting pricked by garden thorns because everyone had been using antibiotics like sweets. And who told them to use them like sweets? Who told them to pour them, unnecessarily, into farm animals to fatten them more quickly and supposedly to keep them healthy? The people who made them and sold them. It was only after the new generations of anti-bacterials had been discovered by companies, cynically speaking, who wanted to make more money that we got a bit safer. The great pandemic of 2020 when millions died of a coronavirus around the world just showed what can happen if there are not the right drugs about. Before that people said mercury was safe, arsenic was safe, X rays were used to measure the size of your feet for goodness sake".

Lottie added "at least the drugs we use have to be tested intensively on animals and humans before they can be used routinely though. A lot of the chemicals used in things we use and eat every day have never been tested on anything though".

"Ok so there may be issues about chemicals and other things that may or may not cause us harm but the point here is that no-one has died because of this radiation that all this tech activity is supposed to be producing", Harvey felt he was losing the argument and wanted to change it back to what he thought was safer ground.

"Yes there are a couple of things there. Maybe, just maybe and I am not saying it is true but maybe the radiation does not kill people directly but what about the possibility of the radiation indirectly causing the death of people", he paused "and anyway there are things just as bad as dying, maybe even worse and they could be caused by high doses or constant low doses of radiation".

"Like?"

"Right come with me on a bit of a tangent" announced Wil. They were beginning to get used to the winding roads of arguments that Wil kept taking them down. "So once upon a time naughty kids were called naughty kids given a slap and sent to bed or put on the naughty step".

"Well I have been on enough naughty steps in my time to agree with that", supported Lewis.

"Yes but now...."

Wil cut Lottie off in mid-sentence. "Well now the naughty step is off-limits and no-one would dare clip a child round the ear now so now their behaviour is diagnosed as a medical problem and they are medicalised. They are all labelled as having attention deficit disorder, or autism, or they just cannot accept or recognise authority and the numbers of kids diagnosed with these things have sky rocketed and they still are rocketing."

"Are you saying this is because of radiation?"

"Bit of a coincidence isn't it. Increase in radiation and increase in all these brain centred disorders. And now the amount of radiation is going to go through the roof. And, arguably, a life blighted by some of these really debilitating conditions could be worse than dying".

"But it is a coincidence. No-one has proved otherwise that there is a connection between the two," said Lottie.

"Nothing has been written but the conspiracy theorists are all over it".

"And that proves diddly squat", Lewis was still not convinced.

"So why did they ban mobile phones in schools and put restrictions on the amount of time people spent on their phones?"

"That was to stop addiction though and trying to get the little blighters to concentrate on their lessons and not because of health issues".

"I beg to differ. It was a bit to do with addiction but also there was still suspicion of exposure to radiation at close quarters to the brain. Well the bans are still in place and now instead of the fairly localised risk of radiation from a unit held close to your own body there will be a massive amount of radiation smog surrounding everyone, everywhere, all the time. It's not just phones but everything else that requires radiation to work. It will be like an invisible and ever increasing electronic smog that will surround everyone all the time and I think it will cause more brain damage."

"But ADHD and the rest could be anything. It could be genetic".

"So suddenly within a generation genes get changed. Something that can take millions of years gets changed over a generation and only in some countries? "

"Well, yes but I suppose Darwin's survival of the fittest did suggest that genes should only change to benefit the person or animal and a lot of these changes like ADHD, if they are genetic do not benefit", conceded Lottie.

"It's a bit like obesity then. Everyone said that fatness was due to genetics, especially the fat people, and the genes must have changed pretty quickly to make everyone so fat so fast and fatness is certainly not beneficial". For some reason Harvey found himself reaching for the chocolate biscuits but realising what he had just said he pulled back just giving the packet a rueful glance.

"Quite, evolutionary genetic change is very, very slow and should improve the creature it takes place in but radiation doesn't cause genetic damage is that it?" asked Lottie.

"Well ionising radiation does cause genetic damage but all this stuff about in the atmosphere is non-ionising. It is supposed to be safe and not do any cell damage or flip genes".

"So they say but there were rumours about phones and they were safe because they had low power outputs but now with drones, planes, trains and billions of calls on the system the power output has to be much higher".

"Well not that much higher" offered Lewis not really knowing but feeling a bit left out.

"Yes it is, we are talking 15 or 20 watts for a train and more for an aeroplane".

"But there aren't that many planes".

"I beg to differ, there are huge numbers of passenger planes at the minute and the numbers are growing, but what about the millions and millions of drone journeys? They reckon that in a year there will be 50 billion drone journeys in the US alone", said Wil.

"But if you compare that with all the petrol and, even worse, when they used diesel engines and the couriers delivery staff are all over the place. They took ages getting anywhere and there was huge amounts of pollution. Now the drones go straight there and back with electric motors so no pollution", said Harvey.

"True but a drone generally does one journey, drops its load and then goes back to base back but a van would do loads of deliveries on one round. Admittedly some of the bigger drones can do multiple drops before having to return home or to their mother ship and they are electric. Anyway it isn't down to the engines they used or to the energy that drove the engines it is down to the guidance systems that they all use finding their delivery points and the comms that goes on between them and their bases not to mention the comms to the customer when they arrive. A van driver is sent out with a wagon load of packages and he is on his own. A drone is sent out and has to be monitored continually to make sure it is going in the right direction and isn't hitting anything on the way. Then add that to all the other uses like comms, entertainment, monitoring. It all adds up".

"But even if there was a link could you hold back such phenomenal developments just in case a few people might be affected after all we had cars even though loads of people have been killed in and by them?"

"Depends on what you mean by a few. A few hundred, a few thousand around the world that are affected because of it. A few million that are put on drugs to counteract the effects of radiation. Is that acceptable?"

"Perhaps it could be prevented?"

"So for the convenience of getting things delivered to your door by drone or having a taxi on call a few million people have to be disabled or everyone has to wear some sort of hat made of some sort of material to shield them from the radiation?"

"Well they could be well designed hats", Harvey chipped in sheepishly instantly recognising the weakness of the argument.

There was a little pause as everyone felt the argument had come to its conclusion. Tea and chocolate biscuits were passed around and everyone ate some pretending to think about the discussion they had just had and some thinking if they could get another biscuit without being frowned on by the others.

"So as well as ADHD being rampant what about dementia? Isn't it a bit weird, or a coincidence if you will, that kids are affected by ADHD but that has nothing to do with radiation and millions of old folk and not so old folk are suffering with dementia, another brain based affliction, but no-one knows why but that has nothing to do with radiation either?"

"But then there has always been dementia hasn't there. It used to be called senility or going gaga".

"Yes, and not many people got it because they all died off earlier with something else so didn't get old enough to get dementia."

"True but there also wasn't the amount of radiation about then either. In fact there was no radiation about then. Can you cast your mind back many moons when I was talking about spirits and them having a small electrical charge?"

"Yes and then you went banging on about kissing sharks or something", recalled Harvey.

"Ok suppose you are right and non-ionising radiation, if there is enough of it about, has some sort of effect on the brain. What do you do next, apart from wearing one of Harvey's hats, and are you saying it only affects the brain?" asked Lottie

"That's the problem. Once upon a time smoke from coal fires, factories and power stations killed people so they turned it off and made everyone use smokeless fuels. Just like the electronic smog I think we will have, they had a smoke smog that killed thousands in the industrialised cities and everyone had to wear face masks to try to protect themselves. In heavily populated cities like Delhi and Beijing the pollution became so bad that people could barely see a few metres ahead of them. The air literally turned orange and opaque. Some countries converted to less polluting forms of energy but others didn't. And then all sorts of chemicals were brought into manufacturing and no-one had a clue what the effects would be. After numerous clinical and health issues gradually the effects gradually became known and more and more chemicals were banned. Even sugar was made responsible for obesity and diabetes and gradually taken out of circulation, same with salt."

"Yeah and the trough full of food porkies would eat became irrelevant to them because they had a problem with their metabolism and it was that which had the biggest to their weight".

"Well that's true. People ate too much but sugar and that was held responsible for things like diabetes. Too much salt for their blood pressure".

"True and all the lard arses with diabetes thought it was a badge of some sort and were almost proud to be a band of afflicted but little did they realise the issues they would have to face".

"Anyway sugar was identified as a problem so it was strictly limited. Diesel engines were banned and that was the real start of electric transport. Not to mention things like tobacco that was eventually banned. And then there was the stupidity when they legalised cannabis and quickly had to ban it again because of the damage it was doing to people's brains even though they knew it was damaging. And who promoted it? Those that grew it and made money from it. I'll bet they didn't use it themselves."

"All very well but they are smallish things that could be banned and after a bit no-one would know any better or miss them. Who remembers people smoking now? Apparently people smoked in cinemas, on planes and in restaurants but no-one smokes at all now. So if you find there is something doing harm you can do something like banning it or, at least, restricting it but this is a massive change to everything in everyone's lives everywhere. How could you get rid of electronic communication? It would set everyone back a hundred years".

"Undoubtedly it would set everything back but what is the alternative? Do you keep on increasing the volume of radiation and the power of the radiation and fry everyone's brains?" questioned Wil.

"It wouldn't be quite like that surely", asked Lottie rather hopefully.

"Ok so we carry on as we are, maybe even increase the amounts of radiation, how many kid's brains being fried is acceptable? How many homes for old people with fried brains would have to be built? Who would pay for it all? Would there be some sort of euthanasia scheme to cull out people? Don't forget the numbers of people is going to keep going up".

"And that means more problems feeding them all", observed Harvey thinking back to the chocolate biscuit situation.

"And keeping water available. There is enough trouble already with droughts, floods and people building dams and diverting water courses."

Wil felt they were going off topic a bit but never one to miss a good discussion he added "I think the main problem will not be enough food or water it will be enough jobs so people can earn money to buy the food and water. No jobs, no money and where are they all going to come from?"

"Look, as long as there are enough vested interests in keeping this communication model going, governments, big businesses and the like, as well as people who only plan for themselves, then any research that might link massive increases in radiation to brain damage is going to be suppressed. All these advances can be translated into jobs and jobs keep people happy, fed and watered so they have to be good. Right? And even if anything about it being harmful did get out it would be denied and we will be told that everything is fine and we are safe so there is precious little we can do about it".

"So you said you were going a bit off topic by bringing in ADHD and dementia and saying the amount of radiation would affect these things and make them worse so what is the real topic? What else are we discussing then? What else can the radiation affect?" asked Harvey knowing he had lost the plot.

"The partition".

"What about the partition?"

"Well, and I appreciate this is the same argument that we have just had but I think the amount of radiation is affecting the partition".

"How?"

"So we know that solar flares and increased solar winds can affect the partition by weakening it and even tearing it allowing more spirits to cross over".

"True, we had all seen increased activity when there are flares but are you saying that radiation has the same effect?"

"I am. It wasn't really noticeable in the early days but the concentrations, especially with the new satellites that this ruddy report is describing and the uses that it is being put to and the increased power being used, I think, is going to really stress the partition".

"I suppose it is going to be more affected in areas of highest activity and the areas of highest activity will have the highest population and because they have the highest populations they would have the highest death rates and so have the highest numbers of spirits on the other side".

"Exactly. High concentrations of spirits, high levels of radiation, high levels of partition damage and more spill over into our world".

"So the increased ADHD, dementia and brain damage are the least of our worries?"

"Potentially, yes but I do think that the increased radiation is one, if not the main, cause of these. Dinosaurs probably thought the odd fart was the least of their worries too. Turned out a bit different and the pollution that did for them was the methane. For us the pollution may well be the carbon dioxide but it is more likely to be the electronic pollution made all the worse by the carbon dioxide. Also not forgetting that these examples like ADHD and dementia are all based around organs that operate on small amounts of electricity. Sharks and kisses and all that. Suppose all this radiation is affecting electrical charges in the brain and in the partition".

"And don't forget asthma. So what are we going to do about it? Assuming there is something we can do".

"Assume away. Personally I don't have the faintest idea what we can do" added Wil rather unhelpfully.

"Isn't there anything we can do to strengthen the partition?"

"No, the only tools we have are to repair the partition and even then we are really stretched if there is a large tear. That's why we have always been able to repair it but if the tear is large enough or there are multiple tears we could be overwhelmed".

"And if the tears join up then, presumably, the whole thing comes crashing down and we are overrun by spirits".

"Exactly".

"So is there anything to protect the partition, you know a tin hat for it?"

"Bit difficult to put a tin hat on something that has no substance".

"Suppose a support wall is out of the question?"

Everyone laughed at the idea of a tin wall erected around something that could not be seen and had no boundaries. And how would people manage with a great tin wall all over the place.

"Wouldn't it be possible to make a second partition then to ring round the first one? It would still be invisible, undetectable but would be twice as thick and strong".

"In theory it would be possible but there are not the resources to do it. No-one knows how the partition is made, who made it if anyone did, what it is made of or how it actually works. There are no plans down the library".

TWENTY NINE

"Shit".

Or to be more exact – no shit.

How come you just get yourself comfortable on the throne with the next Sudoku quiz in one hand and the phone in the other when the phone goes off?

It had happened so often in the past that it could not just be chance there must be something monitoring his movements waiting for him to get comfortable in the smallest room and then sending him a message. Piers felt uncomfortable about taking a phone call when ensconced on the throne and video conferences were definitely out when in there. Especially after the last one. But why? Why does it happen every time?

It was something of a relief when he saw that the phone had buzzed an alert that there was a drone delivery was outside his front door waiting for him to collect. Nevertheless he knew he had only sixty seconds to either collect the delivery or, at least, tell the drone to drop what it was delivering and scoot off back to its base station. The throne would have to wait. Things had moved on from the early days when drones would zip back and forth to the warehouse and there seemed to be more time to collect their deliveries. Now so much was delivered by drone that huge ones more like small warehouses themselves would position themselves in a central area and smaller drones would go back and forth to it collecting and delivering but travelling much smaller distances and being able to make many more deliveries. On the other hand, and it had happened to Piers on more than one occasion, his out of control habit of buying over the internet had caused a small queue of drones at his front door all trying to deliver at the same time.

He got up off the throne which automatically flushed and disinfected lowering the cover as he moved away. Taps came on as he waved his hands under them and the soap dispenser did what it said on the tin. As he left the bathroom the light automatically switched off and the extractor fan closed down. He made his way through the house with lights automatically coming on and going off as the motion detectors also did what they said on the tin.

At the front door the locks automatically unlocked and as he swiped his hand over the security sensor and as it swung open he saw the drone designed to look as though it was a smiling face proffering its delivery towards him. He took it, clicked on the phone that the delivery had been made and watched as the drone elegantly banked and flew back to its big brother.

He went inside and unwrapped the delivery. His freshly laundered suit smelling sweetly of lavender which was just managing to hide the smell of the cleaning reagents. Today was an important day so it was important he looked his best and he might just forgive the inconvenient time of delivery.

Not being blessed with too much time he quickly dressed and was back to the front door just as his driverless car arrived at the bottom of the path. He had booked it to arrive and give him plenty of time despite knowing that there were rarely any hold ups these days even though there were many more vehicles on the road at any one time. The blessing had been that most commercial traffic, the huge trucks that slowed things down had been banished to the night hours but as none of them had any human drivers they could operate 24/7 if required. He climbed into the car not now perturbed that there was no driver nor any of the technical and mechanical apparatus that had been associated with driving cars. No steering wheel, pedals, brakes, dials and switches. Just a screen displaying the route to his destination, a print of the time and distance to go and an estimated time of arrival. And the pay slot for his card. An automatic voice welcomed him into the car and asked him to confirm his destination. Confirming it was correct it launched into the same health and safety speech he had heard a thousand times before. He ignored just like he had done a thousand times before.

The car pulled silently away from the pavement as his house put itself into lock down switching off everything that it could and firing up the security systems like the alarms, security cameras and timed lighting bursts. It would wait for him to return and then get everything going again before he stepped over the threshold. The fridge would interrogate itself and automatically order his provisions to arrive when he returned. The entertainment systems would automatically scan all the providers and automatically download any films or music that fitted his selector algorithm. It was such a far cry from the house that Norman had lived in but Piers was nothing if not a fanatical follower of electronic devices.

The trip to the station was smooth and quick and he was soon able to get out of his car and entered into the hall. It was a blend of a small airport and a large taxi rank. The taxis or planes, whatever you wanted to call them, were arranged in stacks at the far end of the property and as they detected your presence cross referencing facial recognition and your mobile phone it sent the one allocated to your journey to the exit ramps. The drone taxis were much larger than most of the delivery ones because they had to lift a humans weight which, sometimes, was not inconsiderable so they had to be strong. When you booked a drone taxi you were asked your weight which was increased by 30% by the operators because they knew everyone lied about their weight, your height and the amount of luggage you would be carrying, again the providers added another 30% because they knew people lied about that as well and it would send an appropriate vehicle to pick you up. The more advanced stations scanned and weighed passengers as they entered the building using hidden weigh plates and video recognition trying to ensure the right vehicle was dispatched. There was nothing more embarrassing than a taxi drone that could not lift its passenger forcing the company to ask the passenger to unload and wait for a heavier duty vehicle to be sent. They also gave a range of specifications so you could go first class with refreshments, scented towels, tinted windows and massage machines or cattle class with a reasonably comfortable seat depending on how much you wanted to pay.

So as Piers hit the exit ramp a large eight rotor drone pulled up in front of him. The glass cabin and the rotor blades were all encased in a lightweight but strong cage to protect the machine and anyone around it. The cabin itself was compact to keep weight down but comfortable so Piers settled in for the two hour flight to Bath. He knew the road trip would take at least three hours, maybe four but this, although it was more expensive would only take two hours at most. Nevertheless he did not waste his time. There were video meetings to be made, documents to be sent to no end of people, others to be down loaded or uploaded, phone calls to make, GPS positioning to be continually relayed to whomsoever was monitoring him and the drone, catching up on the local and international news on screen and in print. No peace for the wicked and enormous amount of power and transmissions to use up.

Indeed ninety seven minutes later the taxi was positioning itself to land on the Lansdown taxi port where Piers could hop into the pre-booked car that would take him into the city.

Now you could not blame Piers for what was to happen he was just one of the billions of people around the world who had accepted the new world with open arms and were using all its power and availability to its limits. Since its inception more and more satellites had poured into space, more and more power stations had been built to service the ever growing numbers and size of data storage units that were storing more data than even the most optimistic people managers could have dreamt of. There were more and more people in the world communicating with so many other people but this was outweighed massively by the numbers of machines that were constantly communicating with other machines. From the home hub collating data from the fridge, freezer and cupboards to compile shopping lists that were automatically transmitted to the supermarkets which automatically picked the order, placed it into scuttle buts or drones and had it delivered to your door without any input from you to the massive engineering or finance complexes that drove the world based on massive multi layers of communication both within and without the complexes. Everyone communicated despite the fact that everyone was actually becoming an island and communicated directly less and less with their fellows.

No it was not Pier's fault, it was the fault of the billions of people using the systems, the hundreds of thousands of people who maintained the systems, the hundreds of people who invented the system and the tens of people who were profiting from it. They were all to blame and would all pay.

THIRTY

It felt a bit like a combination of the dread of waiting outside the dentists before major tooth extraction and the exhilaration of Christmas Eve. Wil felt faintly ridiculous all suited and booted holding his rather battered briefcase looking out of the window waiting for the car to arrive. He had actually been waiting for this day for some time, ever since he had read the report announcing the satellite plans, never really expecting that it would come. The biggest hurdle he thought he faced was that despite the fact that he had tried to contact anyone and everyone who he thought might help who actually knew of him? He was not exactly a household name. Did any of his letters or e mails end up with an aide of an aide who would consign any message to the bin? After all who would believe his story even if they did meet him? But, to his surprise and delight, eventually the call did come and he was half invited half commanded to attend the prime minister, no less, in number 10 and now the day had arrived and he was waiting for the car to come to collect him.

As he started his third round of self-doubt and his fourth thought about going to the toilet just once more before he left the car pulled up outside his house. A real car, electric to be sure but a real car with a real driver. It looked quite impressive, black and very shiny. How it had come all the way from London and still looked as though it had just driven out of the show room was beyond him but it did. He was rather surprised but also rather pleased it was not an autonomous motor but an almost old fashioned car with a driver.

Now was the time. He stood and walked to the front door opening it just before the driver had time to push the bell. They exchanged pleasantries and the driver, smartly dressed in dark grey suit, black shoes, white shirt and red tie, held open the rear door of the car for Wil to climb in. First impressions were grand. Plenty of room, nice smelling air freshener, leather seats, today's newspaper on the seat and no heavies in dark suits and sunglasses with suspicious bulges under their jackets waiting for him. He made a mental note to stop watching so many films. It might just be a nice drive up to London although after a couple of unsuccessful attempts to engage the driver in conversation it was going to be a nice and quiet drive. At least it was better than sitting in one of the transport drones that he hated so much and refused to use on point of principle. He settled back in the seat content that he had not needed a fourth trip to the toilet and wondering whether he could have brought a thermos of coffee and maybe a biscuit. But on reflection felt he would have been in trouble with the driver for making a mess in the back seat. Best to just sit back and behave himself.

Two hours and even more rehearsals of his case later the car pulled into Whitehall and drew to a stop outside the black iron gates that guarded 10 Downing Street. The nervousness that had slightly abated on the journey suddenly reappeared and Wil wondered what he was going to find.

He ran through his mind the content of the many letters, documents and e mails he had sent to the Prime Minister and several of her cabinet colleagues over the previous weeks and months trying to get an audience with them to put his case never really expecting to get anywhere. But one morning he answered the phone at home and was invited by someone whose name he never did remember to come to London, meet some people and put his case. The PM was interested in what he had to say and a car would be sent

As Wil walked past the very heavily armed police guards at the gate and then down the short bit of pavement to number 10 he hoped they would really be interested. He had visions of them bursting out laughing and throwing him out when he told them what he had to tell them. Next might be another trip in the black car to Bedlam. The famous, highly polished and immaculately clean black front door now no longer guarded by a single policeman mysteriously opened apparently of its own accord as he stepped up to it. A seemingly disembodied head popped round it and greeted him as Wil walked in to the large hallway. The door closed silently behind him. He was here. Here goes.

"So what happened next?" Harvey asked getting ever more curious.

It was the day after the big meeting and all four of them had gathered at number eighty six to get the low down from Wil.

"Well, I'm not quite sure how it went down, we will have to wait and see. I am not sure whether they were tolerating someone who they thought was a complete nutter or were actually interested in what I was saying. I did wonder if they had seen a string of other people with all sorts of other ideas and plans about the situation. Maybe I was the first of many, maybe the last. Maybe they were getting fed up of seeing nutters like me who were of no help at all. Whatever it was there was a whole lot of them".

"Mister Kingdon, I presume, welcome to number 10. Would you please follow me", commanded the very smartly groomed head that had been peaking round the door.

He darted out of the doorway and followed the now embodied head that walked quickly to the stair case and started up. Wil followed trying to take in all the scene.

"Would you care to wait in here please sir? The PM will be with you shortly". None of the questions were questions but phrased more like very polite commands. Wil went into the wood panelled room whose walls were smothered in paintings of austere and unrecognisable people. The floor was covered in a very deep pile carpet with elegant swirls and patterns. The two tall sixteen panel windows opposite the door looked out over the immaculate garden and were framed with thick velvet curtains. Every-thing smelled of polish and bees wax. Wil considered it would be highly unlikely to find a spot of dust in the room. He took a seat in a highly polished and very firm red leather wing back chair by the fireplace making sure he was securely enough seated not to slide back out of it. He went to place his battered and highly unpolished brief case on the shiny and heavily polished table next to the chair but afraid of scratching it he placed it on his knees and waited. His mind wandered to the film of the Dam Busters where Barnes Wallis was shown waiting outside government office after government office for hour after hour waiting to be seen about his new invention, the bouncing bomb. He briefly wondered who had sat where he was now sitting and what they were called to see the PM for. But before he had finished the thought an adjoining door that he had not noticed opened and a different head popped round inviting him into the next room.

The leather of the chair squeaked gently as he rose and walked over to the door and the squab popped back into shape as if he had never been there. As he passed through the door into the next room he was quite taken aback by what he saw. It was almost as though he was back in the film world.

This room was very much larger than the waiting room with a long, wide light wooden table in the centre. Neatly spaced along the length were small clusters of water bottles and glasses on neat white cloths. The dozen or more black leather and chrome seats around it were all filled with people who stopped talking as he entered the room and were now looking at Wil silently, suspiciously. Mounted on two sides of the walls of the room, running the length of the room were two banks of large TV screens with more people, maybe twenty or so, looking out of them and down at Wil. He could not help but think of another film, the Harry Potter films with all the paintings in hallways at Hogwarts coming alive and watching everyone walk past. Suddenly Wil felt even smaller and more insignificant than he usually felt and that was quite small.

He recognised the PM sitting at the head of the table and a couple of the ministers to her side but in his confusion he could not think of their names. On the wall behind the PM were three large chrome clocks identified as London, Washington and one which constantly changed time as the name of the capital city below it changed. To each side of the clocks was a union flag and above the London clock a portrait of the king. Everyone seemed to have neatly creased and printed name cards and a small black microphone on the table in front of them. But none of the cards were aligned for Wil to see and he had to fight the urge to see what was on the card in front of him. Obviously a lot of these people were as new to each other as they were to Wil and, possibly, as new to all this as he was. He quickly scanned them all and noted they were all wearing virtually the same, regulation dark suit and light shirt and tie or blouse with the exception of the unexplained large number of military personnel who were all wearing the military uniforms of their own branch. This was obviously a wide audience. Each also had a small computer in front of them and, in at least one case, three mobile phones next to it. Wil could not help thinking, what with all the on line participants, this was part of the problem not a part of the solution.

"So did you find out who they all were?" asked Lottie.

"No. They didn't even introduce themselves to me although if they had I might have still been there and I wouldn't have remembered them anyway".

"Sounds as though it was quite a cross section of the powers that be," suggested Lewis.

"As far as I could make out from what they were asking and what they were saying between themselves there were obviously government people and military people but there seemed to be people from the MI's, GCHQ, power companies and radiation people but I didn't know where they all came from".

"What did they ask you? What did they want to know?"

Wil started to explain that after the PM had introduced him to the people round the table and told them what she thought Wil did they all turned as one to look at Wil. Again he could not help but be impressed how neat and tidy they all looked and how they all seemed to move in unison.

Partly to avoid having to look at the assembled he had taken a sheaf of papers from out of the brief case more for effect than anything. Since he had received the invitation to attend the meeting he had written and rewritten his presentation numerous times and then learned it off by heart. The notes were only there if he really dried up and lost his train of thought but with all the electronic devices in front of everyone else Wil's papers made him look just one step up from cave dwelling.

After a bit of a hesitant start he began to feel more comfortable with what he was saying as he explained what his role was and then, getting into the swing, he started to describe the partition, what it did and what happened when it failed.

"I did play down the bits about the dinosaurs though and didn't specifically mention the farts referring to climate change instead. The bits about ADHD and dementia were omitted as well. Thought it best to stick to the relevant bits. I didn't know how much time I had".

"Maybe you didn't think they were as thick as us when you explained it to us," commented Lewis.

As he spoke he looked at the faces of those listening and was slightly disappointed that as he spoke some faces seemed to switch off or adopted the not uncommon posture of disbelief. He particularly fixated on one face on screen who looked to be a member of the clergy although he did not recognise her or her rank in the clergy but at least she looked as though she could identify with what Wil was saying.

"How long did that go on for?" asked Lottie?

Wil continued describing the meeting saying that his explanation went on for maybe ten or fifteen minutes although it felt a lot longer. After that the PM had asked how Wil felt about the huge new amounts of new technology that had been rolled out world-wide and how he thought it was going to affect the partition and, more importantly, the populace.

"You know the argument about the partition and the effect that all this massive increase in radiation is going to have on it. We have discussed it at length", he said to his little band of followers.

The group cast their minds back to the dinosaurs, asthma, farting and the rest and started to wonder how Wil had got that across to his audience.

"Once I had told them what I, we, did and what we thought was going to happen they started asking all sorts of questions and really wanted proof of what I was saying and that went on for ages with me giving them examples. I had prepared some statistics on a flash drive which I gave someone who had it uploaded onto everyone's screens in double quick time and they gave me a screen to talk from as well."

Just at the right time a couple of staff members had come into the meeting room carrying large silver trays and handed round crystal glasses of water with lemon slices and ice. Wil had swigged his eagerly not realising his throat could dry up so quickly.

"So what was their reactions?" asked Lottie

"It was difficult to tell. They all sat there quite dispassionately and very quietly. Occasionally one would point out something to the person sitting next to them something on the screen but I did not know if that was about something I was saying or they were just pointing out where they were in the game they were playing".

"But they took on board your theories and explanations and that the numbers of problems are going to increase didn't they", she persisted

"That is the crux of the problem. I think the numbers of incidents are going to increase in numbers and in severity but would the government, in fact any of the world's governments, want to accept that and take the actions I think they should take?"

"I suppose if they publicly accepted there was a problem it would cause a panic", added Lewis

"Well, it might do but the real problem would be the solution because there is so much money involved and there would be so much disruption I don't think people would wear it".

Wil paused.

"I guess it was a couple of hours later that the PM thanked me for coming and putting my views to the group. She said they would have to discuss what I had said and come up with some sort of response and plan about what to do next, if anything. That was what worried me so I said I hoped they understood that, in my opinion, not doing anything was not an option and if the radiation continued to increase we could be facing a world-wide disaster".

As Wil stood up stuffing his papers back into his brief case all the faces around the table moved from looking at him to looking at the PM. He guessed there would be quite a lot of discussion as he headed back to Sussex.

THIRTY ONE

As soon as the door clicked shut behind Wil the PM leaned forward, slowly closed her lap top, pointlessly adjusted her phones and picked up her glass of water. She swirled the contents around wishing it was gin and not water. Putting it down slowly she spoke.

"So what does everyone think about this? I am not sure I am on board with the thinking but cannot help but think there may be something in it. Is it something we can ignore? I know it sounds a bit outlandish but it seems more feasible than all the other theories we have heard?"

Pausing for a minute and looking down the table at the closed door she continued "as far as I can see there are four questions that need answers. First is the concept of the partition. Do we believe it exists? Second is the concept of damage being caused if the partition breaks and third, and most importantly perhaps, is how practical are the precautions we are being told we will need to take to prevent a disaster and finally what would the consequences of any actions be?"

Church: from one of the large screens mounted on the wall to the right of the PM an unidentified member of the church that Wil had noticed was first to speak. "PM, from a religious view I would suggest that the concept of life after death is one that most religions would promulgate. For two thousand years the Christian religions have certainly offered life after death and a better life in the hereafter to the community. Having said that there is no way that any religion has been able to say what that afterlife would be. The soul is the thing that departs the corpse and passes over to the other side but there is little or no evidence of what that side is, or what the soul actually is or what the soul would do over the other side or what it would look like. As far as I am aware there has never been any consideration of a physical barrier that exists between us and the afterlife".

PM: "So are you saying that from a faith perspective there is an afterlife, that a representation of the human, earthly body, could be somewhere, we know not where, existing somehow, we know not how and it exists alongside our world?"

Church: "Yes PM, it is all in the faith and to be a bit trite I think it is faith that Mr Kingdon is wanting from us. Having said that I am not sure about the concept of a partition as he described it existing to separate the worlds but I suppose there must be some sort of discrimination between the two worlds or maybe three world. After all most religions seem to suggest a good place and a bad place where spirits might go. We, in the church, have always described them as heaven, above us, and hell, below us. Mr Kingdon is describing a place alongside us".

PM: "Well suppose there is a partition, some sort of structure, and that our faiths are right and there is a place for souls or whatever on the other side of it is there any credence in the assertion that damage to the partition could lead to major issues on this side?"

Church: "Of course Mr Kingdon is saying that this is nothing to do with religion or faith. So I am inferring, according to him, that the notion of religious faith is immaterial. No matter which religion and whether the religion believes in the spirit world or not or even if there is no faith, according to Mr Kingdon, this state exists anyway".

MI6: Without looking up from the table a man in a dark suit and heavy black rimmed glasses spoke. "PM, I don't know about the small examples that Mr Kingdon gave us we can only take his word for them as there seems to be no general reporting of such issues. Even the one he mentioned in Brighton which he claimed to involve a numbers of souls was not reported anywhere and did not come to the attention of any security organisation. Admittedly he did seem to have plenty of examples going back into history and I would not have thought anyone trying to pull a hoax would have bothered to construct such a history. But how accurate or relevant would any of these reports be? We have plenty of reports of unidentified flying objects, sea monsters and fairies but none of them actually exist".

He paused and glanced at the PM before looking back at the table again almost seeming to judge whether he should continue.

MI6: "Having said that", he paused again double checking his thinking. "There have been a couple of things we do know of and seem to concur with Mr Kingdoms record that might fit the bill". Without lifting his head he rolled his eyes upwards and scanned the faces of those round the table and especially the face of the PM.

PM: "Go on", she said not quite knowing what to expect.

MI5: "Well there was the case of the underground train in Westminster where over 500 bodies were found on the supposedly broken down train."

PM: "Yes we remember that but it was put down to either a ruptured gas pocket that enveloped the broken down train and suffocated all the passengers or some sort of unidentified terrorist attack".

MI5: "Yes that was the one except there was no gas pocket found and the train did not actually break down and there was no evidence of terrorism", he paused but could not look at the PM although he knew the expression that she would have had on her face. She was going to worry that she was now going to learn the hitherto unknown truth. He knew that a great many people had been to a great deal of trouble trying to hide the fact that no-one had any idea what had caused the tube disaster and at the time the current PM was a new and lowly back bencher who was nowhere on the very, very short 'need to know' lists. "To be honest we did not know what caused the disaster and still do not. Nothing could be proved but if we were to suspend scientific rigour, which gave no answers at the time, and adopted the faith that Mr Kingdon is right then his explanation could fit the bill. Having said that I am sure I could come up with several equally apparently outlandish and, with respect, unbelievable causes, in fact we did at the time".

Muttering broke out around the table with a mixture of incredulity that none of them had been told that the cause of the incident was unknown and the reason that had been given had been a lie. They began to struggle with the possibility, no matter how far-fetched, that the spirit world might have been responsible.

MI5: "If I might continue PM, there is another example which was also never brought to the public. There was a place called Town, a mining town deep in the Ural Mountains where, overnight the whole village was wiped out and no-one knew why. The place was enclosed by steep mountains and there was a very heavy smog over the town at the time almost sealing the town itself into its own confined space. It was a bit like a town in a bottle rather than a ship in a bottle. The coal miners, who had been under ground, came back from a night shift and found everyone that had been over ground were in their houses or streets dead. The scene was much like the underground train incident. At the time it was a massive issue, obviously in that country, and there were great efforts to keep it quiet. The country involved was much more skilled in hushing things like this up than even we are so it remained secret. All the miners that had come up from under-ground were moved around the country, bribed and sworn to secrecy and the town was abandoned, left uninhabited, a bit like Chernobyl. No-one ever heard of the incident but, again, it is possible that the elements of Mr Kingdon's story would be pertinent. So there are two possible examples which could support his theory".

Still looking down at the table he could feel all the eyes on him all posing the same silent question. What else don't we know that we should about anything let alone this?

PM: "Right so you are saying that there could be some credibility in what Mr Kingdon said."

At the end of the table closest to where Wil had been sitting was a very typical army officer straight out of the Sandhurst catalogue. He sat very straight in his chair and, by the slight look of discomfort, he was very tall and did not fit the chair or table well. His uniform was immaculate and looked to have been painted onto his obviously well-honed frame.

Military: "PM, it might be just the way that the gentleman put the examples to us but there did seem to be some sort of chronology to it. The incidents started off as small and infrequent ones, became more frequent and larger with the two very large ones we have heard about this afternoon. I wonder if there have been more around the world that have also been kept quiet by governments. But it would seem logical according to the accounts we have heard that there is a progression going on and the elements that influence the situation are also increasing. Logically if the stressors increase then the effects will also increase".

PM: "So what evidence do we have that the stressors, as you put it general, are increasing?"

GCHQ: "Perhaps we could help here". The person from GCHQ did not look like most of the others around the table being younger by around twenty years at least. The suit which had obviously been put on as a last resort and at the last minute did not look right and the tie was missing. The lap top in front of him looked far superior to those government-issue ones sitting around the rest of the table and the single phone lying next to it looked as though it had arrived from a science fiction film set. Not being very skilled at interpreting anyone else's thoughts or opinions he had never thought about the superiority of his kit but after one meeting he had been challenged about the superiority of his phone compared with everyone else's. Surprised at what seemed to be a mixture of condescension and scorn at the next meeting he had left his phone in his bag and put an empty baked bean tin with a length of string dangling from it onto the table. The humour was not appreciated and the number of e mail complaints to his managers proved it so for the next meeting he went back to his super de-luxe model and to hell with their jealousy. "As I understand it the guy was blaming all the disruption of the increase in radiation as a result of the massive investment in comm technology in the very recent past with the satellite networks and increased connectivity and communication."

Most of those sitting round the table inwardly winced as they realised this bloke was going to talk jargon from end to end and that they were not going to understand a word or acronym of it.

As if sensing the feeling of the room he made a noticeable and almost painful adjustment in his language as if he was moving from talking to adults to children.

GCHQ: "I think Wil touched on a similar theme when he was talking about the dinosaurs".

Everyone felt much happier when he was talking about dinosaurs. Being some of them themselves they knew about dinosaurs, most knew nothing about non-ionising radiation except that it made their phone work.

GCHQ: "If you were looking for a correlation then there seems to have been an increase in the incidents Wil investigates and that has been increasing at the same time as the increase in the amount of electronic comms has been taking place. But you could say that about anything. You could say the amount of dementia or ADHD he mentioned has increased at the same time as the amount of electronic comms has increased. You could say that rising temperatures, increased pollution or an increase in the number of coffee shops have had an effect".

Department of Health: "Well actually we have been looking at that ourselves. There has been a correlation between the incidence of dementia especially and the rise of electronic communications. In fact, as ADHD has been mentioned, it is noticeable that there has been an increase in these conditions whereas with other, more cellular based conditions like heart failures and cancers, the incidences have been steadily falling".

Several members of the room looked at their phones and computers wondering whether to turn them off.

GCHQ: "Back in the early days there was a lot of work into the potential effects of radiation from phones on people but nothing was proven. They were considered safe".

Department Of Health: "I seem to remember the same was said about smoking cigarettes".

Unidentified voice: "And cannabis".

Another unidentified voice: "And diesel motors".

GCHQ: "Yes, well, there was still no evidence that anything was considered dangerous".

PM: "But all that was research into the direct effect of radiation of the human body. Was there, and I think I know the answer to this, any research done on anything like the partition?"

GCHQ: "Well no PM, mainly because we did not know anything about a partition so there was nothing we could do to investigate it".

PM: "So irrespective of whether the radiation affects ADHD or dementia it is just possible that all this radiation could have effects on things we know not of and even on things we do know of but have not associated with damaging radiation?"

Environment Secretary: "There is plenty of evidence of things we have done that cause damage to the environment and we only find out about these things much later on. Usually when there is a catastrophe. I know it is a long time ago now but look at my own country and the first environmental issue at Aberfan and there have been hundreds since then like Chernobyl for example or Fukushima or Three Mile Island".

Business Secretary: "I think that the implication that radiation based communication and connectivity are the cause for the problems is a massively dangerous one from a financial and economic standpoint. Just suppose it was the cause then what would be the solution? Stopping all electronic communication? Switching off all the satellites? Stopping all computer and IT based activity? Grounding planes, docking ships, parking all road transport or, at the very least, going back to manual systems with actual drivers, pilots and the like? The effects would be massive and we would be back in the stone-age before you could blink".

PM: "So thinking the unthinkable for a minute. Just suppose all this electronic activity is the problem and we have to get rid of it and cease all the activity, presumably for ever unless there would be some way to reinforce this partition, then how would we do it?"

GCHQ: "It could not all be turned off with one flick of the switch. Well, in theory it could be but the consequences would be immense. It would not just be going back to the stone age it would be much worse. Everything is so inter-dependant that civilisation would just stop. If it was to be turned off it would have to be slowly scale down bit by bit with well-planned mitigation processes installed to take the slack".

Home Secretary: "Just a minute, I might be in a minority of one here but are we really thinking we would have to switch off all of the worlds communication networks with all the chaos that that would entail because someone thinks that the souls of our dear departed are going to come back and revisit us when this partition, whatever that is, breaks. Aren't we in the land of UFOs and Loch Ness monsters here like the gentleman from MI6 said?"

MI5: "I am afraid you may well be in a minority of one. After the Town incident and the underground train we were at a bit of a loss. But, as you know we monitor communication traffic for words or phrases that might be of interest, particularly regarding things like terrorist networks".

There was much shifting in chairs as the monitoring of communications was mentioned with many wondering if theirs was being monitored and wondering if they had been saying things they would rather other people did not know they were saying.

MI5: "We did pick up something on Mr Kingdon and started to monitor his communications and it appeared that he had been liaising with people in other countries. It transpired that there are people like Mr Kingdon all over the world, in almost every country, with a few exceptions, and they all seemed to agree that there is a massive potential problem that would, actually, only be an escalation of the problems we have already had. Since then we have been particularly active within the 'Five Eyes' group and Australia and New Zealand have been monitoring activity and agree with Mr Kingdon on the increase."

Several members around the table started wondering again just how much was going on that they did not know about. Suddenly this is not a British problem it is a global problem. They wondered if the other government ministers in these other countries knew as little as they did but they really knew the answer that they also probably knew as little.

Slowly, very slowly, the enormity of the potential problem was beginning to dawn on the folk in the room. But the same meetings were being held in other countries around the world and they were all coming to the same conclusion. We were going to have to wait and see what happens next because despite what was being said it was all still a potential problem and potential problems did have a habit of going away. Maybe the Wils of the world were wrong and the partition, if that was what the problems revolved around, would be able to withstand the radiation pollution and maybe he was just plain wrong.

PM: "Right ladies and gentlemen, thank you for coming to the meeting today. We obviously have a great deal to think about and we all have our various international meetings to attend no doubt to discuss the same issues so I want everyone to report back here in one month unless anything untoward or catastrophic happens in the interim".

She pushed back her chair picked up her phone and left the room by a side door. The rest broke out into chatter and gradually gathered themselves and started drifting out of number 10 with a lot more on their minds than they had when they went in.

THIRTY TWO

All the travel books said the view over Hong Kong from Victoria Peak were spectacular. From a height of over five hundred metres it said you could see over the bay to Kowloon and along the shore of Hong Kong island taking in all the impressive glass and steel buildings stretching high into the sky but still below the viewing points on the peak. Just below the peak the ferry terminals with the Star ferries could be seen shuttling back and forth all hours of the day. There was the Golden Bauhinia square and further along the coast the Royal Hong Kong yacht club and Causeway Bay. Helicopters, looking like small dragon flies, would dart between the peaks landing on platforms high in the sky and avoiding the giant planes heading into and out of the airport. Lower down personal transport and delivery drones dashed down the glass valleys. Lower still the roads that were often clogged with traffic through which the old trams would roll unhindered reminding everyone of the old Hong Kong.

But none of this was possible today. Today was one of the more common days when the pollution generated by the incredibly busy city and its huge neighbour, China, conspired to close it all down giving the viewer from the Peak Tower a glorious view of smog with only the tops of the very tallest buildings piercing the layer. It was very often bad but it was particularly bad today. The clouds were very thick and white with the sunlight bouncing off them making them look solid. Looking down onto them it looked as though the city had suffered a huge snow fall, nothing could be seen through the layer. Beneath the clouds was another layer of smog, yellow almost orange smog that dipped low down so that it was almost within touching distance of the people. As the visitors on the peak could not see down so the pedestrians could not see up. With the sea on one side and the mountains and tall buildings on the other and the thick, impenetrable layers above them the protestors were almost in a small, sealed box stretching almost the length of the business districts of the island.

The eight minute almost vertical launch of the immaculately clean green Peak Tram with its hard wooden slatted benches full of tourists had burst through the smog layer swapping the views of the bottom of the buildings and the dirty grey layer of pollution for the view of the sky and the tops of the buildings. It was suddenly warm and bright inside the cars and the air was actually breathable.

Folk who had been disappointed not to see the travel book description of the city were waiting patiently in line at the top of the hill. They were ready to be packed into the descending tram to descend back through the clouds, out of the sunshine and back to the packed pavements below. As the tram car poked through the clouds they started to wave at the strangely silent and no longer expectant folk packed into the ascending tram.

The people in the queues started screaming before the tram actually stopped at the top station. Looking like something from a horror movie the previously quiet and orderly queue erupted into screams and gasps and they started pushing back from the barriers and onto the peak again. By the time the tram had actually stopped the queue had disappeared with the screams following it.

As soon as the tram had stopped and the operator had seen the contents of the tram he decided to send it straight back down to the lower level and flicked the switch setting it on its way. Four minutes later the trams had changed positions and the one with the dead tourists who should have alighted at the top and taken their positions looking down over the city had touched the bottom station. The other tram that should have been full of tourists departing the peak was empty. As soon as the tram arrived at the ground level station the automatic cut-off switches came on and the lifeless operator would not have seen the system grind to an emergency halt.

Hong Kong was always an exceptionally busy place, so little space and so many people and the people were very happy today. Celebrating was almost a national hobby and it did not take much to get people out, usually with their multi-coloured umbrellas, marching up and down the wide streets with their chants echoing off the giant buildings to the right and left. Even the folk on the peak could hear the commotion down below. Today was no exception. Despite the pollution and the need to wear face masks partly in the vain hope that they would clear the air being breathed in and partly as a disguise to fool the hundreds of facial recognition cameras installed all over the city thousands were out in the streets. Banners were held aloft all celebrating in English and Cantonese. But all their mobile phones were turned off since they learned that the state could and still did track every one of their citizens through their phone knowing exactly who was celebrating and where. The irony of the situation was lost on all concerned.

As far as one could see there were crowds of people packed together, all along Harcourt Road and past the City Hall and Mandarin Oriental. In the other direction Gloucester Road and Convention Avenue and around the Convention and Exhibition Centre and past the sports centre almost to Victoria Park was crowded with more in the side streets trying to join the main throng. It was impossible to tell how many people were there, thousands, tens of thousands and everyone single one of them dead. The silence was deafening. There was no traffic because of the throng of people but there was no traffic on most of the side roads either even the trams were closed down. Far distant from the crowds cars in normally busy roads were almost at a stand-still as others tried to find ways around the protestors but otherwise silence. High up in the tower blocks there were hundreds of faces looking down from their high vantage points onto the scene below. Some had come down from their offices to see what was happening but they quickly succumbed and fell to the ground. It did not take long for those still in the offices to realise they were trapped and fear that whatever had killed those in the streets below would soon come for them as well. Fearing gas all the doors were closed, lifts turned off, fire doors sealed and the windows that could be opened were closed.

On the periphery crowds were running not quite knowing where to run to or what they were running from but the sight of thousands of people gasping for air and collapsing in front of them was enough for them to take to their heels. Those just inside the periphery were trying to crawl away and escape the disaster but further into the mass there were just piles of dead bodies covered with thousands of brightly coloured umbrellas.

Police cars, lights and sirens blazing, screeched to a halt as they arrived at the human barricade of bodies and the occupants raced out of the cars and tried to drag the struggling few to safety but they were not to know that the cause of the disaster was mobile and many groups of rescuers were enveloped and started choking.

In some places around the extreme edges people, as suddenly as they were covered and they started choking were uncovered and carried on trying to save people as if nothing had happened.

Soon drones and helicopters started flying over the scene sending pictures back to the government offices and round the world and it was those that the British PM had seen.

THIRTY THREE

"Get them all here and get them here now!" The PM was racing around her office barking orders at the secretaries that were dodging her movements. "All the cabinet, all the ones who were at the last meeting about this business. Set up video conferencing for the ones that can't get here in time. Prepare the bunker room, there isn't going to be space in the COBRA room. Get all the information about Hong Kong that you can get and load up all the plans that had been discussed if this was ever going to happen. Now! And another thing get that Kingdon chap up here. Blue light him if necessary."

No sooner had Wil answered the phone to be told he was wanted in London than the doorbell rang. Typical, just when you need to get a move on then the Jehovah's witnesses or double glazing people turn up at the door. So he was a bit surprised when he opened the door and there were two large and very obvious police officers in rather superfluous Hi-Viz jackets standing there.

"Mr Kingdon?" asked one.

"Yes".

"We have come to take you to London so could you get your things together apparently it is rather urgent".

"Blimey, the phone has only just rung telling me to come up to London and you are here already. Give me a minute or two to get my bits and pieces up together."

"OK but if you could be quick please sir, we really need to get going," replied the larger of the two policemen.

Wil disappeared back into the house and collected his boxes and notes he had made since the last meeting. Not thinking it would be appreciated if he offered the officers a cup of coffee he followed them down the path and into the police car.

"I suggest you buckle up tight sir", said the passenger cop "we will be going quite quickly".

As if the click of the seat belt buckle was connected to the cars accelerator the engine suddenly surged into life. The flashing blue lights and sirens followed and the police car ploughed a track down the centre of the road forcing all the other cars to one side as they sped towards London. The fact that the police car's computers could communicate with all the vehicles around them and cause them to move to the side of the road just as they arrived certainly helped. A27, A23, M23, A243, A3, red traffic lights all flashed by in instant and the two hour, eighty mile journey was done in forty seven minutes. They were going so fast Wil started to feel sick sitting in the back and started planning where he was going to vomit. The briefcase did not look vomit tight and there was nothing else. He closed his eyes and tried to focus on something, anything but at least he did feel strangely safe. The driver was certainly good and this was absolutely nothing like travelling in the so very sedate autonomous electric cars. He did not notice his knuckles turning white as he gripped the handle set into the roof with one hand and the lowered seat divider with the other hand but he did notice the front seat passenger was lightly gripping his roof top handle while calmly chatting into his radio. It was taking quite a bit of effort to stop being thrown from side to side and his back started to ache and he started to wish for the sedateness of the autonomous cars.

In a ridiculously short period of time he found himself stepping rather unsteadily from the car wishing his legs would stop trembling and that some blood could find its way back into his face. In a slightly unsteady voice and without looking directly at them he thanked the policemen for the drive. They dutifully acknowledged him and looked as though they had thoroughly enjoyed the experience. Briefly he wondered how he would get back to Eastbourne and hoped he would be allowed to take a bit more time over the return. Dodging the other black limos that were pulling up outside the gates he made his way through security and towards the now more familiar black door that once again mysteriously opened on its own.

"Good morning Mr Kingdon, please follow me," said the same voice from behind the door.

Expecting to go for the staircase Wil was surprised when they went down the short corridor and then through a door and down stairs. He was shown into a gigantic room that made him think of the operations room in the film Doctor Strangelove and then he thought, yet again, that he must stop watching so many films and comparing them to real life even though the drive had been very fast and furious. Stop it. In the centre of the room there was a huge round table with some people sitting at the regulation computers and some in little gatherings discussing something or other. At one end of the room was a matrix of video screens some with the heads of participants and some showing empty rooms waiting for their occupants. Wil was ushered to a seat and he sat down.

Everyone seemed quite preoccupied and no-one gave Wil a second thought. After a couple of moments looking round the room and feeling a bit more composed he decided that rather than just sitting there like a sack of potatoes he would actually do something so he reached into his briefcase and took out his wooden box and put it on the desk in front of him. Next came the lap top which he opened and switched on. Moving it to one side he positioned the wooden box in front of him and removed the polished brass one which he opened. As soon as he did he could see the particles moving quickly about the black surface. They would pause momentarily and then start moving again forming another pattern and then another. Wil quickly noted down the patterns on a bulging and well used notebook with an equally used pencil until he had a list of at least twenty numbers. Gradually he seemed to be getting a larger audience from the others in the room but he did not notice.

Moving to his computer he started typing in the numbers one by one writing down the geographical location that appeared. Just as he was getting to the end the Prime Minister walked in and started towards her chair at the top table but on seeing Wil she changed course and headed for him.

He was still engrossed in his work when the slightly unsettlingly strong smell of perfume wafted into his personal space accompanied by the PM herself.

"Good morning mister", she paused.

"Kingdon, Wil Kingdon", he introduced himself again attempting to get to his feet.

"Yes, Mr Kingdon", answering as if she was confirming that what he had said was correct "glad you could come today. May I ask what this is that you are doing?"

"Well", Wil paused not quite knowing how to address the PM, "PM, I did not really have too much choice with two police men at the door and a Back to the Future type ride up here. I am pleased to help, if I can".

"Good, so what is all this you have here?" She repeated

Wil noticed that the room had become quite quiet and everyone was looking in his direction.

"Well PM the best way I can describe this is that it is a kind of very ancient GPS", gesturing towards the wooden box. "It tells me where there are break downs in the partition".

"And are there some?"

"Oh yes. Obviously the biggest one has been the one in Hong Kong and there are still very many smaller tears happening in the region and that is very concerning but there are many small and mostly insignificant ones all over the world. Some in this country".

"Why so?" asked the PM as she made her way to her chair at the head of the table sending all the other people scuttling for theirs.

"Well for a number of reasons really. The first, the one in Hong Kong, is the biggest tear we have ever seen. Now you might not be surprised about that," he said looking towards the PM.

She did look surprised and with a definite hint of disbelief. "So, and let me get this right, you are saying that the problems they have had in Hong Kong are caused by the partition, as you describe it, has torn and large numbers of". She paused not knowing quite which words to use.

"Transients, they are transients or spirits," helped Wil.

"Thank you. So large numbers of spirits have leaked out across the partition, occupied all the space under the pollution and between the sky scrapers and suffocated all these poor people. Am I right that is what you are saying?"

"Yes, that is what I am saying. It has been made worse because the tear is so big that they are having difficulty repairing it and getting the spirits back to the other side".

"They? Who are they?"

Wil briefly wondered if he was going to be wasting his time explaining all this when there was going to be a heap of scepticism if not pure ridicule coming from some of those around the table who would not believe what he had to say.

"The partition is maintained from the other side. We do have the ability and resources to mend small tears and ruptures from this side but the big repairs are beyond us and have to be done over there," he waved his hand as if indicating where the 'over there' was. "Our role, on this side is mainly to shepherd the spirits safely back to the other side. The problem here in Hong Kong is that the tear is so big and so many people poured across it is difficult to repair it because it keeps on tearing and the pressure of the numbers of spirits make it hard to knit the sides together. It's a bit like trying to keep too many wet mushrooms in a wet paper bag."

He quickly replayed what he had said in his brain not quite sure where that analogy had come from and whether it was appropriate but he knew he had definitely had problems with torn paper bags and mushrooms falling on the floor in the past.

Moving quickly on he said "but the other problem is that the whole area is so weak that there are other tears occurring all the time. Most of them are small and discreet so can easily be repaired, some might even repair themselves but others might join up and make for even bigger tears. Also it is very difficult shepherding so many spirits at one time to get them back through ever smaller gaps as the partition is repaired. Altogether it is a," he just managed to stop himself swearing "nightmare". A mucking fuddle he thought. A super giant mucking fuddle but not as big a fuddle as there may be in the future.

"OK so what are the problems they are facing aside from trying to fix the partition?"

"Well there are a lot really. Obviously you are aware that the death toll is due to suffocation because the spirits are space occupying and they displace all the breathable air. It's a bit like ship being launched and it displacing all the water that it floats in. The spirits displace all the air they are occupying even though they do not have any real mass themselves. Until they can be returned to the other side they will mill around where they are making it impossible to safely recover the bodies of those that had died. Also the mass will move around and may affect areas of the city that have not been affected yet. Of course the partition might rip more and allow more spirits across compounding the problem. It doesn't help that this is an island so the spirits are trapped on it and cannot spread over the water and disperse, bit like what would happen here. On the other hand it is good because the break can be contained to just the island".

As they spoke they could see live TV feeds on two of the screens on the wall showing drone and helicopter footage of people in haz-mat suits with breathing apparatus loading bodies into ambulances and ferrying them away.

"Another problem is that the mass of spirits will move around a bit so there will have to be quite a big exclusion zone around the incident to make sure other people are not involved. Also they will need to give the people trapped in the sky scrapers oxygen masks to get them out and through the mass to safety if they want to get them out now or they leave them where they are until the repair is made and the spirits sent back".

"So how long would it take to repair the partition?"

"Difficult to tell".

Obviously not the answer that was required by looking at the expression on their faces.

"It could be as little as a couple of hours", he thought he might leave it at that hoping it would be a positive enough answer. "I expect there are quite a few people like me working on it".

"People?"

"Well I obviously use the term loosely when I refer to the spirits on the other side. What I really mean is the spirits although there will be people like me over there trying to help and do the shepherding".

"What else?"

"Well there could be more tears in the local vicinity".

"Is that likely?"

"Well the problem is the cause of the tears is not going away and, if anything is getting worse".

"And that is?" The PM asked already knowing what Wil was probably going to say after the last meeting.

"The radiation is the problem and it is not going away unless something very, very radical is done".

There was a lot of shifting in seats around the table. This was not going to go down well. It was all very well listening to explanations that may or may not be believed but if one of the courses of actions was what they were thinking then there could be major, major issues.

After the first meeting with Wil there had been many discussions about causes and effects and preventions based on what he had said but as with all things committee based the dangers were gradually diminished and the dangers of the cures were embellished until the ideal committee decision was made. Do nothing now and wait to see what happens in the future. And now Hong Kong had happened.

Sensing the atmosphere the PM continued "so you were going to tell me what you are doing with your gadgets there".

"Like I said it tells me where there are other tears".

"Would that be in this country or around the world?"

"Both. The last lot I got were for this country though".

"What! You mean something like Hong Kong has happened here?"

"No, not on that scale," he paused "yet".

"What do you mean yet? Is it likely to happen here?"

"Yes it is likely. More than that I would say, quite confidently, it is bound to happen here. All the numbers I have been getting this morning have been from places around the UK but they have all, thankfully, have been away from the big cities. There have been a couple in Scotland, one in Cornwall and several in Yorkshire. The biggest has been in Sussex but none of them have affected people and our people have been able to close them down quite quickly but it won't stay like that forever. It's a bit like a space craft breaking up in the atmosphere. Most bits will land in uninhabited places, or the sea, others will land on cities. Except in this case there will be nothing over the sea, it will all happen on land It is bound to hit a big city sooner or later. Maybe London". He briefly thought that if he could get them to be afraid that they might be directly affected they might actually do something.

"So what is the solution?"

"Shut down world-wide electromagnetic comms right now and for the foreseeable".

The room went quiet. Verbal communication stopped but non-verbal communication soared.

THIRTY FOUR

"So last time you spoke with us, Mr Kingdon, I have to be honest we treated what you had to say with a deal of scepticism," started the PM.

"Really, I would never have thought that", thought Wil not feeling bold enough to say it out loud.

"You probably appreciate that hearing something like what you were telling us is difficult to take on board and understand, especially with little evidence".

Wil bristled a bit about the lack of evidence thinking back to the piles of incidents that had been recorded over the centuries. He was in two minds as to whether using the dinosaur arguments that he had used with Lottie and the rest back in Eastbourne would be a good idea. It did happen rather long time ago and, admittedly, it was difficult to prove and there were lots of competing theories that might be more believable even if they were wrong. A meteor strike was much more believable and understandable, even climate change or a disease of some sort would be more believable to a disbeliever than the partition.

"Nevertheless, as a government we are bound, as a primary function, to ensure the safety of our population so we do a lot of contingency planning for various events. These may be things more likely to happen like a disease pandemic, terrorist attacks, a war, floods or loss of utilities but we felt, in this case and at this time, it was necessary to try to plan for this eventuality even though we were not sure what it actually was or what it would actually cause. I have to say the initial response was to wait and see and not actually do anything straight away but I felt we should perhaps do some initial thinking. So perhaps I can call on our GCHQ representative to tell us, first, about the issues as they see them".

GCHQ: "Thank you PM. As you said this is quite an unusual scenario and we started with the assumptions that the problem was the breakdown of the partition and that the breakdowns were increasing in frequency and intensity. After that we assumed that, as mister Kingdom states the reason for the breakdown is the increase in electronic communication. This was very different to anything we have had to consider before so it was difficult to know where to start. So as a starting point we started with what we thought would be the worst case. Well, we thought it was the worst case at the time but from what Mr Kingdon has just said it is probably the only case. Therefore we assumed that the only course of action, the only solution was the very draconian step of shutting down all comms. Also from what I understand the shutdown would have to be world-wide and not just this country for example and it may have to be permanent or, if a safe level could be identified perhaps, once the emergencies had stopped, some functionality could be resumed. Perhaps I could ask Mr Kingdon a question? If the breaks and tears in the partition can be repaired can it be strengthened? We are assuming that even if all comms were shut down and the partition repaired as it is then as soon as the comms started up and returned to current or even higher levels the tears would start again?"

"Yes, that's right. If nothing else was done to limit or stop activity as soon as the radiation levels went up again the tears would start happening again. Also depending on the loss of life this round of tears would cause there would be very many more spirits to be contained on the other side. Just to be pessimistic and in my opinion there could be millions or even billions if the comms are not cut".

PM: "So we need to reinforce the partition if possible? Is it possible?"

"The problem is that I do not know if it has ever been done before. In the past it has always been a case of smoothing over the tears and filling them in. A bit like sewing a surgical wound. The two edges are brought together and resealed. As far as we are aware there is no such thing as a patch that could be put over the tear like a plaster or a skin graft that could be put over a wound. But the fear here is that there are not just tears happening but the partition material itself is being eroded, as if the skin was thinning and ageing, and if it is we cannot replenish what has gone and there is less likelihood of a repaired tear holding. It is likely to be much weaker than before the tear".

PM: "And that is because?"

"Because we do not know exactly what the partition is made of and, like I said before, we, on this side, cannot repair anything but small parts of it. The major repairs and restructuring can only be done on the other side."

"Excuse me PM", asked a voice from one of the screens "can I ask if anything has ever been done to analyse the fabric of the partition, if I can put it like that?"

"Yes, in recent years as technology and science has progressed we have tried to sample the partition and analyse it but it is almost as though it is a living thing. It seems to be a cross between something like a very fine, but strong mist and a piece of your imagination. As soon as you try to take a sample, if you can take a sample, it seems to die or at least visibly change from what it was. It is a bit like trying to hold a snowflake in your hand. Its there but as soon as you touch it it disappears. But that, of course is assuming that the thing we are sampling actually is the partition. It very well may not be. It is a bit ironic to think that the thing that contains the dead is a living thing itself but it does appear to be something akin to living so we have never been able to analyse what it is. Even if we could I am not at all sure we could fabricate more even less sure we could patch it into the existing partition".

GCHQ: "Ok, so we assume that there is a catastrophic, world-wide breakdown of the partition and that it may or, more likely, may not be repairable and even if it is then it is not able to be strengthened. The other assumption is that it is the radiation from all the communication services that have multiplied across the world that is causing it and that is a bit of a stretch without evidence. How do we know that it is the radiation that is causing the breakdown? Could it be something else?"

Wil struggled to stop bringing up the dinosaur fart argument again being pretty sure it would not help his argument so he continued "throughout history the tears have all been small and almost always down to a temporary thinning of the partition to a point where it tore but it was always small, easily repairable and unlikely to cause much damage and that will undoubtedly continue. But", he paused, "but the numbers of tears have been increasing in the twentieth century, we reckon by over five hundred percent and it has to be down to something and we do not think it is the numbers of coffee shops". He felt the coffee shop line would be more acceptable than the dinosaur fart line. "It might be coincidence and I might be wrong. But I do not think it is and I do not think I am wrong".

PM: "If you accept that for every action there is a cause then there must be a cause for the tears but even if there are more tears but why is it radiation that is causing them?" She checked frowning a touch as she tried to recall if the sentence she had just constructed actually made sense.

"Because it couldn't be anything else and plenty of other reasons have been put forward and tested". Thinking that was a bit of a simplistic statement Wil felt he needed to expand. "Since the growth of radiation based communications there have been increases in the numbers of tears. They were usually concentrated in the more developed parts of the world where there was the most traffic as you might imagine but they were still generally small with a couple of exceptions. Of course it could be down to the increase in numbers of coffee shops or just coincidence but I believe it is down to radiation, and to be honest PM you haven't got much time to decide what the cause is and to do about it".

PM: "Yes, I understand that. Last time you were here it was mentioned about the underground and the Town examples last time. But there have been no other large scale issues since then, until Hong Kong?"

"No, well, at least none that we know of. Not all countries are quite as open about what happens in them as we are but we are fairly sure there have been no others. We tend to pick them up on these", he gestured towards his wooden box, "whether they admit it or not. Of course there could be a couple of ways this goes. We could accept that the cause is not known and continue with the levels of radiation and accept that there will be, from time to time, incidents like Hong Kong, or hopefully much smaller incidents and do nothing. Or we could do nothing and there could be a single catastrophic break of the partition which, effectively disappears completely and all the spirits are released. This would be life ending as there would be no way of repairing the partition and the numbers of dead on this side would go into the billions, wiping out huge sections of the population and exacerbating what is actually no longer a problem. If the loss of the partition happened there would be next to nothing, no, absolutely nothing we could do".

Feeling the intakes of breath from the rest of the room and seeing the faces slightly whitening he continued "the least bad scenario is that individual tears will continue to happen. Well they already are and always have done and always will but these could be massive and frequent. Today London, tomorrow Beijing, next Saturday New York or number 10. No-one will know where or when or how big but just imagine, for example, one happening in Mecca when thousands of pilgrims if not millions are concentrated in a very small space. If a tear happened there it would be catastrophic. Would that be acceptable for the sake of increased communication?"

Home Secretary: "So if you are saying you would not know where they are going to happen there would be no point in trying to evacuate people just in case they were evacuated into a place where the tear happened?"

"Quite. Sometimes we can get a bit of idea if a situation is going to happen. My colleagues the Lawns, for example, slightly anticipated the tube incident in London and were quickly on the scene to help get the spirits back. If they hadn't there might have been many more casualties in the rescue teams. But that ability is quite rare and could not be relied on. It is a bit like trying to predict an earthquake or volcano. In fact evacuating people and concentrating them in one place might concentrate the use of comms and stress the partition even more."

Home Secretary: "So it would be counter-productive".

Chancellor: "Counter-productive and expensive".

PM: "Not to mention the panic it would cause. So just going back to the cause why could it not be something else, other than communications?"

"Well air pollution is, or was, one potential suspect and, to be fair, we think it has been the cause of major failures in the distant past. But although there may be examples of that happening in the past in recent decades the actual amount of pollution, air pollution that is, has at least levelled off and some has declined but it still is probably not helping the situation and may well be making it worse. Just going back to the radiation issue I said that it usually had happened in the more advanced countries but ever since the new satellite systems have launched the whole of the world is covered with a huge increase in radiation. Even the deserts have levels of radiation that was never heard of before. With a single rocket being able to launch hundreds of these satellites space is becoming very crowded and the increases in numbers of base stations and data storage centres has happened everywhere."

Wil sat back in his chair feeling slightly pleased with himself for not bringing up the dinosaur based air pollution.

PM: "Well at least we are doing something right about pollution but is there anything else?"

"Solar flares used to be a suspect and there have been more recently and some of them have been bigger than before and there is a suspected correlation between flares either erupting or hitting the Earth and tears. So really, apart from pollution and possibly, but rather unlikely the rising Earth temperatures there are not many suspects".

The PM turned back to the GCHQ rep. "So you were going to say what plans or consequences there might be if we shut the systems down".

GCHQ: "OK so we assume radiation is the culprit. What do we do? If we shut everything down with a flick of a switch then there would be chaos. Everything that relied on communication would stop. No drones, deliveries, autonomous cars, planes, ships. All commercial and financial functions would cease. No telephony, no streaming, no social contacts. We would be back to the 1950s or earlier and undoing the knot of systems stopping and reverting to paper systems would be horrific. Except, of course we could not revert to mid twentieth century practices overnight. Everything would have to be re-invented and re-engineered. The economy would collapse, trade would stop, communication of all sorts would stop".

He paused wondering if he had laid it on a bit thick. Looking at some of the faces around the table he could not decide if they were all shocked into silence or scared that they did not understand or appreciate the situation and were wary about making any sort of stupid reaction.

PM: Mr Kingdon, what would be the result of a total shut down on the partition? Would it stop the tears?"

"Difficult to say PM. It would certainly help but it might not stop the tears happening as they had become so weakened and, as I said before, it would not restore the integrity of the partition. Just to be really alarmist, we might have reached or at least be approaching a point of no return where the breaks happen faster than they can be repaired and we end up with a multiplier situation that cannot be stopped". Wil felt there was nothing to lose by ramping up the level of threat. Maybe that wold focus their attention.

PM: "So according to your theory we shut everything down, the world stops and there is enormous disruption. Food production and delivery stops, all communication stops, transport stops, anything based around computers stops. And then we find that, either that you were wrong and it is actually something else going on here, or you are correct but the tears continue and whatever we do cannot stop them or that the repairs take so long to make and the restitution of the spirits takes so long civilisation, as we know it, stops. Alternatively you are right and the tears top, the spirits return and we start again in the early nineteen hundreds. Quite a gamble. What other effects might it have on the country, or world for that matter? Home secretary?"

Wil interrupted "or I am right and the tears stop and the partition is restored and we go back to normal, without the enormous levels of comms that we are experiencing now".

Home Secretary: "Well our plans were really two sided. One was the home situation and the other the international. Internationally there would be a security problem. How would we keep up our security systems? Anything that was based on tech would be instantly disabled. No air cover, all planes would be grounded including civil and military. There would be no computer systems but if it affected the whole world then there, at least, would be no danger of hackers and IT based warfare. Assuming all countries were affected in the same way. If they weren't there could be offensive IT approaches. All systems like radar, missile systems, and deep sea cover like submarines would be lost. We would be back to world war one communications within the military although as they are used to working in difficult situations they may be able to cope better than most which would be just as well".

PM: "Why?"

Home Secretary: "We would be assuming civil insurrection. Just imagine what the public are going to see. Mass extinction events like Hong Kong and us saying they are going to continue and, probably, get worse and that you, mister public may be next but you will not know what, when, where or if. We have seen runs on the shops in times of crisis before and this would be worse because all the supply lines would fail, all delivery systems would be disrupted, stores would not be able to order goods or process payments. The cashless society would be slaughtered and we would need to go back to cash but there is little cash in the system now. Depending on what Mr Kingdon says if it were to happen in separate areas, Birmingham for example or Glasgow then we could perhaps contain the initial problem if it could be repaired but nationally we would still be suffering the problems of loss of comms and in the site affected the loss of life as well."

Military: "If I might just step back a moment and add PM that not all forces hostile to this country or any other, for that matter, rely on high tech weaponry. The loss of high tech might give the less sophisticated terrorists the opportunity to launch low tech assaults on any number of targets around the world. There are numerous governments at permanent threat from small terrorist groups with basic armaments but high levels of determination. There is also the potential for IT governed weapons systems to not only fail completely but, more worryingly, there could be glitches that could launch missiles where there are no fall back, fail safe mechanisms to stop them. "

PM: "So what else would you plan for?" She asked GCHQ

GCHQ: "Well the next plan, assuming there was not the catastrophic and complete failure of the partition that Mr Kingdon describes, is for there to be isolated cases and as the Home Secretary says these could be coped with in much the same way as if there was a flood, albeit a massive flood. The problem here is that a large number of small or medium sized tears or incidents might be as crippling as one large one not to mention unsettling for the population. Of course if this happens world-wide then there are great implications for the food supply chain and other imperatives like medicines".

PM: ""So on one hand, and in the extreme, we have what seems like a civilisation ending event and on the other hand we have an unpredictable and, probably, increasing number of isolated events affecting few or many and both are possible if we do not reduce comms?"

GCHQ: "Yes but, again according to Mr Kingdon".

Wil started, for the first time, to feel the pressure of being the centre of all these plans and projections. Although he had thought many of the thoughts that were currently being aired he had never really thought it would all actually happen but apparently it could and was happening and he was being put front and centre. It suddenly felt rather warm in the room and he wished

Norman had been with him to reassure him he was right.

GCHQ: "According to Mr Kingdon this is all happening because of the amount of radiation in the world is dissolving the partition. He suggests that the only solution is to close down the whole operation. The problem with that, as we have heard is that would cripple the world. Rock and hard place come to mind. So perhaps there is a mid-way where we shut down some comms and see what happens. Can we get away with a reduction in radiation enough to allow repair and restoration with no increase unless and until we can reinforce the partition"?

Wil's face adopted the potential validity of the solution and the GCHQ man noticed and was encouraged.

GCHQ: "The trick would be knowing how many layers of this system could be unravelled, how much it would cost, how it would impact on everyone and when we would know. Ideally we would want a scenario where this could be applied. We have tried it in simulation but I don't think it is the same. At least there we could identify stand-alone systems that could be shut down but everything is so inter-related in the real world identifying anything that does not impact on a multitude of other systems is next to impossible. Also we need to get the whole world to agree to the proposals and for them all to actually carry them out. Herding and cats spring to mind".

"One problem would also be how to measure the effects on the partition if say ten percent of the communication was closed down. Would that stop the problem? Would it stop ten percent of it? Is there a direct correlation between the amount of radiation and the effect on the partition? What if we shut down ninety percent but we still had some breaks?" Wil felt he was doing absolutely nothing to help the situation but felt he needed to make it a bit more complicated than the room was thinking it to be.

PM: "I totally agree the trick would be in getting all the countries participating in these schemes to also agree and I just know that there are a lot of them out there that would rather believe the moon is made of cheese than believe what we have been told recently. There would be many not happy to obviously suffer the consequences of lost business and functionality on the mercenary grounds that it would stop the loss of life".

Foreign Office: "I can support that view. Not all countries have the same belief systems for example. How would we prove to them that the cause of these multiple fatalities are down to their ancestors spirits? Some believe in nothing after death, others in reincarnation and even if we could how would we convince them that the comms are the reason? It might have to be that we get some of the major countries to agree and then use the threat of force to make the less committed countries toe the line"

GCHQ: "So, to go back to our modelling, we started to look at the layers that perhaps would be stripped away perhaps one by one to see if there was any effect on the partition and the effects on any other layers."

PM: "And they would be?"

GCHQ: "Well Mr Kingdon seems to suggest that the real problems happened when the satellite systems were turned on". He looked towards Wil who although not looking at him was nodding.

"So if we started with some of that. Of course there would have to be international agreement and a good deal of contingency planning and preparation before anything went off line".

PM: "Ok so if we went that way where would we start?"

GCHQ: "Perhaps the hungriest applications are the transport ones. So we could ground all things like drone delivery systems, robot ground based delivery systems, drone taxis, autonomous road transport, driverless trains, buses and planes. The problems being that there are a lot of nations and people who are now dependant on these systems partly because they did not have anything like that before and there are others that did have systems before these but since their inception that have run them down or got rid of them altogether".

Wil looked around the table and saw representatives from the departments of industry, transport and finance all busy tapping away at spreadsheets sending out orders to minions to start working out what the effects would be of any of these measures and how they would be mitigated. All round it looked like a colossal vote loser and elections were only a matter of months away. The only ones that looked disconcertingly calm were the military representatives who could see their workloads escalating exponentially but they looked not in the least concerned. The military can always deliver.

PM: "And if it doesn't work? And, Mr Kingdon, if everyone did this how would you see the issue developing? Would there be a reduction in events, in your opinion?"

"I'm afraid I haven't a clue. I am hoping it will have a positive effect but how much is anyone's guess. All that can be done is to try it and see if it works. The snag is that although we can monitor tears we cannot predict where they will happen so even if the damage is limited there is nothing to say that major cities anywhere in the world will not be affected. Also I do not know how long it would take to repair the current tears or if there would be a time lag between the comms being turned off and the partition being strong enough to stop breaking down."

PM: "So if it doesn't work completely what are the next measures?"

GCHQ: "Well all the monitoring of people would have to stop. All the CCTV, all the monitoring of personal phones and computers and all the storage of the data that is collected".

Home Secretary: "Well I can see that being popular with all sorts of folk. Population monitoring has never been terribly popular outside of the real totalitarian states".

Round the table there was a lot of head nodding with the exception, Wil assumed, were the heads of the state security organisations who loved to keep an eye on everyone.

PM: "I have to say that after our last meeting and after a couple of briefings about what we should do there were several G7 and G20 meetings to discuss the issues. Again I have to say there was little or no agreement. Most of the heads of state completely dismissed the notions and refused to countenance any potential problems and absolutely refused to consider any reductions in the comms traffic. Many refused to believe the possible presence of a partition".

Wil winced at the reference to a 'possible' partition. Perhaps Hong Kong might change that.

PM: "Perhaps what is currently happening in Hong Kong might change this".

Foreign Secretary: "PM, may it not be possible that they will still not accept the potential for the partition and spin this event, if I might call it that, to some other explanation that their public will be more likely to believe?"

Well perhaps a 'potential' partition reference is better than a 'possible' one but Wil was worried about trying to convince people of the cause. Only once they accepted the cause might they be persuaded to accept the solution.

"Have any of the heads of states consulted with people like me in their own countries?" asked Wil.

PM: "Mixed picture. Some have and taken on board what they said, some have and disbelieved it all, some refused to meet with your colleagues and, I have to say, some of your colleagues took to the hills in case they were accused of witchcraft or trying to undermine or subvert the governments. Some regimes are pretty intolerant of people they would identify as subversives or heretics".

Military: "So what do you want us to do prime minister?" a voice asked after a couple of minutes silence.

Wil felt the meeting was coming to an end but was worried that nothing much had actually been decided.

PM: "For now I think we will continue with our contingency planning, for the worst case scenario but also for a potential down grading of our comms systems. We will wait to see what the explanation the Chinese come out with for the Hong Kong situation. If nothing else they can be quite imaginative about this sort of thing. And then we just wait. I think the only way we will get any movement from other world leaders is for this to happen again".

"And it will happen again. Again and again", chipped in Wil.

The meeting closed.

THIRTY FIVE

As Wil packed up his box and computer he felt deflated. It all seemed so obvious to him. What was happening was explainable and what needed to be done was highly unpalatable but it had to be done and he could not see why everyone was not jumping to it and getting it done before Hong Kong two, three and forty six happened.

The taxi pulled up outside the gates to number ten and Wil climbed in. The electric motor whirred into life and the GPS effortlessly and safely took him along Whitehall round Parliament Square and down Victoria Street to Victoria station. He watched all the other driverless cars whizzing about all cleverly avoiding each other all talking to each other and to their guiding computers. They also manoeuvred expertly around the thousands of visitors milling about almost all looking more often at their phone than where they were walking hoping to catch sight of someone famous. He wondered how people would adjust to having to go back to cars that had to be driven and how the fact that hundreds of thousands of people did not know how to drive and had never driven would go down. How would they cope with no transport at all? Above him delivery drones zipped about following their delivery instructions and also all expertly avoiding each other. Other wheeled delivery trucks also weaved between people following their dedicated lanes which guided them away from other traffic and to their destinations.

The computer controlled, driverless electric train was in the station waiting to go. Time keeping and punctuality was the by word now overseen with ruthless efficiency by the computers. The huge electronic notice board listed trains, destinations, departure times and platform. Information that was also beamed to mobile phone apps ensuring people either caught their trains or missed them by moments. Wil checked through the gates using his phone and made his way to the nearest carriage and settled down. Silently the train pulled away from the platform and out into the sunlight. As they crossed the river Wil saw one of the thousands of giant, power hungry data warehouses that was storing all the data and driving all the functions that kept the world turning. All the world apart from Hong Kong.

A couple of days after his visit to London the little Eastbourne group had met at number eighty six and Wil was telling them what had happened and what he hoped was going to happen next. What did happen next was the doorbell rang. Since the last time it rang and he was whisked off to London in double quick time Wil had become nervous to answer the door so he took a deep breath and feared the worse as he opened the door.

To his relief there were no policemen on the step but there were two bodies he did not recognise. He scanned them quickly trying to work out if they were from some sort of secret agency that he should be wary of but they looked reasonably normal. He looked past them half expecting to see other people milling round watching him.

"Mr Kingdon?" asked one of the pair.

"Yes, that's me. Who are you? What can I do for you?"

"Mr Kingdon, can we come in? We have a few questions to ask, perhaps you can help or maybe we can help you", said the other voice.

Wil was intrigued. Others offering to help was a new experience. Best to see what they had to say.

"Yes, do come in then".

He opened the door wider and showed them to the rear room. Best not to show them his nerve centre upstairs until he knew what they were about. As they made their way to the back the other three came downstairs and joined them.

"Who are they?" Lottie whispered to Wil.

"No idea, but they say they can help. We'll see".

"Please take a seat". They all pulled chairs from under the table and sat around it.

"Mr Kingdon, perhaps we should introduce ourselves".

That would be a good start and tell us why you are here as well thought Wil.

"My name is Paul Gates and I have been asked by the PM to liaise with you and your team", he cast his eye over the other three at the table "and try to formulate a plan that she can take to government here and to the other world governments to try to find a solution. My background is in IT and communications and I did a lot of work on the satellite systems so I do have a lot of background knowledge about the systems and what we thought the effects might be".

He paused "and this is my colleague".

"Good morning Mr Kingdon, my name is Ann Dromeda and my background is, how shall I say, in the spirit world".

"Well good morning Paul, Andromeda".

"No it's Ann, first name and Dromeda, second name. My parents thought it would be funny".

"Apologies Ann, as you know my name we also have my friends here, Lottie, Lewis and Harvey. So what do you want from us?"

"Well to start with we have obviously caught up with your theories about the partition and I have to say we do see a lot of sense in them and we agree with your diagnosis and, I also have to say reluctantly, agree with your views on addressing the situation. So we would like to explore the notions a little further if you don't mind. Firstly, can I ask you if you have ever noticed any sort of pattern to the breakdowns of the partition?"

"No, they always seemed to be quite random at least in this country and, as far as I know, everywhere else".

"Right, you don't think that has changed at all?"

"No, not that I am aware. Why?"

Ann picked up the discussion. "We have been looking at the current and historical data you gave us and then started looking at where the new incidents were happening. You are right there did not seem to be any particular pattern, certainly in the older data, but now we are not quite so sure. Do you have any more data on any other incidents in the last year or so whether they are big or small?"

"Well, yes we have the co-ordinates on all of them pretty much, big and small and all over the world. As you have seen we have them going back hundreds of years".

"Great, that is just what we need, so perhaps we can concentrate more on the ones in the last fifty years shall we say" she continued "can you give them to us?"

"Of course they will be on my data bases upstairs. Follow me".

Feeling as though these people might be on his wave length and be of use he felt less wary.

As they walked into the back bedroom Paul and Ann's eyes popped open seeing all the screens and shelves of files. Paul recognised the brass box that Wil had taken to one of the meetings at number 10 where he had attended through one of the screens on the wall.

"Right, so can you give me a file with the co-ordinates on it and I will try to plot them and see what comes out".

As Wil was constructing and sending the file his heart sank a little as he thought it would take a long time to plot all the co-ordinates and there were hundreds of them from all over the world on a map but he was soon proved to be wrong.

No sooner had the file been transferred than a map of the world was projected onto one of the walls from a small grey box that Paul had taken from his case and red spots started to appear as the co-ordinates were located. In no time they had all been plotted and the wall was awash with red spots.

Paul stepped back from the computer and reviewed the map with a highly satisfied look on his face. He exchanged a smile with Ann.

"That is terrific, much more than we could have hoped for." He focussed in on England. "Do you see what we see?"

"No I can't see anything except a jumble of dots," admitted Lewis.

"There is a pattern there. There seem to be some lines which the dots are aligned with," offered Harvey. "Is that what we are supposed to be seeing?"

"Absolutely. There are a lot of what we will call outliers but then, according to Wil, they have always occurred but can you see that with the most recent ones many of them fall into a pattern?"

He zoomed into a more detailed section of Sussex and Kent.

"They do and I think I know what is coming next," added Wil.

"Presumably you know about ley lines then?"

Oh yes, they all knew about ley lines and they recalled their discussions what seemed like decades ago when Wil was explaining what he did.

"Well ley lines, like you can see on the screen now, or as the Chinese call them Dragon lines seem quite important. They have been discovered all over the world and all civilisations seemed to believe in them although with different names. We had them, the Chinese had them, the Incas had them, and the Australian Aborigines had them so civilisations remote from each other in terms of time and geography believed in them. The one thing they all had in common was that the civilisations believed they were spirit lines or spirit paths although some saw them as death roads. Whatever they called them they were thought to be tracks for the movement of spirits".

"Yes, we discussed the ones in this country especially the one that went through Beachy Head and Sussex," added Harvey.

"Good, well look at this".

With a flourish he pressed a key on the keyboard and overlaid on the map projection were global ley lines.

"Brilliant," exclaimed Ann and high fived Paul. They both looked at Wil and beamed.

Wil could not believe what he was looking at although what he was looking at seemed to make perfect sense and validated a lot of what he had believed and preached over the years. He quietly wished Norman had been there to see it and could not believe they had missed it.

With a number of exceptions the majority of incidents fell either on or within a couple of hundred miles or so of the ley lines. They passed through Town and Hong Kong even though there was quite a time difference between the two events and they only occurred over land masses. Ley lines crossing water showed no incidents, only those on land.

"You know what that means?" asked Paul.

"Well I assume that if the majority of these incidents happen on lines we could predict which cities are most at risk although we couldn't really tell them when they were most at risk".

"True, and the problem is that if we did tell everyone who was at risk that they were at risk there would be panic and pandemonium and possibly with no reason. Annoyingly they do not all fall on ley lines. Many are but many are also close, using the term fairly loosely. So you could say city A was at risk but you could not necessarily say city B was safe and if the tears increase in size the chances of city B being safe will reduce." added Ann.

"Right, and the other thing is that perhaps we can surmise that the lines are actually lines of weakness and they are affected by the radiation of the comms industry more than other areas but the other areas could still be at risk. For example an area of high activity that is nowhere near a ley line could be at risk merely because of the activity. Of course an area of high activity that was on a ley line would be at the most risk".

"So if the most likely to be affected are on or near ley lines then we could perhaps reduce the levels of radiation in those areas and prevent more breakdowns?"

"Yes, prevent breakdowns but also we could maintain the rest of the comms and satellite networks so not everything would need to shut down. We could, perhaps, divert a lot of activity to places where we think the partition is stronger. The trouble is that there are hundreds of lines and, as you can see, not all the incidents happen exactly on the lines. Big cities that lie off the lines could still be affected," enthused Paul seeing a reprieve for his industry.

His phone rang.

"Get back here right now mister Gates and bring mister Kingdon with you there's been another and its serious".

THIRTY SIX

1600 Pennsylvania Avenue, Washington D.C. certainly lived up to its name this morning as the bright red sun rose slowly into the sky. The White House was truly white as it sat under a thick layer of snow that merged it into the garden scape. If the White House had had a shed at the bottom of the garden it too would be white shed today. Despite the computer power, satellite measurements and legions of meteorologists predicting what the weather was going to be like ten years hence they failed to predict the couple of feet of snow that the winds coming from the north east dumped onto the city overnight. But being America thousands of workers with hundreds of snow ploughs and snow blowers had been dispatched to clear the streets of, arguably, the most important city in the country. Everywhere plumes of snow being processed through the blowers glittered in the bright morning air as they gently fell back onto the pavements blocking the path of the few pedestrians that had braved the land scape. Car owners pointlessly tried to uncover their cars knowing full well they were not going to be driving anywhere today. Power line workers were desperately trying to clear frozen ice and snow off the overhead cables before the weight brought them down. Heavy four and six wheel drive vehicles patrolled the almost deserted roads looking for vehicles that had left the road and were causing blockages pulling them to one side and then moving on to the next. Stranded buses and coaches were neatly sacked at the side of the road.

Inside the White House however things were very different. The temperature had risen considerably and one very angry president was storming into the Oval Office screaming at the aides who were following him with arms of paper work that, despite the inexorable rise and rise of computers, could still not be dispensed with, and computers. Everyone seemed to be shouting into their phones as they dashed about.

POTUS: "What the hell do you mean we have had a Hong Kong here? What the hell does that mean? Speak to me".

First Aid: "Well Mr President". He was interrupted.

POTUS: "Get me the vice president, chiefs of staff and whatever the guy that is running the space department is and get them here now," he demanded.

Second Aid: Immediately wishing he had not been quite so negative said "it might be a bit difficult to get them here soon because of all the snow, sir".

The president looked at him with what amounted to a death stare and the aid dropped his head and rushed out of the office to perform miracles.

POTUS: "And get me the British PM on the phone, she seems to know more than me about these things. And where the hell is my breakfast?"

The President swept through the Oval Office and into the large meeting room off to the left where the actual work was done. He flung himself into his chair half wondering where his staff were and half wondering where his breakfast was. "Okay, tell me what the hell is happening here someone".

First Aid: "Well Mr President we were alerted early this morning", he flicked through his papers "at, let me see, seven twenty seven actually, that there was a problem reported in Texas, Laredo", he flicked through more papers "yes, Laredo. Actually the northern neighbourhood of Laredo. A call was put through 911 to the local police to say there were a number of dead bodies in a factory. When they attended there were indeed fifteen people dead in a small room in the factory but none of them had any obvious signs of why they died".

POTUS : "Ok so fifteen bodies. Was it some sort of mass shooting or something?"

Second Aid: "No, sir. There were no gunshot wounds or wounds of any sort. But the investigating team did think of the issue they had had in Hong Kong those weeks ago and this scene fitted the bill".

As the president started to speak the door opened and in rushed the VP and the three chiefs of staff with the head of the National Security Council but still no breakfast.

POTUS: "Look fifteen dead people is bad enough but why all this panic. God knows we have been here enough times before?"

First Aide: "Well, sir, that was not the end of it. While they were investigating the scene in Laredo there came other calls from Webb and Callaghan north up the interstate 35 highway. There were reports of people falling dead in the streets there. So far we have had reports of over sixteen hundred".

POTUS: What!" He screamed fifteen hundred dead in the street and no-one knows why?"

First Aide: "Sixteen hundred sir, and it looked like the same cause as the deaths in Laredo. No physical injuries or obvious reason".

POTUS: "So what is the reason? That sort of number of people do not drop dead without a reason". He lowered his voice to a whisper, tilted his head down and looked through the tops of his eyes. "It's not terrorists, is it?"

National Security Chief: "No sir, we do not believe it is terrorists. There does not appear to be any bombs, no explosions, no gunfire and, so far, we have not been able to detect any poisonous or noxious gases. The great majority were out in the streets or in their cars. It was rush hour so everyone was going to work or school. There seems to be limited cases inside the homes possibly because of the weather, even in Texas, people were closed indoors. Of course as soon as they ran outside to help they were affected as well".

POTUS: "So, again, what is it?"

First Aide: "Sir, we do not know the reason but just before we met we had reports of another incident".

POTUS: "Oh my God what now?"

First Aide: "Well there were reports of a couple of deaths in Artesia Wells. A bit further up the inter-state 35 although there had not been anything in the towns between it and Callaghan. So far all of this has only been reported locally and not picked up Texas wide or internationally".

POTUS: "And?"

Chief of Space Operations (CSO) chipped in via video link from Vandenberg: "Sir if I might interject. We have a time line here going from Laredo, through Webb and now Artesia Wells. If this thing is progressive, whatever it is we might be looking further north again and that would take us to San Antonio, then Austin or Dallas. If the same thing happened there we could be in for a heap of trouble. Laredo is 181 miles from San Antonio and San Antonio is 274 miles from Dallas so there may not be much time before it, whatever it is, hits the metroplex".

Before they could all digest the potential one of the aides passed a phone to the POTUS and whispered "it's the British PM Sir". The PM flashed up on one of the giant monitors fixed to the office wall.

POTUS: "Good Morning PM thank you for coming on line. Have you heard what is happening here?"

PM: "Yes Mr President I have and I have gathered my team again. I have to say it sounds very much like Hong Kong only, potentially, much worse especially if it spreads north. I have spoken to my expert on this and he says he has been in contact with his counter parts in the US and he is of the opinion that you are experiencing the same as Hong Kong and other places but on a much, much larger scale, at least in terms of area covered if not in terms of the numbers of people affected".

Chief of staff: "Yet".

POTUS: "And that is what exactly?" asked the president glaring at and then looking away from the chief.

PM: "He is saying that you are experiencing at least one massive tear in the partition and several smaller ones along a line. The worry is that all the little ones either multiply or, even worse, they all join up to be a single enormous tear that could stretch for hundreds of miles. Of course, where the tears are occurring the spirits are coming across, displacing all the air in the locality and all the victims are being suffocated".

POTUS: "Oh crap, not all that again. And what does he say we should do about it?"

PM: "Frankly there is nothing you, we, you can do about it right now. We have to leave it to the other side to try to repair it and hope that they can before it breaks down completely. You have a bit of an advantage because the state is so big that, if the tear is slow enough, it might be repairable before it hits any other major cities. But the problem is not necessarily the tears that happen where there are people although that is bad enough. The problem is that tears occur anywhere, if it is in a deserted part of the country all well and good for the time being, but if they all start joining up you are in trouble and, of course, you are a big country so it could spread coast to coast and even north up into Canada or south into Mexico".

POTUS: "And if it cannot be repaired or the number of tears stopped?"

PM: "Then I am afraid there are going to be a lot more casualties".

The door to the office flew open and breakfast came in along with another aide.

Third Aide: "Sir we are getting reports of a number of deaths in San Antonio. They started south of the city but have increased and moved north through Alamo Plaza and through Fort Sam Houston, Terrell Hills and Alamo Heights. There are hundreds of casualties".

National Security Chief: "So no need to tell you that the next stop is Dallas Fort Worth metroplex with nearly eight million people. If it hits there we are in deep shit".

POTUS: "PM put your expert guy on for me to talk to".

Wil looked to the PM with the look of a startled rabbit. Hang on a minute, the other day I was pottering around Eastbourne gathering data and watching what was going on and feeding the ducks in Hampden Park and now I am talking with the most powerful man on Earth about saving the world. How has that happened? Where's Norman when you need him? Then he thought that Norman was on the other side watching what was happening as well and trying his hardest to stop it happening.

POTUS: "Hello, what's your name?"

"Wil", Wil paused not knowing whether to call him sir or Mr President or your worship or something.

POTUS: "OK Wally". The decision was taken out of his hands. "Tell me what you know about this and what we are going to do about it".

"Ok, Mr President, sir" Wil decided that too many titles would probably be better and more respectful than none. "It's Wil actually and I think you are aware of the topic of the partition and my belief is that what you are experiencing is what Hong Kong experienced a while ago but yours is more serious over a longer tear that seems to be continuing for longer combined with a multitude of smaller tears which seem to be following a line".

POTUS: "Well I know that but what is going to happen next and how do we stop it happening again?"

"There is nothing you can do to stop it at the minute".

The President butted in "what do you mean there is nothing we can do! The goddamn thing is heading towards Dallas and then, presumably it will go further. We have to do something before it starts hitting the really big northern cities".

"There is nothing we can do from this side but there will be those working on the other side to stop the tear and marshal the spirits back. There are two problems though. One is the tear seems to be progressing like a tear in a sheet of paper and I expect it is going along a line of weakness, probably a lay line."

POTUS: "And the problem is?"

"Well there are two or three problems".

The President slumped back in his chair with a look of exasperation. Two or three problems are three and four problems too many.

POTUS: "No, I don't want two or three problems. I want two or three solutions".

"One problem is that the tear will keep going along the line it is going and it will hit Dallas and then, maybe go on after that. The second is that the point of the tear that started, I believe, in north Monterrey will start tearing and going south back through the city and on south. The third, and most serious problem would be if the tear started widening. At the moment I think it is only a few hundred yards wide but if it started getting wider and longer it could, in theory, envelope the whole country coast to coast and up through Canada and down through Mexico and even further south".

POTUS: "Yes, yes, yes I have already heard that. But you cannot be serious". As soon as he had said it he wished he had not but there it was. "We have to get this stopped. Is there really nothing we can do?"

"No, nothing we can do, except".

Grabbing at any ray of hope the President jumped in "except what?"

"Well we can leave the repairs to the other side. As I said a problem would be the tear widening but it appears it is not, yet. And that gives them time. The other is hope that Dallas is far enough away from San Antonio and Austin that they can build up the strength there to stop the tear going on. A bit like a bit of nail varnish on a nylon stocking". Wil made a mental note that that was probably not the best example. "If they can stop it spreading north and reinforce it from spreading south and if it does not widen then they have a chance of repairing it without a great deal more damage".

POTUS: "There are a lot of 'ifs' there but I suppose, if there is nothing we can do we just have to hope and try to evacuate people along the line to perhaps a distance of ten miles". He looked at his chiefs of staff and particularly to the National Guard who all took their cue and as one stood up and left the room. "Is there really nothing else we can do?"

"Well there is one thing but you won't like it".

POTUS: "Look mister whatever your name is, Wally, there is damn all I like about any of this so one more thing isn't going to make one damn bit of difference. Let's have it."

Wil was a bit disappointed the president had forgotten his name again but chose not to remind him even many thousand miles away he was still quite intimidating and he did have other things on his mind.

"You are probably aware that I believe the main cause of these tears is the huge increase in radiation caused by all the communications traffic. I believe Texas, in particular, is quite a hot spot for all of this."

The president looked at the Chiefs of Space Operations and the Office of Science and Technology who both nodded in agreement. The Texan cities had been very proactive in building the huge data information and storage systems and there were more concentrated in and around the four big cities in Texas than anywhere else in the US.

"So one thing you could do is switch off all the communications in this area. That would stop the stress on the partition and help those that are repairing it".

POTUS: "Don't be ridiculous we can't just turn off all the comms in Texas just like that".

"Not necessarily all the comms but enough to reduce the stress. Stuff like the cars, ground the planes, stop all the surveillance, stop the entertainment networks and the pointless comms".

POTUS: "Can we do that but keep up the comms we need to marshal the people?"

Chief of Office of Science and Technology: "Well we can do some of it by perhaps closing down the satellites over part of the area and ordering the entertainment companies and others to stop working for a period of time. But one issue will be trying to explain it all to the population who are just not going to believe it. There were all sorts of rumours, mis-information and fake news after the Hong Kong incident. I do not need to tell you, Mr President, that it will all be your fault".

POTUS: "Oh I know that only too well. It's my fault if we do something, it's my fault if we do nothing and it's my fault if we do the wrong thing or the right thing for that matter. But. Do it. Shut it all down. Now. And we will see what happens. Thank you Mister Kingdon for your help. Please make sure you keep in contact we might need you again". The last of the breakfast disappeared but the president did not feel any better.

Wil added "Of course one issue is that if you shut down much of the electronic traffic across Texas much of it may be diverted to other centres and then they will be exposed by the excess radiation".

POTUS: "Well from what you say we don't have much of an option and we haven't got time to think it all through. Let's go for it and see what happens. Surely it cannot make it worse".

Wil was not sure that it could not make it worse but he was pleased that someone was actually linking cause and effect and was prepared, from his point of view anyway, to gamble on a solution.

THIRTY SEVEN

Within minutes all over Texas the VTOL drones stopped in their tracks and after a seconds hesitation started their flights back to head-quarters forming orderly lines as they closed in on their base stations. On the ground workers rushed to unload the ones that had landed feeding conveyors that disappeared into the giant warehouses before other drones took their place waiting to be flown off and stacked ready for use again. Winged drones described elegant turns as they also headed back to head-quarters also circling patiently awaiting their turn to land and unload. On the ground scuttle buts about turned and headed home with their loads still intact. In San Antonio and other affected areas they had to swerve and steer around the dead bodies, crashed cars and other obstacles that had appeared but they diligently ploughed on. Autonomous, driverless cars were allowed to deliver their passengers before having to return to their garages as did the large people carrying drones. The only things moving on the roads were the few old fashioned vehicles with drivers and the only things in the air were craft with pilots.

Security chiefs winced as their facial recognition screens went blank and their population monitoring ceased. Bang goes people control. People winced as their film and music downloads terminated before completion and were no longer accessible. Entertainment was no longer available and this was no time for enjoyment. The only communications were texts and emails hitting devices and radio and TV announcements telling the populace what was happening and trying to explain why it was happening. Social media shut down and shared communication sites blacked out.

Communication systems were allowed to remain functioning as were the finance and healthcare systems but they remained under threat as anything that required non-ionising radiation was turned off.

POTUS: "How long do we think this is going to take?" He had reluctantly decided to take the decision to shut things down and blame it all on a massive glitch caused by the same unknown thing that was causing all the deaths.

Chief of Staff: "If what we are told is correct, and believable" he added with more than a hint of sarcasm and doubt "then it might only be a few hours. I assume it would not be more than a day. At least I hope not. And I hope it can be limited to Texas".

POTUS: "Can it be?"

Chief of Space Operations: "It should be possible to restrict it to Texas only, maybe even to the San Antonio area if needs be. The satellite systems are quite dense so each one covers a small, limited area so a number can be turned off paralysing only smallish areas and Texas is quite big. The problem is that Texas ends up being a black hole in the communication networks so nothing that would be coming in can come in and things that would be going out and interacting with the wide world isn't. It's going to look like Texas just disappeared".

POTUS: "Right let's see what happens".

On the ground in San Antonio there was a lot of activity. Through the remaining communication systems residents in the city and on the projected route of the tear had been told to evacuate to the west and east for as many miles as they could manage. Under no circumstances should they evacuate north or south. National Guard and military vehicles drove around districts with loud hailers telling people what to do. Other transport vehicles were positioned to collect the majority of people without their own transport. The highways agencies noted that the roads were getting busier but the police were reporting a lot of resistance from people because they either did not know what they were evacuating from or they did not believe the reasons for them having to evacuate.

Along the length of the tear mortuary trucks, ambulances and police vans were collecting the bodies and taking them back to the local hospital mortuaries and hastily requisitioned ice rinks for documenting and identifying. Fire trucks put out the burning cars and crews tried to extricate bodies from them. Police and National Guardsmen were shepherding people away from the areas that were obviously affected into areas that they thought and hoped were safe but as none really understood what was happening they were acting in the dark. Looters that invaded the affected areas were soon affected themselves causing the levels of crime to drop dramatically.

Overhead helicopters from the radio and TV news agencies were filming the activities and reporters on the ground were trying to find and interview witnesses.

On one corner in Terrell Heights one reporter from TSTV started their report.

"Good morning everyone. I am standing here on Terrell Heights in San Antonio and can show you all the activity going on over a stretch of the city from north to south and over five hundred yards wide. It is a sight of devastation but without any apparent reason. I have here with me Mister Dean East who witnessed what had happened. Mr East can you describe what happened".

"Well, man, I was working in my front garden and looking down the steep hill we have here when I started to see people in the street down below seeming to choke. They were holding their throats and gasping for air. Then they started to fall to the ground and cars and vans with their drivers also choking ploughed into them running down some who were choking and some who were not. It looked as though no matter how hard the autonomous cars tried to steer around the bodies they could not and ended up running into each other. It was crazy and I didn't know what to do".

"So what did you think was happening?"

"I didn't have a clue and was really scared that whatever was happening to them was going to happen to me. I didn't know whether to try to go and help or to run but I didn't know where to run. And then I saw them".

"Sorry, you said you saw them. Who did you see"?

"Well I don't know really but there seemed to be thousands, hundreds of thousands maybe".

"Who?"

"Not really who more what. They looked like people but they had no facial features, no obvious clothes they just looked a bit like a silver, grey shadow in the shape of a person that was suspended a foot or so above the ground but in a huge pack that was enveloping the people in the street."

"So this mass was surrounding the people who were collapsing in the street. Did you see anything else?"

"It was surrounding them and intermingling with them. Sometimes it looked darker and sometimes a bit thinner. It looked like a huge grey cloud had dropped out of the sky and onto the ground".

"Did you see anything else that might have given you a clue? Do you hear any explosions or noises?"

"I didn't really see anything else and there were no noises. It did look as though the cloud or whatever you would call it was coming from one or two places. It looked a bit like a crowd of people coming off a train at rush hour or maybe off of a ferry. If you could call it a crowd. One thing I did see and that seemed quite clear in comparison was a shape that looked like a large dog.

I started running away from the scene as it seemed to be moving quite quickly up the road with more and more of these things appearing and more and more people collapsing. Even people who ran to help the people who had collapsed also started collapsing so people stopped running in. It was almost as if it was a gas cloud but there was no smell of gas. It was weird".

"Is there anything else you can add?"

"Only one thing and that there seemed to be a great air of sadness about. I don't know what it felt like down there but even up here I just felt so sad and it wasn't just about the deaths. I don't really know why but I just felt so sorry for the whole thing. So sad".

THIRTY EIGHT

"So what was it like talking to the President of the United States?" asked Lottie as she reached for yet another chocolate biscuit. The group had met at the house as soon as Wil had returned from his latest jaunt to London eager to hear of his experience.

"Well, to be honest, I was really nervous but I'm not sure why".

"He is the guy with his finger on the button. The most powerful man in the world. One wrong, move from him and we are all toast," chipped in Harvey.

"Yes he is that but actually he was really nice. He was polite, to me at least, and listened and seemed to want to hear what I was saying. Except the bit about shutting down all the comms and radiation. I saw a bit of a wall come down then. He did seem to cheer up when his breakfast arrived though".

"Did they believe what you were saying though?" asked Harvey.

"Not sure. Well, actually, I am fairly sure they didn't or at least didn't want to".

"But at least they did act on what you were saying," added Lewis.

"Yes and it looked as though it worked. The tears did seem to slow down and eventually stop and they must have been able to get the spirits back," said Harvey.

"And it even seemed to stabilise after they started switching the comms back on," added Lottie not wishing to be left out.

I think they were just damn lucky there," added Wil. "I don't quite understand how it all did not go off again when they did turn things back on".

"Perhaps they did manage to reinforce the partition when they repaired if," offered Lewis.

"I don't think that is likely. I think it is more likely that they did not turn everything back on and that the levels of radiation did not go back to where they were before it happened".

"What about that person who said they had seen the spirits in San Antonio. That was quite a revelation wasn't it?"

"It was but, again, I'm not sure they believed it. They probably thought it was another nutter jumping on the bandwagon".

"It was the first time we had heard the descriptions though and I was quite surprised even though we have heard of umpteen tales of ghosts in different sorts of clothing haunting places. Why do they all look the same as well, people don't?"

"Forget about them being people. If you line people up they all look different. Men and women, old and young, black and white, able and handicapped, Muslim and Sikh you can tell them all apart. But then there are other things that you cannot use to differentiate just by looking for example intelligence, skills, and beliefs. But then if you go deeper, for example examine all the people's internal organs, their livers or heart for example are all the same and by looking at them you could not tell black from white, clever from stupid and the same is true for the soul or spirit. It is exactly the same for everyone and you cannot tell people apart by looking at the soul and that is why all the spirits look pretty much the identical. Also it doesn't much matter what you believe there are souls and spirits and they do exist across the partition".

"There are no 'things' with them either. No clothes, no jewellery nothing," said Harvey.

"No, we have no evidence of material things from Earth going across the partition. We presume it is only living, or in this case, dead things that can cross".

"So all the Egyptians and the rest who filled tombs with gold and silver and stuff were wasting their time," added Harvey.

"Yes, but maybe the horses and in some cultures the wives who were buried with them went across with them so they might not have been completely wrong".

"Well the wives would certainly have gone across as well as any servants that were executed to accompany their master. Same as anyone murdered would go across as well".

"It was interesting when he said there was a feeling of sadness about it all," commented Lottie.

"It was but probably because the spirits knew what was happening and they did not want it to happen so they were sad and upset and communally the feeling was picked up by Dean. I have always had the impression that there is no sadness on the other side".

"So what do you think is going to happen next?" Asked Harvey

"Don't think that is going to be difficult to guess" said Wil. "Even though they reckoned over 95,000 died in the states and over 28,000 died in Hong Kong as soon as the panic is over in Texas and they switch everything back on again they will stress the partition again and they will be back at risk. That is assuming the tear is repaired and the spirits returned. So I think there will be more incidents and they were lucky in Hong Kong that they managed without turning off all their comms but that might have been because so much had been turned off or at least wasn't being used because of all the demonstrations".

"But there have only been two perhaps there won't be any more. Perhaps they have fixed the other side permanently".

"There have only been two that we have been told about".

"You mean there have been more" asked Lewis incredulously.

"Well I know of at least two that have happened in China that they have completely hushed up. Anyone trying to report it have been mysteriously disappeared and all the comms in the area have been closed since they happened".

"Were they just small outbreaks then?" asked Lewis

"Hardly. We reckoned there were at least one and a half million deaths, maybe more, we cannot be sure but we know there were a lot".

"Wow that is a lot. So maybe two million world-wide" commented Lottie

"So far but it is not going to stop. Mark my words".

THIRTY NINE

Wil checked himself as he threw more newspapers onto the ever growing pile in the front room of eighty six. He recalled what the place looked like when Norman had passed over. Piles of newspapers everywhere held together with dust and not much else. So many thousands of them that it took many skips to clear out and here we are again with the grey, dusty shoots of a blossoming new pile of rubbish. He made a mental note to make sure it did not get out of control but was pretty sure Norman would have made the same mental note and that got nowhere. In some respects the house had changed quite a bit since Wil moved in. There were obviously the big changes to the back bedroom and the clear out of the rubbish but other rooms were still the same and seemed to be trying to revert to their former selves. One thing that had remained constant was the main diet which still seemed to centre around tea and chocolate biscuits especially when Lottie came to visit.

The current newspapers though were a depressing read. After Hong Kong and then again after Texas the papers were full of reports but mainly full of speculation and unanswered questions about what had happened and what might happen in the future. They were particularly scathing about the shut-down of comms in Texas concluding that it was a coincidence that the disaster had come to a conclusion just as the comms were lost. They were all oblivious to the fact that the comms were shut down on purpose as they were all led to believe that there was a coincidental failure in the regional comms system. Immediately after the incident the secret service departments were busy flooding all the information networks about the failure of the systems and the heroic efforts, in the light of the emergency, of the comms staff to get the systems back up and running.

The unanimous decision of the media, not entirely impartially, was that the comms explosion would continue and continue it did. More satellites were launched, more data centres and power stations were built, millions more people signed onto millions more apps and the radiation smog grew and grew invisibly but caustically.

Report after report from issued from various countries groups reinforced the position:

The G7: We consider the incidents in Hong Kong and Texas to be one off natural disasters and do not consider that they will be repeated. We support the growth of the information and structural technology apparatus and do not consider it to be a threat to world health.

The G20: We consider the incidents in Hong Kong and Texas to be one off natural disasters and do not consider that they will be repeated. We support the growth of the information and structural technology apparatus and do not consider it to be a threat to world health.

The Security Council: We consider the incidents in Hong Kong and Texas to be one off natural disasters and do not consider that they will be repeated. We support the growth of the information and structural technology apparatus and do not consider it to be a threat to world health.

ASEAN: We consider the incidents in Hong Kong and Texas to be one off natural disasters and do not consider that they will be repeated. We support the growth of the information and structural technology apparatus and do not consider it to be a threat to world health.

NATO: We consider the incidents in Hong Kong and Texas to be one off natural disasters and do not consider that they will be repeated. We support the growth of the information and structural technology apparatus and do not consider it to be a threat to world health.

ANC: We consider the incidents in Hong Kong and Texas to be one off natural disasters and do not consider that they will be repeated. We support the growth of the information and structural technology apparatus and do not consider it to be a threat to world health.

EU: We consider the incidents in Hong Kong and Texas to be one off natural disasters and do not consider that they will be repeated. We support the growth of the information and structural technology apparatus and do not consider it to be a threat to world health.

USAN: We consider the incidents in Hong Kong and Texas to be one off natural disasters and do not consider that they will be repeated. We support the growth of the information and structural technology apparatus and do not consider it to be a threat to world health.

Commonwealth of Nations: We consider the incidents in Hong Kong and Texas to be one off natural disasters and do not consider that they will be repeated. We support the growth of the information and structural technology apparatus and do not consider it to be a threat to world health.

The media which had initially swamped the news outlets with stories about the incidents continually asked pointless and unanswerable questions:

"What happened?"

"Why did it happen?"

"Whose fault was it"?

"Who is going to resign over it?"

"Will it happen again?"

"Where will it happen again?

"When will it happen again?"

"How many more people will die"?

"What are you going to do about it?"

"When are you going to do it?"

"Is it due to spending cuts"?

"Why are you not being clear about what you know?"

"Why are other countries doing this and that and you are not?"

"Why are you doing this and that and other countries are not?"

"What is the message you want to put across?"

"Why is the message not clear?"

"Why is the message confusing?"

"Why do you keep changing your mind?"

"Why don't you change your mind when you should?"

And now the weather forecast.

Eventually the media realised that no-one in authority they interviewed could or would answer any of the questions posed so they all moved on to the next subject to obsess about.

Soon different, new, news came to the fore. Wars started here and there, big companies made more and more money, the weather turned hot or cold, there was a flood here or an earthquake there. Memories of the losses of people in Texas and Hong Kong were forgotten or at least put on the back burner. It was a one or two off, maybe a four off if the tales from China were right but it was low figures and it was over now and the little incidents could be ignored.

Over and over again Wil read in the newspapers that countries all agreed with each other that all the crackpot and ridiculous theories about what had happened, including Wil's, should be dismissed as unbelievable nonsense that should not derail the massive strides being taken in technology and communication. Money was to be made, power was to be assumed, influence gained, second swimming pools could be built, bigger swimming pools could be built, posher cars bought. And indeed all the theories were dismissed and the developments carried on apace.

The Eastbourne group met frequently at Wil's house and they studied the map with all the locations of the breakages carefully catalogued and displayed. Some days or even weeks there were no new significant breaks and Wil hoped rather than believed that perhaps he was wrong and there was no increasing effect on the partition. Or maybe they had been able to strengthen it and there was no more danger. These thoughts were quickly dispelled on the days when multiple incidents occurred. This is not going away and it is not getting any better.

One day though Paul Gates and Ann Dromeda came back to the house and they all went upstairs.

"Wil, we have come down today because we are concerned there have been some developments in this situation and we are rather disturbed by them so we want your opinion".

Wil looked worried. It looked as though he might have missed something that was relevant but he could not think what.

"Look at the map and tell me what you see" said Paul.

"It's the same as it always has been isn't it. Dots everywhere, more often in the more populated areas and often close to or on the ley lines," chipped in Lewis

"I am afraid that is the point, it isn't the same as it has always been," answered Ann

"So what is the difference?" asked Wil

"Well do you remember when I first came down and we plotted these incidents and then overlaid the maps of the ley lines?"

"Yes. They seemed to match quite well and backed up the idea that the ley lines might be weak spots" answered Wil.

"Absolutely, they did but there is something new and we wondered if you had spotted it yet".

"What is it?"

"Well we began to think that more of the incidents were happening off of the ley lines and appeared to be happening randomly so we looked for other patterns and found one".

Paul hit a button on the computer and another set of lines appeared on the screen and they seemed to join up many of the incidents lying off of the ley lines.

"It seemed that there was some sort of pattern so we switched off the ley lines and put another grid onto the map".

"They certainly seem to show some sort of pattern. What are they?" asked Lottie

"Now that is the problem and we might have some trouble selling this idea. All these new lines are the top or most used communication lines. Lines where there is the most activity".

"And the most radiation" added Wil. "That is brilliant. Well done". Wil slumped back in his chair cheered by the proof that seemed to be being put forward. There was a direct correlation between radiation activity and the loss of the partition. No-one could argue against it now. Surely not?

"Exactly, this seems to show a direct correlation between the lines of comms, the density of radiation and the likelihood of a break in the partition," said Ann

"The lines have taken over from the ley lines as points of weakness and there are hundreds of them and they are strengthening all the time," confirmed Paul.

"So that means instead of monitoring the ley lines in case the tears happen along them they could actually happen anywhere in the world," observed Lewis "The grid you are showing us here looks to be much more complex than the ley lines grid".

"Right, so now the whole world could be at risk. Tears could happen anywhere and the more activity there is the more likely there is to be a weakness and the more likely there is to be a tear and a disaster and there is still nothing we can do to predict where it might happen".

Wil added the logical conclusion "I presume that the heaviest use is going to be associated with the densest populations where, if there is a tear, the most people are at risk".

"Exactly, but how do we get the powers that be to see it and understand the risks they are taking" said Paul.

A wave of blank looks swept around the room and then back to Paul who looked as if he had more to tell.

He did. "There was one other thing that Dean, the American, said when he was being interviewed about the Texas incident and I wonder if any of you picked it up".

"What was that? Lottie asked, "I don't think I heard anything else of importance".

"When he was describing what he saw and the reporter asked him if he had seen anything else he said he thought he saw what looked like a dog. That comment wasn't broadcast with the interview but we had a copy of the full conversation and picked this up".

"Oh my God did he? I completely missed that," observed Wil. "That's terrible if it is true".

"Like I said it was not included in the broadcasts so there is no reason why you would have picked up on it," reassured Paul.

"Why is it terrible?" asked Harvey

"Well it could mean that the partition between the human environment and the animal one is breaking down as well which would mean…."

"All the animals on the other side could come across as well as all the humans," Wil completed the sentence.

"Correct".

FORTY

"And that is the end of today's news so I will hand you over to Dick Lower in the weather studio to tell us what we can expect tomorrow. Dick over to you".

"Thank you, good evening everyone. Before I tell you about tomorrow's weather I would just like to tell you of a huge amount of activity on the sun's surface we have been monitoring over the last couple of days. It is being predicted that the biggest solar flare since the first huge one in 1859 was seen is likely to occur so keep your eyes peeled for it. It could be seen, to the naked eye, as a bright white light back then. But remember to protect your eyes and do not look directly at the sun. Now…"

"Bloody typical", exclaimed Wil to Lottie "not only have we got all this radiation on the planet but now the sun is going to chuck even more this way".

"Didn't you tell us that the solar flares might be damaging to the partition?" asked Lottie.

"I did and it is. So as well as the radiation and the pollution now we have solar flares to make things worse".

"So what are they and why will they make it worse?" asked Lottie.

"Solar flares are huge eruptions from the sun where plasma can be ejected at millions of miles an hour from the surface and into space and if that comes this way there will be huge amounts of electromagnetic radiation hitting us".

"What can it do?"

"Well the powerful ones have been known to knock out terrestrial power grids and disable satellites and therefore communications so if they did do that it is not all bad. If it did take down communications it could help the partition and give more time to repair it. But, on the other hand, we also think the radiation from the flares can damage the partition itself. So it is six of one and half a dozen of the other. Will it damage the electronic infrastructure more than it will damage the partition?"

"I suppose we will just have to wait and see".

"We will but the partition is so fragile at the minute that any more damage could really rip it apart. It also depends on the sizes of the flares. They may be wide and cover the whole of the Earth or smaller and only cover small parts. It also depends on the time over which they are released. If it were a quick burst it might mean only the face of the Earth that is exposed to them as they pass would be affected. If there is a stream over a long period then the whole rotation of the Earth might be affected. And more than once".

FORTY ONE

Despite thinking that he had fairly high tech IT equipment in front of him as he sat in the chair that he had inherited from Norman at the desk that he inherited from Norman on the carpet that must have been in the house when Norman's parents moved in he felt rather insignificant. After all he was, essentially, in his back bedroom playing on his computer. Millions of lads and lasses must be sitting in their back bedrooms playing the latest computer games or engaging with other lads and lasses in back bedrooms around the world playing their games and here he was with his in his back bedroom. But that was where the similarity ended.

He was at his computer, true, but the room he was looking at on his screen, although it could have been a computer game invention, was a real room. But just the fact it had walls, floor and ceiling did not make it an ordinary room. For a start it was huge. Wil couldn't make out how big it actually was partly because all the surfaces were black and there were no lights but it gave every impression of being enormous. He was able to access cameras in the room to look up and down its length but he could not see an end to it. So it was long, very long, and it looked to be quite narrow. Along the wall to the left of the room there was a huge screen and lined up in front of it were three tiers of rows of chairs with people sat looking up at it. Each chair had a small desk swung over the lap of the attendee on which they had their own computer. Wil could not make out who the people in the room were as they were only illuminated by the light coming from the wall screen and their personal computers and there were no name badges this time. On the wall behind them there was another bank of screens with a person looking down into the room from each one. Wil was slightly surprised to see himself in one of the screens.

The major screen running the length of the room in front of all the people was a massive map of the world. It was slightly amended in that the poles were not visible and the oceans had been shrunk making the position of the countries looked more like what Gondwanaland had been like. Waiting for the meeting to commence Wil could hardly help himself trying to fit them even closer together.

There was no writing on the maps but Wil could surf around the image of the map on his screen and click onto areas which would display the name of the country, the capital, the president, king, queen or ruler, the contact and their position and, more importantly, the numbers of incidents being recorded and the numbers of people being affected. Wil knew that the last statistic was a misleading because it included all the people who were evacuated from an incident site as well as the casualties but it was one that the majority of leaders had insisted on. It was the number of people affected and not the number of deaths although they were often one in the same but rarely very accurate. Some countries were better at collating the data than others and some did not want to reveal the true state of affairs in their country. At each spot he could zoom in closer and show regions in more detail with statistics for each of the small areas being viewed. Below the map there were displays showing the total, worldwide numbers of incidents, the numbers of people being affected and the numbers of incidents being resolved. Wil also knew that the numbers of incidents being recorded were the ones that the people on the ground experienced. He knew from the data he collected from his own instruments that the numbers of incidents were far higher than the ones officially recorded. Many of these caused no harm and were repaired before they were noticed but Wil knew that the situation was worse than those in the room were aware of.

As an incident occurred a light on the map came on. If there was a single incident the light was green, if there were two incidents in the same area the light went amber. More than that, or if it was an especially large incident, it went red and flashed. There were very many green lights scattered over almost all countries. Some largely uninhabited areas like eastern Russia, the deserts, parts of the Australian outback and Canada had few, if any lights, but, disturbingly there were many lights in a few highly populated areas. As Wil watched more lights came on. China, India, Europe, Brazil, Mexico all showed several amber lights and a small number of red.

On the wall opposite the map were what must have been at least 100 large screens with the face of the countries representative in sharp focus. Wil could not help but sigh when he noticed that the back drops behind the talking heads seemed to be entering into some sort of contest to be the most impressive. Bookcases were popular, artworks of varying authenticity, views out of the window across beautiful countryside and the sea were popular. Wil realised he had a backdrop of his back bedroom curtains which, on reflection, could have done with a bit of a launder before being exhibited to the world.

Similarly the desk at which the representatives was sitting looked as though they had been specially designed to send a message to the world. Many had a little flag of the country, some, rather pompously had the name of the country on a small plaque, there was a variety of expensive looking crystal decanters and glasses, the odd blotter pad and pen which looked so out of place when practically no-one wrote anything with a pen any more. Wil had managed to whip his half eaten pack of chocolate biscuits and a can of cola off his desk before the cameras displayed to the world his weaknesses. Apart from them there was nothing on his desk.

The meeting had been going on for over an hour now and it was quite obvious that tempers were getting frayed. Somewhere there were people moderating the meeting but they were not in view and had not been identified but they frequently had to intervene to ask people to calm down, stick to the point and keep their comments relevant or they resorted to cutting them off completely. Screens would occasionally go black and the sound lost as moderators moderated. The recriminations went round and round. Few people would accept what Wil and his counterparts in all the respective countries had been telling the leaders and were frequently abusing Wil and blaming him for making all this happen. When they got fed up of blaming him they started blaming each other. Wil could not help thinking it was like some sort of weird Eurovision song contest where blocks of countries that were friendly to each other would blame other countries with whom they were not friends. Occasionally the arguments subtly changed and friends suddenly became enemies and unlikely alliances were formed although only for a short period of time. Universally the dire situations that they found themselves in were obviously either the fault of the USA or Britain. China and Russia were completely blameless, North Korea had never had any problems and if anyone tried to blame them they would consider it an act of aggression and attack them, African countries could not have caused it because they never got enough aid from the west. The Middle Eastern countries did not believe the basic principles so it couldn't be anything to do with them.

Every reason was brought forward to try to explain the situation. Land grabs by this country, water grabs by that country. Some sort of chemical warfare released by this country, mass hypnotism by that country. Something in the air, something in the water. Alien invasion, virus invasion, bacterial invasion. Or maybe it is a giant con. Every reason was touted except the real reason. Wil tried time and again to argue his point but he was usually shouted down until the shoutee was moderated into silence.

Wil despaired that they would not accept the cause and if they would not accept the cause they would never accept the solution. Several times he had listened to the noise while staring disconsolately at his chocolate biscuits wishing he could just sit there and eat them until all these bloody idiots had argued themselves out and then seen reason. He did wonder what the other heads would think if he got his mug of tea and a plate of biscuits and just sat there eating and drinking while the hot air and stress levels rose. Maybe a nice plate of fish and chips.

Wil was not quite sure why he had become the representative of the group of people who actually understood what was happening and had the solutions. He knew full well that all countries had people like him but the fact that he had been seen to be central to the

United Kingdom's team and had spoken with the President of the United States seemed to have catapulted him into the frame. Now everyone wanted to talk with him. It was just so unfortunate that rather too many of them did not believe what he was saying and just wanted to find any reason to discredit him.

It seemed to Wil that the main problem with the lack of acceptance was the association of the principle of the spirits with religion and, more to the point, the outright denial by many religions of the possibility of the spirit world. No matter how many times Wil had tried to explain that this had nothing to do with religion they would not accept it. The denial of religious belief or the acknowledgement of another's religious beliefs dogged every argument. Some spirits went to paradise, some came back as other living creatures depending on how they had behaved on Earth, and some believed death was the end of it all. The fact that the existence of spirits was, and always had been, a matter of fact just as the presence of chocolate biscuits was a fact was unacceptable to many. But it was not a belief, It was a fact and the fact was the thing that was killing the world. Even more unacceptable was that the thing affecting the fact was the great advances and benefits brought by the communication systems that had swept the world. The fact that the breakdowns of the partitions had started soon after all the comms had surged was of no consequence to the faces on the screens. The fact that the solar winds had exacerbated the issues was just a coincidence and had no bearing on the matter.

FORTY TWO

The astronomers had no idea, they had never seen anything like it before. The solar flares were reaching thousands of miles into space, leaping from the surface of the sun. Some were as though they were rockets launched from the surface blazing a straight line from the surface into space before falling back. Others seemed to be like unrolling Catherine wheels and yet others were like explosions with showers of flares stretching hundreds of miles across with multiple flash points. From pole to pole of the sun there seemed to be some degree of activity and it had been going on for days. If the astronomers did not know better they might have thought that the sun was self-destructing but it wasn't it was just boiling with flares launching particle heavy winds into space day after day and flinging them towards the Earth at thousands of miles an hour.

In contrast to all the activity on the Sun's surface the waves of flares and winds had no effect on the Earth. No-one apart from the astronomers knew or particularly cared that they were being bombarded. But the partition knew. The partition was being very badly affected. Day after day waves of radiation swept over the surface of the planet. Pulses of high activity were followed by pulses of low but the Earth kept rotating through them and it was behaving like a pig on a spit with each part being brushed by the flare activity. Even when the flares on the surface of the sun had eventually stopped leaping from the surface the waves kept pouring over the Earth for days until, at last, they faded and stopped. The partition had been battered, ripped and torn by the massive increases in non-magnetic radiation created by the massive surges in electronic communication and this was mightily exacerbated by the Sun. Everywhere tears were appearing and it was getting more and more difficult to repair them. There were so many and they were, often, so big. Wil and his mates had been going out to all the local incidents despite there being so many. Fortunately all the ones they had detected were quite small and had had little effect on the Sussex populations but other places in the world were not so fortunate.

The lights on the giant atlas in the, now deserted, black room had started to light up more often as the flares swept past the planet. Data being gathered by each country continued to be fed into the central data base and through a time lapse display covering the previous weeks it was noticed that the numbers of incidents that had been slowly growing prior to the flares had massively increased as the solar flares had increased. The astronomers had been questioned by the media on an almost hourly basis about their calculations as to when the flares might stop but they were as much in the dark as the politicians and could not give any concrete answers. One of the theories that enjoyed some popularity and which Wil had heard was that all of this was due to the Sun's activity and the flares were just exacerbations of the problem. The hope was circulating that when the flares stopped the incidents would stop, or at least slow down long enough for a solution to be found and that the whole thing had nothing to do with the comms activity on the Earth. It was all the Sun's fault.

The meetings in the black room became frequent and long. People would drift in and drift out but some stayed resolutely fixed to their screens. Behind the faces on the screens the governments of the world who were minded to believe Wil were trying to grapple with the problem and explain it and their response to their increasingly panicked populations. Some tried to downplay the emergency, some tried to explain it and describe what they were going to do about it. Most blustered and bluffed while trying to look statesmanlike and on top of the problem. Government oppositions said that whatever the government was doing was wrong and that they would do it better but they never offered any ideas or solutions. Some blamed 'outside interference' which was not a million miles from the truth, some blamed the opposition parties, the right blamed the evil left and the left blamed the evil right. Whenever anything was done it was claimed that it was too late or too soon or should never have been done in the first place. If it was done at the right time it was the wrong thing to do and something else should have been done instead. Those that had been badly affected had a hint of panic and those that had yet to be affected were complacent and found spurious reasons why they had been spared. Statistics were offered by everyone showing how badly or how well they were doing. When the statistics started to be uncomfortably bad they were removed or manipulated until they showed good news. Badly affected countries showed statistics that showed other countries were even more badly affected and that whatever the government was doing was working. All leaders and countries were united in two major areas. The first was that they had no idea whatsoever of what was happening and why it was happening. The second was that they refused to believe the real reason and the much less the unpalatable solution.

The whole situation was made worse by the rolling news media around the world. Whenever they appeared on screen they, wherever they were in the world, claimed their country was suffering the most, that their government had no ideas about solving the problems and that the situation was far worse than the leaders would have the population believe. Talking head after talking head appeared offering their own interpretations and condemnations. Self-declared experts, made Wil laugh out loud when they displayed their total lack of understanding, but they were asked endless, pointless questions to which they had no answer. Nevertheless they waffled on as if they were experts using the latest buzz words and populist ideas. This all led to pointless speculation and uneducated guesswork which led to more and more confusion and dissatisfaction. Many years earlier the notion of fake news had been invented and the situations being experienced lent themselves to fakery. Endless spokespeople appeared on news and discussion programmes all with twenty-twenty hindsight stating categorically that whatever had been done, and not much was, was wrong and they knew it was wrong but, again, offered no solutions going forward.

But, while around the world governments flapped and media accused them of being ineffectual the populations were suffering. In numerous places around the world the sound of sirens and the sight of blue flashing lights on top of, usually white, wagons with the word ambulance spelled out in dozens of languages dashing about the country to the latest scene of casualties became common-place. TV screens showed seemingly endless pictures of mechanical diggers, earth movers and people digging ever larger pits in which to bury the bodies who were now only being buried in white shrouds. Carpenters were no longer able to keep up with the demand for coffins.

There was a complete lack of predictability. The notions of tears only happening along ley lines had eventually been dropped by Wil and his fraternity and even those governments that had some faith in Wil had dropped the idea. Even the notion of activity along lines of electronic activity had been dropped once the solar flares had arrived. Tears could and were happening everywhere and they were completely unpredictable. People who had concluded that they were only at risk when they were at ground level and moved to higher floors were horrified to find that tears could happen at any level and no floor, not even the floors of the super sky scrapers were safe. They did not realise that the partition was three dimensional and spirits could move across it and up it. Space, as it was on Earth, would have become an issue across the partition if the spirits could only occupy what could be considered ground level so they, too, could occupy higher levels.

Multiple sites across the big cities were being flagged. Dozens of sites in the mega cities like Beijing, Delhi and Mexico City were being recorded. Citizens around the world were panicking and deserting the cities and going to smaller villages in the vain hope that they were safer there. But whole, small villages and towns were being affected, even small farms with only a single building and a few people were being hit. People were afraid to go out and gather in groups in case they were hit but they were also scared to stay in their homes in case they were hit.

There were scenes of mass panic when there was a tear and people started to be affected. Everyone in the area started to run from where they thought the epicentre was but, unlike a tornado, there was no obvious centre so they often rushed to areas of more danger raising the casualty levels. People going to their assistance were often engulfed as the cause had no boundaries and spread over large areas. It was not unusual to see a single dead body on the ground though. There were cases of road traffic with their occupants dead in their cars stuck at their destinations and unable to move on as the passenger had not signed out releasing the car to return to its base store. Other autonomous cars were stuck in the grid lock of people trying to escape contributing to the congestion. Many ran out of electrical power going many miles off their planned routes trying to avoid congestion and stopped at the sides of the road far from their destination or base.

Although there was no formal acceptance about the cause of the problems people were learning how to behave around it. They no longer rushed to try to help people struck down and left it to the rescue teams wearing breathing apparatus who, almost always, arrived too late to help most people. Nevertheless because the spirits were unlikely to be able to swiftly re-cross the partition because the partition could not be repaired as quickly as it used to be the breathing apparatus teams were still required to retrieve the dead bodies. Then there was the problem of the area being declared a dead zone as if the spirits did not return to their side of the partition no-one could enter the areas they occupied. This was further complicated by the fact that the groups of spirits could move, split apart, remerge and, effectively, become a land based cloud that could affect areas around the initial spill.

All the while the numbers recording the numbers of incidents and the numbers of casualties in the black room rose. Past the thousands, past the millions, past the tens of millions. The only number that rose very slowly was the number of large incidents that had been resolved. The larger ones that continued to appear and merge with others continued unabated despite the repairers trying to concentrate on the large ones at the expense of the smaller. This was in the knowledge that although the large ones presented the immediate danger the smaller ones could easily merge together to make more large ones.

Wil stormed around the bedroom taking kicks at imaginary cats or stones or heads of states muttering to himself and the others.

"What the frig is the problem with these people? Why can't they get it into their thick heads what the issue is here? Why can't they see what they are going to have to do?"

"Is this just going to get worse? I mean what is going to happen in the end?" Lewis asked not really wanting to know the answer.

"So, the way I see it is that we were getting into deeper and deeper trouble with tears being caused by the EM activity and that was not going to stop either until the EM sources were shut down".

"Which was going to be unlikely," contributed Harvey as he carefully carried a tray of tea cups into the room.

"Which was going to be definitely unlikely because too many people would lose too much money and or face. So it was going to keep getting worse unless the other side would be able to step up their repairs".

"Which I assume was going to be unlikely," added Lottie.

"Which was going to be impossible. But then there has been this kick start with the solar flares which could not have happened at a worse time".

"So are you saying that the flares have accelerated the breakdowns out of all possibility of it being repaired?" asked Lewis

"Yep, no chance now".

"So what can be done?"

"Well one hope is that now the solar flares have passed there will be no more exacerbation from them. That will be one source of damage removed".

"But that still leaves the increased EM," pointed out Lewis.

"But that still leaves the increased EM", Wil checked himself aware that he had started repeating what the others had said back to them and resolved to try to find a new way of answering them. "I don't see any way of even trying to repair the partition, even if that is possible, until all the EM is shut down".

"Hang on, what do you mean 'even if it is possible' do you mean that there may be no way back, that the partition may never be repaired and that the spirits will be on our side for ever?"

"Well, I didn't really want to go there but the worst case scenario is that all, or at least large parts, of the partition may be beyond repair and that masses of the spirits will be on this plane for ever".

"And that the cases of suffocations and everything will go on for ever?"

"Well, that is the possibility. Using rather coarse terms clouds of spirits will waft about the Earth, much the same as they do on their side, and, of course, they will affect us on this side. No-one will be safe anywhere and even if they shut down all the EM it might be too late".

"Tell me you are not predicting the end of civilisation".

"Maybe not the end but there could certainly be a massive and perhaps a drop in population numbers that is not survivable".

"Jesus, what the hell can be worse than that?"

Just then Will was distracted by his black box which had been constantly charting events. He went over to it and clapped both hands to his face.

"Oh my God!"

"What is it?" asked Lottie fearing the worst.

"Cows".

"What do you mean cows?"

"What I mean is it just got worse. Much worse".

"How?"

"Remember that American guy who said he thought he saw a dog in the spirits? Well it seems that he almost certainly did and that was a sign of forthcoming issues. Seeing the gizmo here I reckon that the partition between us and the animal world has just broken and now they are coming across too. It could be possible that billions and billions of them could be able to get across to our side".

FORTY THREE

"But why is that such a problem? If they start swilling about they are going to be smaller than us so they shouldn't cause us any harm surely?"

Wil sighed and looked at Lewis somewhat disbelievingly. "Don't quite know where to start here, Lewis. There are so many problems here".

"Like?" Lewis added still not quite on the same wavelength.

"OK so how many animals do you think are on the other side? For the sake of argument how many farm animals that we eat? How many do you think there might be?"

"So, probably a lot. Millions, maybe billions", offered Lottie.

"Billions is right, maybe a billion every year for the last God knows how many years," Wil stressed the every year.

"But as Lewis said they are small".

"Ever seen a small cow or horse. Granted sheep, pigs, chickens are small and dogs, cats and the like so they are not going to be suffocating adults but they all take up space so they will squeeze the human spirits into smaller areas. Also cows might not be adult size but they are child size so a herd of cow spirits could wipe out a school of children but leave the adults unaffected. Sheep might wipe out a kindergarten or play school."

"So we all take precautions in those areas as well. It's obviously bad but it could be catered for, couldn't it?"

"I suppose so but there is the problem of repairing the partition. Obviously there are problems, maybe insurmountable problems fixing our partition but now they have to repair the animal to human partition as well. Even if they can fix the partition efficiently there is the problem of getting the spirits back. The human spirits are usually very compliant and understand the need for them to go back to their side but getting animals of different types to go back is a whole other story. They have no idea of what they have to do and just might not want to obey what they are being told to do".

"Are they likely to affect living animals as well?" asked Harvey suddenly and unaccountably concerned for his cats.

"Of course. We have seen animals wiped out by human spirits so they could just as easily be wiped out by animal spirits".

Wil paused not really wanting to pour more grief into the situation. "There are two other problems".

The other three looked at each other wondering if they were ready for more bad news.

"All the deaths are increasing the pressure on the other side because all the new deaths result in new spirits so the numbers are increasing exponentially. And."

The others were not quite sure if they were ready for an …and.

"And there is going to be the problem of food shortages if this goes on. We have seen that there are problems in the shops with people panic buying but with if the numbers of people keep falling then harvests will be threatened and even if they are not the processing and distribution networks might start collapsing because people will not want to go out or there will be just too few people to do the work".

"I suppose if the animals start being killed off there will be no meat. We will all have to go vegetarian".

"If there are any vegetables," contributed Lottie.

"Exactly, and this is happening all over the world".

"But, at least there will be fewer people needing food," Harvey contributed, immediately wishing he hadn't.

"The only upside is that the internet activity and the like will slightly decrease but it is not going to be enough to stop the disaster. Something has to be done and we know what it is but it is getting those idiots in charge to understand that is the problem".

FORTY FOUR

After twenty two days the instruments the astronomers and physicists were using to measure the solar winds slumped back to normal levels. A few days before the readings fell the observatories and even people watching with the naked eye could see that the level of solar activity was slowly dropping. Everyone hoped that soon the levels of solar winds would start to fall and disappear and, just maybe, what they were being told by Wil and his groups would prove to be right. The fall in solar activity and solar winds would reduce the numbers and the severity of incidents that were happening on Earth.

And it proved to be the case. Slowly the effects of the solar flares could be discounted but the dangers were replaced by the break-down of the animal to human partition and the increasing numbers of tears that involved huge numbers of animals. The fact that there had been no reduction in EM activity ensured that the incidents would keep happening. As a consequence the numbers on the counters in the black room kept rising. They did rise a little slower post solar flares but the millions started into the tens of millions. Population centres were being cleared of people both through tears in the partition and flight out of them by scared citizens.

Wil, who had been elevated from local Sussex nerd to national expert was now being hailed as the world authority despite the fact that those on the screens he kept addressing would not believe him. But gradually he felt there was a wave of acceptance that just maybe he was right. Certainly on the streets people, when not fleeing or panicking, were organising themselves into protest groups. Wil had been on numerous television news channels around the world. Eastbourne had become the epicentre of news broadcasting and all down his road there were multiple outside broadcast teams speaking to their audiences in every language under the sun.

FORTY FIVE

"So what you are saying is that everyone seems to be accepting that the problem is the amount of electromagnetic radiation being generated?" enquired Lottie.

Despite all the activity in the road outside the house and Wil's elevation to partition guru the group still managed to meet at the house. Eventually all the reporters outside had realised that it was only Wil that they needed to interview so the rest were now able to slip through the gangs of TV vans without being harassed.

"Well I am hoping so. We have been saying it often enough," stated Will with a degree of frustration. "There has been enough time now for everyone to test out their own favourite theory and try to implement it and, so far, they have all found that nothing they have tried has worked". Wil did find a crumb of comfort in what he was saying. At least no-one had been able to come up with a plausible theory that would have displaced his and no-one had actually disproved his despite many, many desperately trying. Especially the hi-tech companies at which his finger had been pointed from the beginning.

"But even if they do accept it what are they going to do about it?" asked Lottie

"Well they could try what they did in Texas and if they are going to start cutting down the EM traffic there seems to be a couple of obvious ones like the autonomous cars, that must take a huge amount of energy," chipped in Harvey who was no fan of the autonomous cars and harked back to the time when people drove cars and not computers.

"It might be obvious and I know you liked driven cars but the problem is that if you took all the autonomous cars off the road people would not be able to get around. There are few manufacturers that make non-autonomous cars anymore so there are not many real cars, as you would call them, about. Even if there were then there are millions of people who could not drive them. There would be no way we could get old cars out and train people to drive them in less than loads of years". Lewis looked crushed as Wil explained the situation to him.

"What about drone taxis?" added Lottie hoping to placate Lewis a little.

They all nodded and agreed that drone taxis could stop making people either travel on the ground which required considerably less computing power or make them stay at home. There was silence as everyone tried to think of ways to cut electronic traffic.

"What about cutting the amount of drone traffic delivering stuff ordered over the internet," offered Lewis.

"Possible" added Wil, "but if you cut all the drone deliveries and stepped up road deliveries would everyone be able to get what they wanted. Back in the day when there were physical shops you could nip down to one of those but with all the internet buying most of the shops have closed down, even the food shops. So where would everyone get their stuff from. We cannot magic up loads of shops and the hubs where it is stored now could not cope with thousands of people descending on them".

"Even if there was enough food to stock them," mused Lottie gloomily.

"They could set up warehouses to distribute packs of food and stuff and chuck them into people's cars as they went past," chipped in Lewis

"And what did we say about cars?" spoiled Wil.

"True. A real problem isn't it?"

"They could send in their orders and the hubs could send them out in more vehicles, possibly autonomous, or maybe driven vehicles".

"And how would they do that if we had to close down the internet?"

"What about rationing people's use of autonomous cars so they only get so many trips a week?"

"Yes", added Lottie "you could set a limit on the number of purchases anyone can make using drone delivery".

Will looked despondent "whatever we do there are going to be riots. No-one is going to like any of it".

In a moment of rationality Lewis piped up "but whatever you do people will moan. Do something and they will moan, do nothing and they will moan. Do it now and it will be too soon, do it later and it will be too late."

"All they have to do is look at the alternative".

"My dad always used to say to people moaning about their lives that the alternative as much worse".

It all went quiet again as everyone began to realise how much of their lives had been taken over by computers.

Not believing she was saying it as she was one of the biggest users Lottie offered that all social media should be closed down. Surprisingly everyone agreed being united in the condemnation of it as a complete waste of time, a sewer, a machine for dumbing down, winding up and aggravating people. They moved onto downloading of films and entertainment but began to realise that there was no other way of accessing such things. The old methods of DVDs or CDs or cinemas were long gone and were not going to be revived any time soon.

"Population surveillance. Get rid of that. Everyone hates it anyway. Perhaps that is something we could agree on. Well, everyone except the government. And the police."

"But whatever we get rid of how long will we have to be rid of it?"

"Good question" said Wil. "Who knows?"

"Not such a good answer then".

"Assuming we cannot make the partition any stronger we cannot go back to where we were so some things will have gone forever unless different ways can be made to make them work. How long it would take to repair the partition is difficult. Some tears are huge and spread over a huge distance. Smaller bits are easier to knot together but large bits that might still be breaking down as they are being fixed is much more difficult." Wil observed.

"And all the time it takes more people are going to be killed".

"Correct".

"But, at least with the numbers of people dying there must be a steep decline in the amount of electromagnetic communications and that must help to stop damage being done to the partition?"

Wil tipped his head in slightly begrudging agreement "that is true I suppose but we do not know if the decrease is actually having a protective effect on the partition. The damage might already be too severe and the damage might just be compiling with tears making other tears without any levels of radiation".

"You mean that even if we turned off all the communications right now there damage might continue?" asked Lottie.

"It's a bit like a hole in a river wall. Once water starts getting through, unless it is stopped, the hole will keep getting bigger. If the partition opens more will pour though damaging the sides and putting stress on it. It might flex and tear even without pressure so, yes, the damage could be self-perpetuating and might end up irreparable".

"And if it cannot be stopped or repaired?" asked Lewis not really wanting to know the answer.

"You don't really want to know the answer to that do you?" said Wil.

"No, but tell me anyway".

"Worst case scenario?"

"Worst case scenario".

"Worst case is that the damage is so severe that even if we stop all transmissions right now and keep it off forever the damage not only cannot be repaired but it keeps going avalanche style continually breaking down until it breaks down completely and every spirit comes across".

"And if every spirit comes across the death rate keeps going up".

"With the exception of those that are remote enough from any spill-over point that they can survive. But, of course most of civilisations support systems will be destroyed so how could they continue to survive".

"So you are saying we will die out".

"Yes, we are the latter day dinosaurs and we will leave the planet for the next inhabitants to come along and start all over again. Maybe."

"And go", finished Lottie.

"And go, yes".

FORTY SIX

It was coming up to three in the afternoon on a fine December day. The clouds were gathering and it was getting a bit darker. People were generally rushing home or finding a place to sit and watch the news on their devices. It was a warm day, the sun had been out but despite being a couple of weeks to Christmas it was warm enough to just wear a thin jacket. There had been no snow for many years and frost was very rare. Winter temperatures rarely fell below ten degrees centigrade even in north Yorkshire where the Davisson estate was located. Lights were being turned on and people were waiting. There had been news bulletins all day with reporters endlessly trying to guess what was going to be said and what the effects of what was said would have. Endlessly they interviewed each other and wheeled in experts or people just out shopping. But all they really knew was that the Prime Minister would be addressing the country that afternoon and that leaders of countries all over the world would be giving the same address at the same time. This was going to be important.

In the library of the great house the broadcasters were setting up their equipment ready for the all-important speech to be given by the prime minister at three. The scene was repeated in countries across the world. After innumerable meetings within countries and between countries, after every conceivable cause for the emergency had been investigated and eliminated and after begrudging acceptance of the cause of the disasters everyone was agreed all countries that agreed to broadcast to all their populations despite many being in the middle of the night. To Wil's eternal surprise and gratification the great majority of countries had also agreed to the solution. There were many countries that were in violent disagreement but enough big hitters eventually over-ruled them and decided on the next actions which would be implemented without the agreement of dissenters. Might was right and the threats of military interventions to shut down national systems eventually worked. Only a handful of countries who were not in agreement were not broadcasting the vital information despite being affected by the actions. They were rehearsing their attacks on the rest of the world and how their actions were going to have a serious effect on their country.

At three o'clock the Prime Minister started.

"Ladies and gentlemen, thank you for joining me today. I regret to say I am the bearer of very bad tidings and have to say we, in this country and around the world, are faced with a crisis more severe than any the world has had to face. This is worse than any war, any disease pandemic and any natural disaster.

As you will know from the news broadcasts of the previous months that there have been many, many millions of deaths due to causes that have been little understood. Many potential causes have been put forward and many solutions considered. Many, indeed, have been trialled and tested but all have, so far, been found to be ineffective. We are therefore confronted by such a serious situation that, as yet, is uncontrollable that we expect many more deaths in this country and across the world and that the whole infra-structure of society will be put at risk. We have already seen food shortages, which we fear, despite our best efforts at maintain supply chains will get worse. Transport, as a whole is failing and we are at high risk of essential utilities like electricity and water being severely rationed unless drastic measures are taken".

As she spoke Wil had one eye on the screen in the black room and watched as the numbers of cases increased steadily. The numbers of deaths leapt sporadically as information from different countries was fed into the system. The numbers of lights indicating incidents increased although there had been so many coming in that they only represented incidents where more than a thousand people had died. There were many more red lights than there used to be, many more large scale incidents.

"One of the theories put forward regarding the emergency is that the causal effect is the amount of electromagnetic radiation that is generated by the way that we live. The theory has been hotly contested around the world and, as yet, there has been no proof that it is not correct".

"No proof that it is not correct!" Wil leapt from his chair and repeated the PM's comment at number eleven on the loudness dial. "No proof. Not correct! What is the matter with the bloody people?"

"Hold on Wil, at least she is not dismissing it yet", counselled Lottie.

"Yet!" and Wil threw himself back in his chair.

"In fact", the PM continued "in a couple of instances when action had been taken to limit the amount of EM in the air there did seem to be an improvement in the local situation which enabled it to be managed. Also, in a negative way the burst of EM from the recent solar flares did seem to make things significantly worse. So taking those two elements it may be that the solution to this is to limit the amount of EM, at least in the short term to see if we can manage the situation and stop all the deaths".

"Calm down Wil", Lewis had been watching Wil as he listened. "She does seem to be creeping up on the idea that you are right and there is going to have to be something drastic done".

"We'll see" said Wil disbelievingly.

"Therefore, I can announce, along with all the other leaders across the globe that as from midnight tonight GMT there will be an almost total shut down of all EM based communications. All transport that requires EM will be grounded, no planes, ships, drones or, autonomous vehicles. They will all be disconnected from their grids and grounded. I appreciate this will cause, potentially, severe hardship not least in the ability to transport, deliver and purchase essentials such as food but we are all of the opinion that this amongst other measures are essential. Where possible transport will be provided by the remaining non IT dependant vehicles. Needless to say this will be limited and dedicated solely to the most essential functions. The one potential glimmer of hope is that if this is successful and we do see a drop in the numbers of incidents then we will have proven that our approach is correct and we might be able to refine it to be better able to support populations".

"Good start, good start", said Wil encouraged.

"In addition all social media will be closed down and all data storage hubs taken offline and all non-essential stored data will be deleted. All social communication platforms will therefore be no longer available although one to one telephone communications especially those based on land lines will continue. No entertainment access will be permitted and no on line shopping will be available. Only one television channel will be allowed to broadcast and then purely for information transmission, there will also be only one radio channel. All other channels will be closed down, and again, I stress that this will be for as short a time as possible after which we hope all will be reinstalled, on a very gradual process starting with the purchase and distribution of food and other essential items. That is assuming the actions prove to be effective".

Lottie wondered how many chocolate biscuits were in the cupboards downstairs. There were usually many packets so she was comforted to think they would not go short.

"I am also announcing that all surveillance initiatives will be closed down, temporarily. All CCTV will be turned off, all facial recognition and movement tracking will cease. Financial and commerce systems will remain functioning as the lack of physical money would grind all financial transactions impossible.

To shut all these systems down the satellite systems on which they are all dependant will be temporarily suspended so anything that requires communications to a data hub or between systems via the satellites will be suspended. I appreciate I am sending us all back to the Victorian times and possibly further back in time but I can say that most of the rest of the world is also taking these steps. It has to be said some more reluctantly than others but once the satellites systems are taken off line then all countries whether they agree or not will be in the same position. I will also stress that, we hope, these measures will be temporary. If they work and we see an improvement in the world wide situation we will review and reinstate. Thank you for listening and for your co-operation and I sincerely hope we can all see the solution to this problem and can all get back to normal as soon as possible".

"Well that depends on what you think is normal", sneered Wil.

"But if it does work and they can start turning things back on then we will get back to normal. Won't we?" enquired Lewis.

"Not a cat in hell's chance will we return to normal. It is what everyone thought was normal that caused all this."

"You notice that he did not say anything about the partition? I think he is hoping that everyone will believe that the cause of the problems is the comms systems themselves. He didn't want to explain about the partition and the spirits did he?" commented Wil

FORTY SEVEN

Wil monitored the screens for days and weeks following the PM's broadcast with increasing desperation. Around the world many of the comms systems were initially shut down plunging the populations into all kinds of chaos. There was no transport to speak of, no communication and the food situation got progressively worse. Power and water services became intermittent and often non-existent. Health care vanished. Support services and charities tried to help but were overwhelmed and eventually vanished. After some initial compliance there started to be riots with people demanding the restoration of services. Some became violent. Protestors claimed the situation was not acceptable and the solution to the problems they did not really understand was worse than the problem itself. Indeed the original problems did not seem to be going away. There were more and more incidents with increasing numbers of casualties.

Wil could not understand it. Even with lots of non-compliance there was some, in fact, a great deal to start with but there seemed to be no end to the numbers of incidents. Populations were being decimated and the ones that survived moved in huge numbers but often moved to areas of even higher risk and they too succumbed.

"Surely we should have seen some improvement shouldn't we?" Harvey asked Wil hoping for a positive reply.

"We should. We should have seen at least a bit of an improvement. Even if we only saw a levelling off then it would have been something. The way it is does not look good."
"How do you mean?" asked Lottie

"My fear was that this had gone too far and that the cure had been too slow in coming and even then not good enough".

Wil paused.

"It is a bit like a cancer. If you catch it soon enough and treat it then it can be survivable. But if you leave it too late then no matter what you do the cancer has gone too far and it cannot be treated".

"And the tears are the cancer?" added Harvey.

"Yes, and the treatment is too late. Is that what you are saying Wil?" asked Lottie.

"Unfortunately that is what I am saying. It might be too late even with all the switch offs".

Wil turned to look at his screen and as he did he felt a tingling in his lips.

FORTY EIGHT

Time had never really meant much to Adam. Today, although he didn't realise it meant even less. All he knew was that it was early in the morning and he had a long way to go. The sun was already quite high and the ground was heating up although even though Adam was barefoot he did not feel the heat or the sharpness of the stones. He had made the same walk many times in his young life so the barrenness of the landscape, the sheer burning heat of the sun and the lack of water meant little to him. It was home and he was comfortable in his surroundings no matter how harsh they were. He could manage it all very easily.

As he walked he felt almost pleased that he was alone in the solitude of a beautiful country. Of course he did not realise quite how alone he actually was. Not so very long ago when he had made the journey he had shared the planet with almost ten billion other people but now most had gone the way of the dinosaur.

He remembered the day the computers were turned off, the desperation of the people who were unable to buy food, unable to work to earn money to buy the non-existent food. Very little moved on the roads and nothing moved through the air. Communications were minimal and solely based on government controlled outlets while there were government controlled outlets. They had been told the shut downs would be temporary, that the power would soon go back on and they would all return to normal, that everything that could be done would be done. But there was virtually nothing that could be done. The whole infinitely delicate structure that kept life going on the planet was falling apart. Lines of communication, of supply, of life were fractured and incapable of repair. Crops died in the fields or in warehouses close to the fields. Most never reached the cities where they were desperately needed. Cattle were not slaughtered because they could not be transported to slaughter houses, milk was not collected. And it only took a few weeks after the computers were turned off that it all came about.

Governments argued about reinstating the communications networks but, as Wil witnessed, even after the shut down the lights on the big board in the black room continued to light up. Calibrations changed from a red light meaning thousands to tens of thousands to hundreds of thousands. Some countries tried to turn systems back on but the inter-connectivity meant that one system was so reliant on shared infrastructure that the local systems would not work. Tears in the partition kept happening and it became increasingly obvious that the damage to the partition had been done. Tears that had happened and were still being repaired or waiting to be repaired increased in size. Repairs became increasingly impossible. Gradually day by day the whole fabric of the partition broke down with longer and wider tears being irreparable. The animal partition continued to break down exacerbating the problems. The spirits trying to repair the human partition were doubly stretched trying to repair the animal partition. The millions upon millions of deaths occurring because of the breakdown added to the problems as there was nowhere for the recently dead spirits to go. They just joined the milling throng of those disgorged from the partition. As the numbers of dead increased the ability of any country to not only bury the dead but to function as a social community collapsed. As well as food shortages the decreasing populations meant that local utilities like the neighbourhood nuclear power stations shut down, water supplies failed as sewage works failed, desalination plants failed, and pumping stations failed.

All around the world countries became susceptible to failures. Cold countries suffered because of the lack of heat, hot countries suffered because of the lack of water, all countries suffered because of the lack of food. And all the while the partition continued to break down. The world was ending, not as everyone had imagined in a world war four, not due to a meteor collision as was supposed to be the end of the dinosaur world but due to rampaging greed and blithe disregard for the natural world.

Only Adam and maybe a few thousand other people in remote, desolate and deserted places on Earth were left and before long they, too, would only be history for the next inhabitants of the planet to discover at some stage and wonder about. The 30 million years or so between extinction events had passed and the Earth was waiting for its next inhabitants.

Adam shielded his eyes from the sun and his lips tingled.

Cast of Characters:

Susan Roads	Wil Kingdon	Gill Dredge
Jev	Piers	Rosie Lands
Harvey	Matt Combe	Mead
Norman Bay	Phil Ching	Holly Wells
Lottie Bridge	Gail Sham	Helen Lawns
Rod Mills	Wes Lawns	Hugh de Beachy
Alice Park	Albert Praed	Paul Gates
Ann Dromeda	Dean East	Dick Lower